Her Night in Shining Armani

Lisa Wells

Cover art: Kim Killion

Editor: Holly Atkinson

Contents

Her Night In Shining Armani

Blurb

The Manhattan Knitters' Club invites you to apply to join them for Friday Night Knit Club. If approved, and that's a big IF, you agree to bring the following to each meeting: tiara, bottle of wine, and knitting supplies.

By day, Wendy Travis is a stone-cold-accurate proofreader of contracts for individuals whose deeds bend toward the peculiar. By night, she's the out-of-date fashionista president of the Manhattan Knitters' Club. The club's motto: What happens at knit club stays at knit club!

When the new upstairs neighbor interrupts her sleep with his nocturnal shenanigans, she's suddenly not so accurate in her job. With the backup of her knitting friends, she confronts Mr. Can't Keep It In His Pants.

Land developer, Jackson Adler, is in the wrong place at the...right time. When a posse of tiara-wearing, needle-wielding misfits—including one very animated, very sexy, and slightly tipsy woman—mistake him for the tenant of Apartment 5C, he doesn't correct their error. Instead, he suggests a quid pro quo agreement. He'll pipe down if Wendy agrees to buy him at an upcoming bachelor-auction...on his dime of course.

Wendy counters wither her own quid pro quo offer because she intends to find out if those late-night moans and squeals of pleasure are fake—or stone-cold accurate responses.

Conventional? No. Worthwhile? Time will tell.

DEDICATION
Thank you to my child who understood when her birthday celebration was postponed because I was in deadline hell.

Thank you to my husband who volunteered to be my assistant and didn't quit when he realized the things I needed assistance with had nothing to do with inspiration for sexy-time scenes.

Thank you to the Portal Plotters. They hang out with me daily, inspire my plots, and keep me focused on the task at hand.
Big shout out to my Zoom writing buddies – you make this author's life a lot more entertaining.

Holly Atkinson thank you for the editing magic you work on my manuscripts.

Kim Killion thank you for the beautiful cover.

1

Wendy cleared her throat, successfully garnering the attention of the other Manhattan Knitters—Eddy and Abigail. Tonight, she planned to do *it*. She would temporarily lower her principles and spill all the juicy details of the contract she had recently proofread at work for the Angelino family.

"Dollface, that's the second time you've cleared your throat. Do you need medical attention?" Eddy asked. "Should I call the hunky firemen brigade?"

Abigail giggled. "They can attend to my needs any day."

While the lowering of her principles wasn't on Wendy's Things To Do Before Turning Thirty list, if she didn't tell the Manhattan Knitters about the booty-call contract, her brain was at risk of exploding. And that would not be a pretty sight. "So, you know how I never—"

A loud boom of thunder caused them all to yelp.

Wendy's gut, a prim and proper thing, took advantage of the interruption to tell Wendy's mouth to shut the daylights up. She ignored her gut. "You know how I never tell you—"

Lightning cracked right outside her living room window, resulting in more squeals.

"Wow, that's some storm out there," Abigail said. "Maybe—"

"Oh! Oh! Oh God! Yes! Yes, baby! Don't stop, baby!"

"Fuck," growled a deep baritone voice.

The surround-sound exclamations came from the apartment above Wendy's. They filtered through the ceiling tiles, through the ancient pipes, and through the air vents. Her rude neighbor appeared to be entertaining...again.

Were the sexual murmurs the universe's way of telling her—if you refuse to listen to your gut, then listen to me? *Work Secrets, no matter how titillating, should stay unmentioned.*

"Yeeeessssss," screeched a female.

Wendy dropped her knitting, jumped up, and grabbed her broom, frustration tangling in her like a ball of yarn in the paws of a cat. She knocked the handle vigorously against her ceiling. "Try having a quiet orgasm like the rest of us."

The female moaned even louder, the voice breathy and higher pitched than whoever her neighbor had been entertaining last night.

Wendy glanced at the other two members of the small but vastly fun Manhattan Knitters' Club. Eddy had his phone out to record the sex noises, and Abigail's mouth hung open.

"Sorry," Wendy said to her friends. "The show usually doesn't start this early." Three a.m. seemed to be Mr.

Upstairs' favorite time to quote Marvin Gaye and say, "Let's get it on."

"Sugar, are they newlyweds?" A blush stained Abigail's freckled cheeks. She looked about fifteen but was twenty-two, fresh off the cobblestone streets of a small, quirky town in Missouri.

Wendy scoffed. "Nothing that romantic. If my ears can be trusted, he never nails the same woman twice."

Eddy put his phone down and repositioned the tiara he wore. A prop from the Off-Broadway musical he'd been an understudy in last summer. "Who is *he*? What does *he* do?"

"I've never met him. The only time he's up there is when he's doing someone." Wendy adjusted her own tiara. Eddy had ordered one for Wendy and Abigail the night their club was born.

That night, Wendy had brought her knitting to open mic at a newly opened comedy club. *You know...just in case there was time to knit between sets.* Upon arriving, Wendy had immediately spotted another knitter in the club—Abigail—and had requested permission to sit with her. Then Eddy had waltzed in with his hot-pink knitting satchel, and they had waved him over.

The tiaras weren't his only addition to the club. He'd also suggested they try a different wine at their weekly meetings. More of an insistence. Said he couldn't knit a lick when sober. Tonight, they were drinking Broke Ass, a smooth red blend from Spain that had been on sale.

"I used to know a boy who couldn't keep it in his pants," Abigail said with a sweet lilt. "Ended up with crabs, bless his heart. Made me happy I was the only girl he never did hit on."

"The guy obviously needed glasses if he never hit on you," Eddy said, before turning to Wendy. "Spill. Give us all the sordid details and don't leave out anything."

For a moment, Wendy thought he was asking about the contract secret she'd been about to discuss. Then she realized he meant Mr. Upstairs. "The night noises started a little over a month ago." Which coincidentally was also the time Pencil Thin, the cubicle dweller next to hers, had failed to show up for work. On that fateful day, she'd been given his client load complete with all the bizarre shit that went with his very special clients—the Angelinos. Bizarre as in she had to sign on the proofreader line as John Smith when proofing their contracts. She had even been made to practice the signature so that it matched Pencil Thin's. Weird. Weird. Weird.

And her BFFs knew none of this.

"A month! You've had Romeo living above you for a month, and you're just now mentioning him?" Eddy pursed his lips. "Girlfriend, I can't even with you right now."

Wendy lifted a shoulder. "Didn't seem newsworthy."

"Bless your heart," Abigail purred. "Your idea of newsworthy and my idea certainly aren't kissing cousins. Tell us more."

Abigail had lots of sayings that went right over Wendy's head. "Like what?" She really didn't know a thing about her upstairs Romeo.

"Straight? Bi?" Eddy crossed his legs at the knees.

"I'm assuming straight. Only because I've never been bombarded with the wailing of two baritones up there."

"You hear that?" Eddy placed a hand over his heart. "That's the sound of my heart breaking."

"I wonder what he does for a living." Abigail had a thing for men in manly careers. Like firefighters, construction workers, cowboys.

Wendy pointed toward the ceiling with the broom handle. "No matter what he does for a living, this seems to be what he does for pleasure."

As if on cue, a loud moan filtered down to their ears.

A huge smile stretched Eddy's lips, showing off his cranberry-orange lipstick. "Sounds like he's *damn* good at his pleasure-sport."

"Well, *his* damn good is messing with *my* damn good," Wendy replied tartly. She was a proofreader for Contracts R Us. A job that required perfection...as in the company had a two-strike policy. Strikes were given when errors were discovered on a contract you'd proofed. Upon receiving your second strike, you also received your pink slip, and an escort out of the building with whatever of your personal items you could fit in a shoebox.

"*You* have a new sex life?" Eddy laid his knitting needles down and leaned in as if ready for an all-night gossip session. "Dish it with a dollop of whipped cream. Eddy's listening."

"I was talking about my job," she corrected. "I almost made an I'm-too-tired-to-concentrate mistake today on an asinine contract. Too tired because Mr. Upstairs kept me awake."

"Asinine in what way?" Abigail asked.

Wendy was over the urge to talk about the booty-call contract. Between her gut and the Universe, it was obviously not meant to be told. "It was on a contract between the owners of a pair of cocker spaniels who want them to marry and then mate." Can't have any bastard cockers in the world of the rich and insane.

"Oh my God," Eddy squealed. He placed his hand over his heart. "That is so cute, it's gross. I want to go to the wedding. Can you get me an invite?"

"Considering I'm not supposed to talk about my work, that's going to be a hard no." The upside to her job at Contracts R Us was her employer paid her the big bucks because she had a reputation of being stone-cold accurate. Five years on the job and zero errors. Plus, they paid for her to live in this very apartment. Not to mention, she was allowed to use her work cell as her personal cell and thus spend that saved money on yarn.

"But you caught the mistake? Right?" Abigail asked.

"Thank God, yes." If she hadn't, they would have given her strike one and deducted a day's pay from her next paycheck. This harsh repercussion upon receiving your first strike was why, when Wendy had read over the contract to be employed at the company, she'd chosen not to report the error on it. The legal document had her listed as living in the apartment above. For better or worse, she'd kept the mistake to herself.

"I don't think I could handle that kind of pressure," Eddy said. "I mean none of us are perfect. Mistakes happen. Hell, I slept with two of mine. Last week." Eddy was currently the understudy for the star of an on-Broadway show.

A good point but not *the* point. "It's my job to find mistakes, not make them." Her career was her strength. A place she ruled. A place she never blundered. Unlike her personal life, which was littered with missed chances, misplaced faith, misguided love, and misfortune. Thoughts of the latter caused her heart to pinch.

"I want you to pick out my next lover," Eddy said. "Someone mysterious, moody, and meant for *moi*."

"Oooh, me too," Abigail chimed enthusiastically. "Only I want kind, handsome, and not afraid to walk down Wooster Street after dark. And believes in ghosts." Considering she grew up in Mayhem, a town known for its ghost population, that addition didn't surprise Wendy.

"How about you, Dollface?" Eddy asked. "What adjectives describe your dream man?"

"Well, let me see…" Wendy considered the question. "Successful, sexy, honest." Emphasis on honest. Dealing with contracts all day, she'd discovered the world was full of weirdos and deceit.

Ever since the Angelino contracts had been reassigned to her, she'd been plagued with apprehensions that perhaps her place of work wasn't entirely on the up-and-up.

"Gag. Honest. I hate it. I love it," Eddy said. "Add truthful to my man."

"I don't know. I think the world runs better when little white lies are on the table," Abigail said.

The Manhattan Knitters had two things in common. They met every Friday night to knit, and they sucked at the under-thirty dating scene. Abigail was the youngest at twenty-two; Wendy twenty-four; and Eddy was three months away from thirty. Oh, they dated—they just weren't any good at it. Abigail too shy. Eddy too shallow. And Wendy too much of a perfectionist. She could pick a flaw in a man at twenty paces with her eyes closed.

The sound of a door slamming directly above them had them all running to the window to watch who left the building.

A couple emerged. "Do you think that's them?" asked Eddy.

"Maybe." The couple was huddled under an umbrella, making it impossible for Wendy to see what either of them looked like.

The Manhattan Knitters simultaneously sighed, turned, and went back to their drinking and knitting.

An hour later, a sound from upstairs had them all pausing their needles. Heavy thumping, but no vocal noises.

"That's odd." Wendy cocked her head to listen harder. "He normally doesn't come back."

"Do you think he brought back a different woman? A quiet one?" Eddy asked.

"Maybe." Wendy didn't think so.

Eddy tittered. "He's such a fabulous T. R. A. M. P."

"That's a nice way of describing him." *Man-whore* would have been Wendy's choice of word. Who would have ever thought she'd wish for her old Mr. Upstairs to come back? His major crimes had been farting loudly and playing his music after ten p.m.

Much like Pencil Thin, old Mr. Upstairs had simply disappeared. One day he'd been up there farting, and the next, the new Mr. Upstairs had been up there making women squeal.

The sound of a thud and maybe a male grunt came from above.

"I don't thump during sex," Abigail said. "Do you guys thump? What do you think is causing the thumping?"

"Maybe he's into kinky sheets," Eddy said, "and the sound effects are a result of some type of dungeon stuff."

"What are kinky—"

"Do you do dungeon—"

A thunder-like thunk shook the pictures on the walls.

"Oh, for crying out loud." Wendy jumped up from her chair. "That's it. I'm going to give him a piece of my mind."

"You go girl." Eddy clapped his hands twice.

Wendy yanked at the bottom of her T-shirt. "If I'm not back in ten minutes, send in the cavalry."

Eddy stood and slipped on his heels. "Oh honey, you don't get to have all the fun. We're coming with you."

2

Jackson Adler let himself into apartment 5C. It wasn't his apartment in the sense he lived there, but it was his apartment in the sense he had recently purchased the building. His sister, Annie, trailed inside with him.

It was pure bad luck she had been visiting Jackson when Mitch had called—out of the fucking blue—and asked to cash in an IOU given to him during their last encounter. Hell, Jackson hadn't even known Mitch rented from him, let alone still had his contact information.

Jackson's initial response had been to tell the asshole hell no. The IOU had been to pay Mitch's medical bills for the broken nose Jackson gave him, not help the guy out of a bind. But that hadn't been stipulated, so Jackson had agreed to Mitch's request, with the added caveat that he promised not to call *her*. Her being his sister.

Unfortunately, despite his best efforts, Annie, who had been listening to his side of the conversation, had put two-and-two together, and realized her brother was talking to the guy who'd once upon a time ghosted her. She had insisted on coming with Jackson to *help.* Like he couldn't find a wedding ring lost during sex.

A *bigger glutton for punishment had never been born.* His sister, not Mitch.

Against his advice, Annie had once dated Mitch. This after Jackson had politely introduced them when they had all run into one another at Starbucks.

At that time, Mitch had been a street vendor outside Jackson's office building, Adler Towers. Nice enough guy, but not a guy you wanted your sister to date. To his dismay, they had hit it off standing in line, and Mitch asked her out.

According to Annie, the date had been magical. Mitch had not only never called Annie for a second date—he'd moved his cart. One day, after work, Jackson had run into Mitch and confronted him. Mitch had made up a bullshit story about a jealous husband shooting him in the foot the day after his and Annie's date and that had been his wake-up call that he was in no way good enough for Jackson's sister.

Jackson had punched the guy in the nose for hurting his sister, then given him his business card to send the medical bill for the broken nose. After which, he'd told Annie about the incident so she'd stop pining for a guy who wasn't the perfect man she'd built him up to be in her brain.

"I can't believe Mitch is seeing *another* married woman." If she'd said this once, she'd said it twenty times on their way from his office to the building.

What he couldn't believe was the pure bad luck to discover the man lived in the latest building he'd bought to flip. What were the fucking odds? "Some men have a learning disability when it comes to women."

"Like you?" she said.

She wasn't wrong. He headed toward the bedroom.

"Did Mitch learn nothing from the last fiasco?" After all this time, her voice still held traces of the insecurity she'd endured at being ghosted.

Hearing that pain made Jackson want to punch Mitch again. At the very least, evict him. He stopped in the bedroom and glanced at his sister. "Men like him want women who don't require romance."

"It's not like I asked him to marry me," Annie snapped. "We simply had a lot of fun."

"But you did expect dates to follow. Married women only want sex, and he's the type that's more than happy to supply orgasms that don't cost him a dime."

Annie folded her arms and tapped her toe on the hardwood floor. "I really thought he might have grown up after being shot by a pissed-off husband."

"I'm going to lift the bed frame, and you look under there for the ring. Mitch thinks she dropped it behind the headboard."

He raised the bed, but Annie made no attempt to search for the ring, so he dropped it.

"You should've broken more than his nose," she said.

"You're probably right. Are you ready to help me?"

She nodded, kicked out of her shoes, and dropped down on her knees to look under the bed.

"One, two, three." Jackson once again heaved the bed. His sister patted around beneath it.

"Got it." She stood up and straightened her skirt. "How can he afford to live in one of your buildings? Even this one?"

He let the *even this one* slide. The building was a new purchase. Major renovations were to come, beginning with insulation. "Maybe he hit the lottery." Jackson let go of the bed frame, and it fell heavily to the floor.

She held the ring to the light. Her mouth dropped open. "Get a look at this thing. It's easily three carats. Do you really think he might have hit the lottery?"

"He's screwing a rich married woman who probably helps him pay his bills. That's a lottery win in his books." Jackson had no reason to actually believe this, but the last thing he wanted was for Annie to fall back into dreamy thoughts of the guy.

"Can you find out the name of the woman who left this behind?" Annie tried to sound nonchalant and failed miserably.

"Why in the hell would you want that information?" How could she continue to carry a torch for someone who'd so easily dismissed her?

She plastered on a too-big smile. "I want to send her an invitation to my charity auction. Who knows? Maybe she'll dump him and buy you."

Jackson groaned. He hated bachelor auctions. They had been bad enough before he had been dubbed one of Manhattan's Elusive Six in a magazine article. Now, they were unbearable.

He gave a firm shake of his head. "I told you, I'm not participating this year."

She sat on the king-size bed and bounced, causing the springs to squeak. "You didn't participate last year either."

"Have you forgotten I'm in a relationship?"

She smirked. "No...you're not. I know for a fact you're single."

Shit. "How? I just found out last night." Damn, he was tired of women who tried to change the rules of a game once the game commenced.

"*Page Six* reported this morning that you're back in the running as one of New York's most eligible bachelors." She poked a finger at him. "That's why I hunted you down after work."

He'd never been one to worry about gossip. Found it tedious and ridiculous. That was until he'd become the source of gossip. Now, he had to read it. Had to know which of his secrets were no longer secrets, and how those secrets had been twisted into something they weren't. "Christ. I wish they'd stop tracking my every relationship." Chasity was a beautiful actress. Built like a brick house. Loved a good time. But no substance. Dating her had been easy.

"Oh, get over yourself. You're handsome. You're rich. And you have a personality. There are worse things that could plague a man."

He grimaced. He hated when she made him sound like an ass. "Why can't I just donate to the cause, instead?"

"What's the harm in letting a woman bid on a date night with you?" She glanced down at her left hand and wiggled her ring finger as if imagining it were occupied.

He bit back a desire to lecture her on how asinine love was. "Because in my experience, only two kinds of women are willing to shell out the hefty ticket price to attend one of your charity events."

"Okay, I'll bite. What are they?"

"One. Married and bored. Two. Never married and looking for husband number one. Neither of those types of women are on my to do list, because I don't do married. Period."

She sighed heavily. "Even if that's true, and I'm not convinced it is, the money raised will be used to bring rescue dogs into the homes of the elderly for daily visits. How can you begrudge a lonely old person a furry visitor?"

He clenched his teeth. As a lawyer, her ability to argue was an asset. As a sister, it was a pain in his ass. "Like I said, I'll donate."

"I know you'll donate. You always do. But I also need you on my auction block. It'll be great for advertisement to have one of the Elusive Six once again up for grabs."

Not quite ready to capitulate, he threw out a monkey wrench. "Aren't bachelor auctions passé in this day and age? All hell would break loose if you put women on the auction block."

Annie slid the ring onto her wedding finger. "Stop being such a spoilsport. We both know you're going to say yes."

He glanced at his Rolex. A gift from his father when Jackson had flipped his first building and cleared five million on the deal. He didn't have time for a full-on argument with his sister. "I'll be your bachelor if *you* promise to place the winning bid on me."

"First, eww." She wrinkled her nose. "That's just gross. And second, I can't afford to buy you at auction." She moved the ring to her middle finger and twirled it. She'd never made any bones about the fact she wanted love, romance, and babies in her future. Too bad Mitch had stolen her ability to trust.

"I'll provide the money." He held out his hand. "Give me the ring."

She reluctantly took it off and placed it in his hand. "You would really be okay with your sister buying you at a bachelor auction? You know *Page Six* would write about it—celebrity girlfriend or not."

"Everyone wears a mask. No one will know you're my sister."

She gave him a sisterly look. One that said I-know-what's-best-for-you. "Why not let loose and go to the highest bidder?"

"I told you, I—" Pounding at the door interrupted his spiel.

His sister slipped her feet back into her high heels. "Is that the married woman coming back for her ring?" She made a move to the door. "I want to get a look. See if I recognize her."

He grabbed her arm. "Stay in here. I promised Mitch I'd be the epitome of discretion." Why he'd given the assurance was beyond him. The woman deserved to be outed for sleeping around. Unless she didn't. Hell, who was he to judge? It wasn't like his life was pristine.

More knocks. This time louder.

Jackson opened it and found himself staring at two women and a drag queen. All wearing tiaras. "Hello."

Was one of them the owner of the ring? *Please let it be the drag queen.* That just might cure Annie of her crush on Mitch.

The cute female in front squared her shoulders, tucked a strawberry-blonde curl behind her ear, and set her chin at a stubborn angle. "I've just about had it with all the...noises coming from this apartment." She waggled her finger at him as she spoke, not looking him in the eyes but instead past him as if to see who else was in the apartment. "You either need to *pipe* down or *move*." She stumbled on nothing and smacked him in the chest as she sought to maintain her balance. The unexpected contact left him with a strange feeling of having been branded.

He'd never been taken to task by anyone not related. And never by someone so adorable. "I'm sorry—"

She took a step back and tilted her head, giving a glimpse of her stormy blue eyes. "Sorry? I don't need sorry. I need sleep, and you're depriving me of my slumber." Her voice would have been melodic if not for the notes of venom.

"Umm." Hell. Should he go to the trouble of explaining he owned the building and wasn't the one who'd been staying here? Considering she was obviously a little drunk, probably not. A sensible man didn't argue with a tipsy female. "How exactly am I depriving you of sleep?"

Her mouth dropped open. "Don't...play innocent...with me." Her tone scalded. "You've been...on top of me...for a month."

Damn if her words didn't cause his cock to twitch. "I have?"

"And I've heard every sex noise this apartment has to offer."

He swallowed hard. She wasn't his type. Not sophisticated enough. Nothing about her said she knew the score. But God help him, he wanted to grab her and kiss her to see what she tasted like. She smelled like wine and trouble. "Sorry about that."

She gave him a sour, schoolmarm look. "I've had enough."

He nodded. "Got it."

She shook a finger at him. "You need to climax quietly."

"Will do." It wasn't like being scolded with a wagging finger was sexy, but coming from her, it felt like fucking foreplay.

"Like me," she said heatedly as if he hadn't agreed. "Have you ever heard me masturbating?"

Sonofabitch, she was killing him. "I haven't had the pleasure."

"That's right, because I orgasm quietly."

Fuck. He wanted to make her come loudly. Hear her sultry, incoherent mews. He glanced at the two behind her. "Are you her support system?"

"Knitting buddies," the other female said, leaning out, making eye contact with him, and then quickly going back to hide behind the queen.

"We're her posse," the man said. "Here to spank ass if needed."

Jackson blinked and brought his gaze back to the fiery beauty standing toe-to-toe with him. On the surface, nothing about her shouted traditional beautiful. But her personality took the term *ordinary*, tossed it into an ocean of glitter, and it came out with the word *extra* dangling from its trunk. Extraordinary. Time to come clean and admit he wasn't her neighbor. "I'll be sure and—"

Annie came up behind him and laid a hand on his shoulder. "Darling, thank you so much for trying and trying and trying," she purred. She held out her hand to the fiery beauty. "Sorry if we disturbed you. You see, it was our first time."

"Oh, I just love firsts," the drag queen said.

His sister smiled at the giant. "Great, then you know how firsts can be. You see, we've been friends for eons. And then, over drinks at the bar earlier this evening, we up and decided to try friends with benefits because neither of us has had any luck in the dating field. And well, between us, things didn't work quite right a few minutes ago. And we had to get creative."

Jackson didn't even blink. He was used to his sister's antics. There was nothing she loved more than a good ruse. Especially if the end result was getting under his skin. And yet, they were close. He'd do anything to protect her, and she'd do anything to annoy him.

The leader of the pack of misfits' eyes widened. "I'll have you know, you got creative with a—"

The drag queen grabbed her shoulder and made a shushing noise.

"What was that you were saying?" Amusement lit up his sister's voice.

Jackson noticed Annie had even gone to the trouble of messing up her hair to add credibility to her lie.

"Nothing," the finger wagger mumbled, sending frosty daggers at Jackson.

He grimaced. Now probably wouldn't be a good time to ask her out.

"Unfortunately, despite the package we had to work with, and his tremendous effort, the sex wasn't up to par," Annie said to the misfit as if they were best friends. "And I simply refuse to fake an orgasm, even for a friend."

Jackson bristled. Common sense said to put a stop to her prank, but ninety-nine percent of the time, his sister was full-on serious about life. Who was he to rain on the one percent when she had fun? Even if the one percent was at his expense.

The drag queen leaned out. "Oh, honey, tell me you misspoke." He flitted his palms as he talked. "The words *fake* and *orgasm* should never be in the same zip code, let alone sentence."

"I wish I had," his sister said. "That's why you heard a lot of thumping but no pleasure. I give him credit for giving it the ol' college try." She opened her purse. "This by the way, darling, is the brochure about the event we were discussing over drinks." She handed the flyer to Jackson. "You're such a dear for participating. Even after. Well. You know." She handed another to the leader of the pack. "You should come." She leaned in and whispered, "There will be men much better looking than him at the auction."

"I can hear you," Jackson said.

Annie stood on her tiptoes and kissed his cheek, whispered in his ear they had a deal, and then sashayed down the hallway to the elevator.

Jackson ground his teeth and counted to ten. Sisters were a total pain in the ass. He glanced at the brochure. Fuck. The thing already had his picture on it. What if he'd said no and stuck to his damn answer? He crumpled it and tossed it toward the entryway trash can. "I'm Jackson. It's nice to meet you." He held out his hand to the fiery one.

"Wendy." She placed her small hand in his palm and surprised him with a firm shake. She pointed toward his sister who stood by the elevator doors. "She has no idea you've had at least three different women up here in an overnight capacity. Shame on you pretending you weren't getting any action so she'd feel sorry for you and agree to be your friend with benefits. It serves you right she found your stroking wanting."

He wanted to explain it hadn't been him, but that would lead to an explanation, and he didn't have time for explanations. He had an important appointment across town. "How do you know they weren't all the same?"

"Really? You can't decipher how I would know that?" Her eyes sparked with indignation.

He grinned. "Enlighten me." So what if he was a few minutes late?

She leaned her head back and closed her eyes. "'Oh...oh...oh...my...God.'"

His dick, which had been at half-mast, stood up and saluted.

She straightened her head and looked him in the eyes.

His stomach did a weird twist. Had this wallflower just faked an orgasm for him?

Before he could reply, she continued, "That was last Friday night's voice. Saturday night's was more like..." Once again, she closed her eyes and tilted her head back. "'Wow. Oh yes. Yes. Yes. Yes. Wow.'" This orgasm was portrayed in a deep, husky voice as Wendy rubbed her hands up and down her body.

Dear God, he wanted to fuck her right here, right now.

Wendy opened her eyes and glared at him.

He cleared his throat. "Saturday night's woman was the same as Friday night's," he explained. "She sounded different because she had a cold."

Wendy straightened her tiara which had gone wildly cockeyed. "Then how do you explain last night's? 'Oh honey, don't stop. Ride me cowboy.'" This orgasm replay was delivered in a syrupy sweet drawl.

He swallowed. Tried not to wonder what *her* orgasmic phrase would be. Hell. "I'm sorry I've been disturbing you. Please, accept my apologies." He'd be sure and have a word with Mitch. He couldn't be upsetting the other tenants.

Wendy straightened, tugged at the bottom of her T-shirt, drawing his eyes to the words scrawled across the chest. *The First Rule of Knit Club...Don't Talk About Knit Club.*

A *knitter.* A little homebody. Sweet and pure as a summer day. Tomorrow, when she was sober, she'd have a titillating story to tell others about the time she told off the cad upstairs.

"I've said what I came to say." Without another word, she turned and marched away.

He watched until she and her shadows stepped into the elevator.

By all accounts, she was plain in her T-shirt, faded jeans, no makeup, and hair yanked back in a ponytail. Nothing that lit a man's sexual fires.

So why did he want to follow her and ask her out for coffee? Or a drink? Or sex?

3

One hour later, the Manhattan Knitters' Club had moved their Friday night gathering to the bar on the corner. Partly because, after returning to Wendy's apartment, they'd found themselves unable to concentrate with no noises coming from the upstairs tenant, but mostly because they'd run out of wine before Eddy had found his knitting groove.

"I know you two are thinking the same, so I'm just going to say it." Eddy took a dainty sip of his third Manhattan. "I smell a rat-bastard in Denmark."

Abigail choked on her margarita. "I think that's just the guy sitting behind you." She pinched her nose and waved her hand in front of her face.

Wendy laughed. The smell of an exploded cologne factory wafted their way from the guy, but that wasn't what Eddy had meant. "I agree," she said to Eddy. "I've been sitting here thinking about it, and the more I do, the more I'm certain there's no way Mr. Upstairs and that woman had just had sex."

"Why?" Abigail asked.

Wendy leaned in and whispered, "Her makeup hadn't been kissed off. Plus, she said he wasn't any good and according to the hoopla I've been hearing, he's damn good at making a woman *feel* damn good." Unless they'd all been faking. But that many award-winning fakers in a row...surely not.

"Exactly." Eddy gave a dramatic sigh. "I could be wrong, but now that I've met Mr. Upstairs, I am certain he is not a lazy lover. In fact, I'd bet my favorite wig he's got a fiery passion burning within that bloody-hot body of his. The kind of passion that could ignite the fire of anyone under the age of eighty. I'm telling you, a guy like that doesn't leave a woman's lipstick on her lips. So why did she lie?"

Wendy's body responded to the idea of her upstairs neighbor having a fiery passion. She could use a little fire in her life. "If they weren't having sex, what was all the thumping about?"

"Why would she say they had done it if they hadn't?" Abigail questioned. She dropped one color of yarn and picked up a new one as she followed an intricate pattern for a sweater. "Where I come from, we don't lie about having the Kool-Aid. We might lie and say we didn't have it, but never that we did. Especially if we didn't. That's just bad manners."

"If they had sex," Wendy said, "there's no way it could have been anything more than a quickie against the wall." Maybe they were burglars. She shook away the theory. Burglars wouldn't have stood there letting them get such a good look at their faces. "Maybe it's quickies that he's not any good at."

Eddy's perfectly plucked eyebrows went heavenward. "You don't do a quickie against the wall with a friend who just allowed benefits to be added to your relationship status." He put his knitting down and surveyed Wendy and Abigail.

"Maybe that's just her personality," Wendy mused. "She did seem a little more uptight than the ones I've been hearing caterwauling night after night. Maybe she's got hang-ups. Maybe that's the only way she'd do it with him. Maybe that's why her dating life sucks."

"Maybe," Eddy said. "Too bad he's not into men. I could find out firsthand if he's all that and a bag of weed."

"I'd volunteer, but I get the impression I'm no more his type than you are," Wendy said.

Abigail made a tsking noise with her tongue. "In Mayhem, we don't have sex just to satisfy our curiosity about a man's abilities. We have to actually like them."

Eddy harrumphed. "Thank God I don't come from where you come from. Half the men I've slept with were out of pure curiosity about the size of their lollipop. What else shall we talk about?"

They all knitted quietly for a moment.

"I have a hottie candidate to join the Manhattan Knitters," Eddy blurted.

Awkward moments of quiet never lingered long around Eddy. He had a big heart and a squirrel-brain. He jumped from subject to subject with ease.

"He's an eleven on a ten-point scale. And I'm sleeping with him. And, bonus." Eddy paused, set his knitting down, and did jazz hands. "He does hair for the rich and famous. I'm pretty sure we could get an appointment with him, and, of course, a killer discount if we allowed him to join the Manhattan Knitters."

"Oh. Are we accepting new members?" Abigail asked. "My new contractor, whom I'm not sleeping with, mentioned he'd like to learn to knit. And I wouldn't mind watching those biceps of his flexing. And I don't know for certain, but I would think he would also give us a discount."

"I'm fine with adding new members, but not lovers." Wendy took a moment to give them a serious look. The kind a mother gives when you've broken her best vase. She took her job as president of the Manhattan Knitters seriously. "Discount or no discount, a love interest today may be tomorrow's scum. New members shouldn't have already seen or ever future see any of us naked."

Eddy flicked a hand at her. "Don't be so stuffy." He glanced at Abigail. "Let's invite your guy and my guy to open mic night, and we can see if we socially click with them enough to ask them to join our club."

Wendy studied Eddy for a minute. "Eddy, your lovers never last. Do you really want to sit around and knit with someone you've humped and dumped?"

He blushed. He never blushed. Was this guy more than a lover? "I can be friends with old lovers. Aaaaaand, don't forget, he does hair for the famous. Did I mention Chasity Kennedy is one of his clients? She is divine, and her hair is a masterpiece."

"I saw she just broke things off with her latest fling. I swear she goes through men quicker than I go through yarn," Abigail said. "I wonder if it's because she's having an affair with the co-star from her last movie. They were seen sharing a limo last week."

Chasity had been great in her film. A dark romantic comedy in which the girl did not get the guy. "And you, Abigail, can you remain friends with an old lover should things heat up and then cool off between you and the construction worker?"

"Bless your heart. I'm from the Midwest. Staying friends with our enemies is what we do best. The kink I see in our plan is, if we ask them to join us during a knitting activity, that might give them the impression they're in the club. We should invite them to a non-knitting activity first and get to know them."

"Knitters don't have non-knitting activities." Eddy placed a palm over his mouth and tittered. "We take our knitting *everywhere*."

"Then how do we get to know them before inviting them to join?" Wendy asked.

Abigail smiled demurely. The kind of smile Wendy had never been able to master. "Well, normally, this is a well-kept family secret, but since Wendy has been known to share shards of her workplace secrets, I guess I can trust you with my family ones. I happen to know a person who knows a guy who could have any and all potential candidates vetted."

Wendy and Eddy's jaws unhinged. Abigail oozed sweetness like espresso oozed caffeine. How in the hell did she know a person who knew a guy about anything?

"Like a background check?" Wendy quizzed.

Abigail went back to her knitting. "Yes, let's call it a background check."

There was a strange vibe coming from Abigail, but since she was concentrating on her knitting, Wendy couldn't read her facial expression for clues. She shrugged it off as one-too-many drinks. "If wannabes have to be vetted to join, it will give the Manhattan Knitters a very exclusive vibe."

"I do like the idea of being exclusive," Eddy said. "After all, one-of-a-kinds shouldn't accept just any Tom, Dick, or Harrietta."

"And you would be okay if your guy doesn't make the cut?" Wendy asked Eddy. Of the three of them, he could be quite temperamental. Once, he'd thrown a ball of yarn at a guy in a crowded bar who'd turned the television from ice skating to football. When it had hit him in the back of the head, a bar fight had ensued. The Manhattan Knitters were no longer allowed in that establishment.

He executed a floppy hand wave-off. "Sisters before misters."

"Abigail?" Wendy waited for Abigail to look at her.

"Yes?"

"Tell us more about your person."

She smiled softly. "My construction worker?"

Wendy shook her head. "Him too, but first, your person who knows a person."

4

T he next day, Jackson's gait had a certain zip to it as he entered Adler Tower, a twenty-story building located in New York City's financial district. In the middle of the lobby, he stopped and breathed in the building's vibe and surveyed his domain like Wendy from 4C had surveyed him last night. Only rather than reflect disdain, he puffed out his chest like a proud dad whose son just signed with a major league baseball team.

The lobby's decorations whispered *lush*, *extravagant*, *rich*. A perfect gateway to the businesses housed within the marbled walls of Adler Tower. His sister's law firm took up space on the nineteenth floor. Jackson's office occupied the entire top floor.

"Good morning, sir." The lobby's receptionist spoke in a perky voice too loud for the subdued setting. "Two Saturdays in a row. You're working hard."

At twenty-two, the receptionist was what his mother would call a work in progress. Then again, Jackson's mother still considered him and his sister works in progress. Mostly because they were unmarried.

"Good morning, Piper. Working hard is a requirement when you're building your empire." Most of the offices in the building were closed on Saturdays, but a few were open. Which meant they needed a receptionist six days a week.

"Your secretary is already here," Piper informed him. "She arrived an hour ago."

Jackson nodded. "She's my office manager, not my secretary. But thank you." He seldom asked Hazel to work on Saturdays. And when he did, he always sent her home at noon and paid her double-time.

Piper's purple lips quirked as if holding back laughter. What was that about? Her moods and thoughts were as chaotic as the spring weather. Hot one day. Cold the next. The only given, she liked to talk. Didn't matter who. Everybody was fair game. Courier. Delivery. Lawyer. Interior decorator. Him. Stop at your own risk. He made it to the elevator without trading further banter with Piper. The door slid open.

"Jackson—my man," said Stone, a guy from the eighth floor. He and his two Marine buddies had recently opened a security company. "You dog, you."

Jackson's gait faltered. The guy usually acknowledged him with a jerk of his head. "Excuse me?"

Stone held up his hands, palms facing Jackson. "No judgment here." He chuckled and kept walking.

As the elevator door closed, Jackson heard Stone say to Piper, "That guy sure knows how to get around."

What the fuck?

When the elevator doors slid open, he stepped directly into his outer office. The domain of his office manager.

She eyeballed him from behind her desk.

He knew that look. He'd done something wrong…again. "What did I do this time?"

She lowered her glasses. "Good morning to you, too."

He bristled. If he had started with good morning, she would have replied, *what's so good about it.* "Good morning." Hazel reminded him of a Sunday school teacher. You simply didn't want to disappoint her with your lack of manners or life choices. "You're looking lovely today," he added to garner some brownie points. "Any idea what has the building buzzing?"

Hazel gave him the stink eye. "As if you don't know." She pinched her lips like she was holding back the rest of her reprimand.

If she *was* holding it back, it wasn't to spare him. She simply wasn't ready to unload yet. "I don't make it a practice to ask questions I know the answer to," he replied.

Hazel had absolutely no filter when it came to her thoughts or opinions. Sort of like Wendy from 4C. The image of her faking an orgasm had plagued his dreams last night and invaded his shower time this morning. Not that he was complaining. A man could do worse for material worthy of a quick jack-off. What was her story? Everyone had a story.

Instead of answering, Hazel held out a clean coffee cup. Her way of avoiding the conversation.

He took the empty cup. "Thank you."

Hazel had informed him when he had hired her that she didn't do coffee. She didn't make it. She didn't serve it. After a heated conversation, which he'd somehow lost, they'd compromised. Hazel made sure he had a clean cup once a week. And he'd bought himself a Keurig which he'd promptly named Hazel. It had pissed his office manager off royally when he would turn it on and say, *Hazel, be an angel and make me a cup of coffee.*

"You're welcome," the human Hazel said.

He didn't move.

"Was there anything else you needed?" she asked.

"An explanation."

"*Page Six*," Hazel said sharply. "See for yourself. I laid a copy of the article on your desk."

For fuck's sake. What did the gossip column have to say about him this morning that had left his office manager in a sour mood?

And the receptionist downstairs smirking?

And Stone referring to him as a dog?

Inside his office, Jackson flipped on Hazel, stuck his coffee cup under the spout, then grabbed the article on his desk. He walked to the blinds, opened them and stood in the sunlight while he read.

Yesterday, we posted that one of New York City's most eligible bachelors was free again. Recent events would suggest it was premeditated. Flyers went up this morning advertising Puppies for the Elderly Charity Ball. HIS TRULY'S face is plastered on the flyer. He is one of their six featured bachelors to be auctioned off. Did he dump the beautiful Chasity Kennedy to get back in the limelight as one of the city's most beautiful and eligible men? According to Chasity, that's exactly what happened. His ego can't allow him to be off the market for very long. He loves attention, and what better way to get said attention than allow himself to be auctioned off to the highest bidder? Especially one for such a good cause. Placing orphaned puppies into the homes of the elderly. We can't wait to see who buys him.

The article left a vile taste in Jackson's mouth. "Son of a bitch." He tossed the paper in the trash. Why in the hell had Chasity spoken to a reporter about their breakup? The whole thing made him irritable and exposed. What had even possessed him to date an actress? His next love interest would be someone low key.

Like downstairs Wendy. The glib thought hit something inside of him. Damn. *What's wrong with me?*

He dated women like Chasity because they knew the score. Their hearts were as jaded as his. Wendy's heart no doubt belonged inside the princess of a Disney movie. That ridiculous tiara she'd worn last night shouted as much. So why did he keep going back to the feeling of her hand on his chest and her accusation in his ears?

He pushed the intercom button. "Get Annie on the line...please." This was his sister's fault. She's the one who had had the flyers printed up with his face before he'd said yes.

"On it."

When his phone rang, he grabbed it. "Have you seen *Page Six*?"

Annie laughed. "I have. Isn't it the most lovely thing?"

"In what universe is it *lovely*?"

"The free advertising universe."

He groaned. "Did you feed the story to them?" Maybe Chasity hadn't been ambushed by reporters. What woman wants the world to know she's been dumped?

"I'm wounded yet flattered. I had no idea you thought *me* capable of that kind of sneakiness."

He sat down and propped his feet on his massive oak desk. "You damn well better keep your end of our bargain and buy me at auction."

A long moment of silence stretched his nerves.

"About that?" she finally said.

He stilled, knowing what would happen next. Knowing it as well as he knew his middle name. His sister had absolutely no follow through outside of her career. Still... "No," he said.

"No, what?"

"No, you can't back out on our agreement." She would never learn personal accountability if no one ever demanded it of her.

"I have to." She didn't sound the least bit upset at having to tell him the bad news. "It's against the rules of the charity. Those in a leadership role can't bid. I can't even buy a man for myself."

He dropped his feet to the carpeted floor. He didn't care if it was against the rules. She was a lawyer. She could find a loophole. "Then take me out of the auction."

"I can't do that either."

"Why not?" He wasn't the only eligible bachelor in New York City. Hell, a lot of the guys loved the process. Got a kick out of women bidding on them. The damn Marines downstairs would no doubt agree to participate.

"Because the advertisement is already out there. You're the face of the auction. If I take you out now, I'll be sued for false advertising. My phone's been ringing off the hook this morning with women wanting to know where they can buy tickets. One of the callers said she had the pleasure of meeting you last night."

Son of a bitch. That had to be the married woman Mitch had banged. God. She'd all but asked him if he was available for an occasional tryst. "Then you better come up with someone trustworthy to buy me at auction."

"Why not let the highest bidder win?"

Hell no. He didn't adhere to the philosophy *whatever shall be, shall be.* He was all about: *most of life's failures occur by people who failed to plan.* "We've had this discussion. I'm not having it again."

His sister gave a heavy sigh. "Because you're afraid of commitment. God. You really need to get over that. Just because Mom's had more spouses than children doesn't mean you or I are going to be the same way."

"Um, I don't see a ring on your finger."

"That's because I haven't found a man I want to wake up next to the rest of my life. That's not to say I'm not actively looking. I am. Trust me."

"Find someone to buy me and sell me back to myself, or I'm not showing up for the auction." He sounded brusque and self-indulgent, but it couldn't be helped.

"Wouldn't that be a splendid little scandal?"

He rubbed his hand down his cheek. "Damn it. Please tell me you have someone in mind, and you're just seeing how many of my buttons you can push."

"How about Hazel?"

Jackson choked on the coffee he'd taken a sip of. "She doesn't do coffee, and I can guarantee you she doesn't do bail-your-boss-out-of-a-bad-situation duties. In fact, she delights in watching me get myself in them and then struggle to get out of them. I think she has a side gig with the devil."

A giggle floated through the phone. "If you'd pay her more, maybe she'd be more in tune to helping you. She's a lovely woman."

"I pay her extremely well." Discretion didn't come cheap. When he made deals, he had to have someone he trusted handling the details. Leaked information could cause a project to drown in less than an inch of water. Which was how he'd purchased the Adler building out from under his competition.

"How about your neighbor?" Annie said in a singsongy voice.

He cocked his head. "What neighbor are you referring to?" He lived in a penthouse that occupied the entire upper floor. "I don't have neighbors."

"I'm talking about the one who thinks you're having sex every night."

His feet hit the floor. "Wendy?" He tried to say her name like he hadn't been thinking of her nonstop since meeting her. Hadn't been thinking about her soft lips on his.

"Is that her name? She was adorable, didn't you think?" His sister sounded casual. Too casual. But why? She didn't know Wendy any better than he did.

"I didn't think any such thing." He shrugged. Having dated an actress, he knew the importance of method acting. If you wanted someone to think you weren't interested, you had to include the body language while responding. Even if they couldn't see your body language, it would come through in your voice. "And I can't ask her. I don't know her."

A sisterly sigh came across loud and clear. One that said she could see through his line of crap. "I got the impression you'd like to get to know her."

Obviously, he wasn't a great actor. "What in the hell gave you that impression?"

"The way your mouth hung down to your belt buckle the whole time she ripped into you. And the fact you didn't tell her she had the wrong guy."

"I did that so as not to ruin your fun." He turned on his computer and waited for it to boot. "Besides, she was drunk and agitated. I saw no reason to excite her further. Being polite to the inebriated isn't an admission of interest." He logged in and opened his calendar.

"Or you thought she was cute all hot and bothered, and you couldn't think of a thing to say, so you said nothing at all."

"More like I had some place to be and didn't have time for explanation." That and he wasn't used to being at a loss for words around a woman. "She's not my type. I prefer blondes."

Annie scoffed. "Your type bores you after thirty minutes. Maybe *not your type* is what you need to give a try." The teasing was gone from her voice. In its place, sisterly concern.

"She belongs to a knitting club, wears a tiara, and travels with a posse of misfits. I'm not asking someone like her out on a date." Even as the assertion settled between them, he had a desire to make a liar out of himself.

"Date? Who said anything about a date? You're thinking about her, aren't you? She got under your skin."

Christ, Annie was annoying with her ability to get information he didn't want to give. "You're wrong. Did you see her?"

"Umm...yes. Adorable. Likeable. Dateable."

"I don't do adorable. I do sophisticated." And maybe if he repeated that to himself enough times, his body would get on board.

"Fine. Don't ask her out on a date. Simply ask her to come to the auction and purchase you."

He tried to imagine Wendy and her gang standing in front of the stage in the massive ballroom of the NYC Vandivort Hotel, bidding on eligible bachelors. No way would they blend in. Not that he cared if they stuck out like daisies at the Rose Bowl Parade, as long as the evening ended with him not beholden to some woman who had bought him with designs on attaching his last name to her first name. Or some woman in hopes of enjoying a roll in the sack behind her husband's back. Like the woman who'd lost her wedding ring under Mitch's bed. "Do you think she would do that?"

"I think the tiara she wears points to a woman who dreams of finding her Prince Charming. She'd find the idea of attending a ball and bidding on a man to keep him out of the clutches of an evil queen a fun adventure."

He rubbed the back of his neck. His sister saw Wendy as a Disney Princess as well. "All the more reason she should be off-limits. She'd probably see herself as the woman the prince falls in love with once she's saved him from the villain."

"You *are* so full of yourself. News flash, not every woman thinks you're all that and a Gucci purse. I'm willing to bet *you're* not *her* type."

"What do you think her type is?" What in the ever-loving fuck was he doing, hoping she said corporate asshole?

"Someone not afraid to be seen with a woman who wears a tiara and rocking a pair of sweats."

"Do you think she really goes out in public in that thing?"

"Probably. Ask her for help. You'd possibly be doing her a favor. I doubt she has many opportunities to attend fancy shindigs."

"Fine. I'll tell her the truth about me, and explain your stupid prank, and ask her. But if she says no, then you better have another plan."

"Don't tell her the truth."

He scowled. "Why the hell would I allow her to continue to believe I'm her rude upstairs neighbor if I want to ask a favor of her?"

"Because wouldn't it be fun to have to work at getting a woman to like you? One who has a bad first impression of you *and* has no idea you're loaded?"

Fun, no. But interesting...maybe. "I'll think about it." He did like the idea of knowing a woman liked him for him before she discovered anything about his bank account.

5

Monday at closing time, Wendy still sat at her desk, staring tiredly at a contract, longing to go home and take a power nap. *Wake up, brain.* The command hadn't worked the first fifty thousand times she'd chanted it today, so she wasn't sure why she thought it would this time.

And it didn't.

Mr. Upstairs had been at it again last night. *So much for sexy assurances.*

Now that she knew what he looked like, the noise had taken on a whole new keep-her-awake dimension. She could see his handsome face as he grunted. Imagine it was her that he was making come again and again and again. And again. Four freaking agains. A bit over the top. But wouldn't it be sublime if Mr. Upstairs... She shook her head. *Holy Devil's Kiss, I should have never gone up there.*

She resisted an urge to rub her eyes. Smeared mascara only worked for raccoons. She took a sip of her sixth cup of coffee since lunch and refocused on the papers in front of her.

The booty-call contract between Penelope and Mitch was getting a face-lift. "Hey, Tom," she said to the guy on the other side of her cubicle. "What do you know about the New York City Angelinos?" Tom never came to work on time, so he never got to leave on time.

"Only that they are related to the Angelinos in Boston."

Wendy's stomach squeezed. Abigail's kissing-cousin comment had hit a nerve with Wendy, and, over the weekend, she'd dug a little deeper to see if the two families were related.

Short answer. Yep.

While on the surface, the New York City Angelinos appeared to be legit business folk and into philanthropy, under the surface, they'd been sent by the matriarch to take over territory from a rival family. Or, at least, that's what they'd said on the true crime podcast she listened to. She really wished she hadn't listened to that episode.

"Why are you inquiring?" Tom asked.

"A friend is naming her child Angelino, and I thought the name sounded familiar."

"I'd tell her to pick a different name. That name could get you killed."

Wendy exhaled a silent breath. It didn't get any juicier than proofing contracts for a mob family. Or scarier. Her boss Mr. Morgenstern's instruction that she use John Smith as her signature sure as hell made a lot more sense in context. He was protecting his asset. Her.

Unfortunately, with knowledge came a heaping dose of trepidation. Odds were high, if she missed something on one of their contracts, her life expectancy would plummet.

She reread the revised booty-call contract, compared the dates and numbers against a calendar, and scanned the notes provided with the legal document. Double-checked the address. Double-checked the spelling of everyone's names. Triple-checked the sidepiece's name. Mitchell Travinni. Two ls, two ns. She left Penelope marked as single. That had been one of the requested changes.

Wendy placed the contract in an envelope and gave it to a mailroom clerk. "Julie, can you see that this goes out today?"

Julie nodded. "I have a courier on his way right now. I'll have him drop it off with the other package going out for the boss."

Part of Wendy felt sorry for Mitchell Travinni. The contract leaned heavily in the favor of the other party. She hoped he knew whom he'd crawled into bed with.

As Wendy turned to leave, she bumped into Mr. Morgenstern, her shortish, weight-challenged, and perpetually sweaty boss. "Excuse me, Mr. Morgenstern." How long had he been standing behind her?

He gave her a long-suffering sigh. "Working overtime...again?"

Wendy glanced at her watch. An hour past quitting time. "Perfection can't always be made to fit into an eight-to-five schedule." As a rule, she insisted it *did* fit between those hours on Mondays, because Monday nights were when she self-indulged. Her way of treating herself for surviving a Monday.

But today she had made an exception due to lack of focus.

On Monday spa nights, she had a ritual. She would order in dinner, drink Devil Kiss martinis, give herself a facial, binge watch the Hallmark Channel or knit or both, and end with some good old-fashioned masturbation. Or as old-fashioned as masturbation can be when one is using the latest sex toy to achieve a quick climax.

It was hard to dread Mondays when they always ended with smooth skin and an orgasm.

Mr. Morgenstern adjusted his tie. "Probably best you did spend some extra time on this contract." A sheen of sweat appeared on his brow.

How in the hell had a nervous ninny like him gotten in bed with the mob? "I triple-checked everything. There are no flaws." She walked to the bank of elevators.

Standing at the elevator, Wendy heard Julie, the clerk, laugh. *Did Morgenstern say something humorous?* Wendy tried to remember a time he'd said anything to her that remotely tickled her funny bone. She couldn't. He was a lot of things. Amusing not on the list.

Just as the elevator doors opened, the woman said, "I heard she's the president of the Manhattan Knitters' Club."

Wendy stiffened and clutched her purse tighter. Not because she was embarrassed, but because they were talking about her. Instead of stepping inside the elevator, she stuck out her hand to keep it from closing and listened.

"Figures," her boss replied. "A boring hobby for a boring woman."

That's not nice to say. Am I boring?

"It's no wonder she racks up more overtime than a lawyer chasing billable hours," he said.

Why was her boss conversing with Julie instead of being his normal buttload of piss?

"She never leaves with the other proofreaders," Julie added.

"Obviously, she doesn't have a life. Do you think she's ever had a date? Or sex?" Mr. Morgenstern asked.

"Maybe." Julie sounded a tad uncomfortable with the turn of the discussion. "I bet if she wanted, she could get a date."

Her boss sneezed and blew his nose loudly. "I'll bet you fifty dollars she doesn't bring anyone to the company picnic this weekend."

Julie didn't respond right away. Like maybe she'd gotten herself into a conversation she wished she hadn't. Then she chuckled. "I'm probably going to lose, but you're on."

Wendy frowned, the nose of her self-esteem plowing into the floor. They truly found her boring. How could that be? She owned two tiaras. *Boring people don't own head jewelry.* She resisted the urge to give them a piece of her mind. Not because she was timid, but because she needed her job. Telling off the boss would be a quick way to unemployment, and until she had another—safer position—lined up, she needed the paycheck.

She stepped into the elevator. Besides, the joke was on her boss. She planned on bringing Eddy to the picnic. Who in the hell was Morgenstern to call her boring just because she liked to knit and was damn good at her job? What an ass.

Two hours later, Wendy sat in her living room with the latest charcoal-craze beauty mask on her face, her second Devil's Kiss of the night in her hand, and the Hallmark Channel coaxing her thoughts away from mob-boss-ordered assassinations and toward romance.

The only flaw in her evening—the new Chinese place she'd ordered from had yet to show with her vegetable fried rice and eggrolls.

What if a hitman hijacked the delivery boy, killed him, and he's now coming here to off us? Eliminate those in the know. Oh God, that could happen.

Ever since listening to the podcast on the Angelinos, Wendy's internal monologue had become quite vocal. Talking to Wendy like a new freaked-out best friend.

Deciding her inner voice had a legit point, Wendy grabbed her phone to call and ask what her delivery person looked like.

A knock at the door stopped her dialing and breathing. Time stood still until her stomach growled, telling her to cut the Eddy-worthy theatrics.

Laughing at herself, she padded barefoot to the door and swung it open. "I was about—" Her words died a quick death. Damn. Why hadn't she glanced through the peephole before swinging the door wide open? "You!" Mr. Upstairs had come downstairs. Did she have her television on too loud?

"In the flesh." He gave her a smile that drew her attention to his perfect cheekbones and gray eyes.

If she could have, she would have responded. The problem was with her tongue. It suddenly seemed too big for her mouth. Had he been this perfectly tall Friday night? Wine-drunk Wendy wasn't all that detail oriented.

He placed his hand on her doorframe and relaxed his stance. "I'm assuming under all that gunk on your face is the *you* I came to see."

She touched her face and horror trampled her. Dear God, she no doubt looked like a monster from a science fiction movie. "What is it you want?" What else could she say? No way would she try to explain her green face. "Were my knitting needles clanking together too loudly?"

An expression she couldn't read crossed his face. "Not at all."

The elevator bell dinged. He pushed away from the door and glanced around as if worried someone might see them chatting.

"That will be my dinner."

No one got off. Wendy's skin twitched. Who stayed on? A hitman for the mob boss's daughter? Had he heard her and realized she wasn't alone?

"May I come in?"

Wendy's brain jumped away from worries of mob hits and back to sexy man. *Speaking of sexy...* She glanced down at her bare feet. Toes not polished. Her bare legs with a piece of toilet paper stuck to her shin to stop the bleeding from a razor mishap. Her tattered robe that covered her skimpy tank top and SpongeBob boxer pajama shorties. Ugh. "If you're here to say you're sorry for keeping me up last night, don't bother."

Here's an idea. Add having your very own booty-call man to your List of Things To Do Before You Turn Thirty. That list could use some sparkle.

Gah. Even her internal monologue thought she was boring.

Jackson's brows squished, which did nothing to diminish his good looks. "I kept you up last night?" He sounded genuinely surprised by the fact. Of course, it was a façade. He'd been there in all the noisy action. He had to know. Probably had done it on purpose.

She wrinkled her forehead which made her mask crack. Damn it. She didn't like for her mask to crack. She liked to peel it off all in one piece. "You and Prissy Moan kept me awake." Prissy Moan had been the most irritating of all the women she'd listened to so far.

He ran a hand down the side of his face. "Prissy moan?" The two words coming from his lips sounded like rocks rubbing together.

She poked him in the chest. "Really? We're doing this again?"

The beginning of a smile tugged at his sexy lips. She glanced away. How old was he? Maybe thirty? Old enough to know how to be a good neighbor. "I guess we are."

Fine. She leaned her head back, closed her eyes, and conjured up last night's disembodied voice. "'Oh, my goodness. Darling, that's a *cupcake* in a world of muffins.'"

"A cupcake?" Mr. Upstairs croaked.

Wendy ignored the interruption. She placed one palm on her chest and the other at the vee of her legs and conjured his face. "'My goodness. My. GOODNESS. God love it, that's the *spot*.'" The woman's monologue had been irritating as hell at four in the morning. "'Ohhhhh, Cupcake. Yes. Yes. Yes.'" Wendy opened her eyes and dropped her hands to her sides. "Or something like that." She really hoped he couldn't tell she'd turned herself on.

Mr. Upstairs looked a little red around the cheekbones, and his lips were pinched. Did he not like having his one-night stand referred to as prissy or did he not like Wendy knowing his package had been referred to as a cupcake?

He cleared his throat. "If you'd invite me in, I'd tell you why I'm here."

"As you can see, Cupcake, I'm not really dressed for receiving company." She spoke in the prissy tone of a high-society woman.

He gave her a thorough look, his gaze stopping in the vicinity of her chest and hanging out there far longer than necessary.

She glanced down to see what the fuss was about. It wasn't like she had cleavage that induced drooling.

Damn it. A chunk of hardened dark chocolate sat like a neon sign at the crease of her boobs. She yanked together the lapels of her robe.

His lips curled. "I think we're way past worrying about proper attire for the receiving of company."

Why-oh-why had he shown up tonight? For all things that were holy, she had gunk on her face. Sighing, she pushed her hair out of her eyes. Her hand came in contact with a roller. *Noooo.* Her ego fainted. Not only face-slime but sporting pink Velcro rollers. *Just call me Ms. Gorgeous.* She took a breath. There wasn't a damn thing she could do about her appearance. Time to get rid of him. "I don't make a habit of asking strangers into my apartment. Goodbye." She tried to shut the door, but his foot got in the way.

"I'm not really a stranger. You know my mating habits. That makes us chummier than all of my closest friends."

She pressed her lips together and stepped back. As he walked by, she took out her phone and sent a text to Eddy. *5C in my apartment. Rescue needed in twenty minutes if you don't hear from me.* A girl had to be safe. "You've got twenty minutes, then the police will show up unless I let my friend know you're gone, and I'm safe."

His lips flattened like he found her safety precautions ridiculous. "Which friend? The tall one or the shy one?" He stepped inside and shut her front door.

"The tall. And just because he wears dresses doesn't mean he can't kick some ass when the need arises. He's a police officer." Technically, that wasn't a lie. Eddy had played the part of a police officer once in a school production.

Jackson folded his arms. "Really? Him? The guy with the tiara?"

She walked over to the couch and pulled a knitting needle out of her knitting bag. She turned and pointed it at him. "I'm not afraid to use this." She owned a gun, a pink BB pistol, but it was in her bedroom. The adorable thing used to belong to her mom. Wendy's stomach twisted. It had become hers the day her parents died in an avalanche while skiing in Colorado. "Believe me, you don't want your junk speared with a knitting needle."

Ouch. Wow. Would we really do that?

If push came to shoving the needle where the sun didn't shine, then yes, she'd do that.

He went a little white. "Noted."

Lucky for him, the guy didn't appear to be planning a murder. She glanced at her watch. "You have seventeen minutes to tell me why you're here."

He stepped farther into the room and leaned against the wall that separated the living space from the kitchen. "I have a favor to ask."

She picked up her drink with her free hand and took a sip. "I'm listening."

"I have been roped into being a bachelor at a charity ball. I hate these kinds of events because of the type of women who are usually doing the bidding."

"And what kind of women would that be?"

"Married or looking to be married."

"And that makes them undesirable in your eyes?" She wanted to make sure she understood what he was saying. Her blood wasn't all going to her brain. Some of it was down south, making her private parts aware of how damn sexy Jackson from 5C was.

"It makes them not for me."

"How do I come into the equation?" Beneath her lashes, she checked him for additional flaws. The obvious one being his lack of sexual social manners. As far as she could tell, he had no physical failings. Handsome. Nice body beneath a fitted suit. What did he do for a living?

She didn't date certain career types. For instance, she did not get hot for police officers the way Abigail did. That career was too risky. The last thing she would ever do was fall in love with someone who was at a greater risk of dying than the average person. Not that she thought she deserved love. She didn't. Ever.

"I want you to bid on me and win me," he said crisply.

She blinked. Lowered the knitting needle. "First, I can't afford to buy you at auction. Second, what makes you think I'd want to if I could? Third, why don't you see me as a marriage-wannabe risk?" The question made her heart squeeze. Did he think her so pathetic that she must have surely given up on the dream of marriage? If he had, he'd be wrong. She liked the idea of marriage. Of deserving happy ever after. But she also firmly believed she didn't deserve those things.

Cupcake gave her a smile, one that simmered with charm and caused her belly to constrict. "I'll give you the purchase money upfront and make the trouble worth your while."

She took another quick sip of her drink and another, and another, not stopping until the glass ran out of liquid courage. "And the marriage part? Aren't you afraid I'd buy you and then go all *Fatal Attraction*-like if you didn't want to marry me?"

He grimaced. "I'm pretty sure you don't even like me. You think I'm a playboy because of my rotating door upstairs. Which you'd be right. I am a man about town. Will probably never settle down. Having said that, I'm sure I'll never make your short list of possible husbands."

"Since a truer statement has never been uttered, I can't think of a thing you could give me to make it worth my while to help you. After all, I asked you to keep the noise down upstairs, and you haven't. Although, I'm sure last night was just you trying to fix your ego after your friend told you that you weren't any good in bed."

"What if I guarantee that you'll never be kept awake again?"

She perked up and then perked down. That was an offer too good to be true.

I can think of something he could give you that would be worth your while.

Wendy ignored her inner voice and walked into the kitchen.

Before you ignore me, hear me out. What if...we asked him to be our booty-call man?

The thought wasn't awful. Wendy mulled it over while she made drinks. "I'm listening." The words were meant for her inner monologue, but when she turned, there stood Cupcake.

"I can promise you no more sex noises from above," he said.

She handed him a drink and stared into the pale orange liquid in her martini glass. "What are you going to do, buy me a pair of noise-cancelling headphones?"

His eyes widened. "Would that work?"

She shook her head. "They bother my ears. Too uncomfortable to sleep in. So, unless you plan on becoming celibate, I'm at a loss as to how you can keep that promise."

He laughed. She found herself liking his laugh. It was part boyish, part sexy man. "You? At a loss? I was beginning to think you had an answer for everything."

That's what her last boyfriend had accused her of. Said no guy could ever live up to her unrealistic expectations. Not true. The perfect man would. "I tend to know a lot." Her dad had been a perfect prince charming for her mom. He hadn't had any of the flaws

Wendy kept finding in the men she dated. "But not everything."

Jackson ran a hand through his hair. "Good to know there are some things you don't have an answer for."

"Being critical of me isn't helping your cause."

"I can't explain how I'll guarantee the noise upstairs will cease, but I promise you it will if you help me out."

She returned to the living room and sat on the arm of her couch. "Fair enough, *but* not enough of an incentive. I have knit club on Friday nights and bingo on Saturdays." She didn't have bingo but wanted to see his expression when she said she did.

Surprise registered in his eyes, followed by something she couldn't decipher.

"How about if I sweeten the deal and buy you a new gown for the ball?"

"Do you *really* think you can *buy* my participation with a ball gown?" It's not like she had buttloads of opportunities to wear a fancy dress outside of the auction he wanted her to attend. And she didn't exactly have a lot of extra closet space to store one for future buy-me-at-auction occasions. "Do I get to pick the gown?"

His lips twitched. "I'm certainly not going to try and pick one for you."

Hell. Maybe she'd say yes. Buy an expensive gown, and then sell it afterward and use the money to help Abigail stock the yarn store she planned on opening in a few weeks. "Any gown?" Or use the money to pad her emergency savings account.

"Any gown."

"An Armani."

He shrugged. "If that's what you like."

She chewed on her bottom lip. Too easy. No way would she say yes—yet. He needed to sweat before she agreed. He'd cost her a lot of sleep. "Do you have any idea what Armani is?" The brand was on her brain because the updated mob contract demanded that Mr. Booty-Call, Mitch somebody, wear Armani suits when he came for their sexy-time visits.

Cupcake drained his drink. "I do believe my sister wore Armani to last year's auction."

She perked up. His sister? How many sisters did he have? Did he have a living mom and dad, too? Any brothers? Those were all details on her perfect-man chart. "Did she tell you how much it cost?" Her perfect man could be a five on a scale of one-to-ten in looks as long as he had a family she loved. Not that the man standing in front of her was a five in looks. Nope. He'd gotten an extra helping of handsome when the angels had dished that stuff out on the day he was born.

Cupcake hooked his thumbs in his pant pockets, drawing her eyes where they didn't need to go. Everything about his suit fit like a glove. The result breath-catching.

"If she wore it," he drawled, "it cost a lot. She doesn't do cheap. I'll buy you an Armani gown if you'll buy me at the auction."

Wendy tore her gaze away and walked to her window. She glanced out at the view of other buildings.

Jackson walked up behind her. "Did you know tenants of this building have one of the best views in the city?"

His deep voice reminded her of a smooth bourbon. And his scent of a summer thunderstorm. "It's pretty grand." She pulled her phone out of her pocket and sent Eddy a text. *All is good.* "I'm kind of surprised someone hasn't turned it into luxury apartments."

Her phone dinged. A message from Eddy. *Honey! I'm dying here. Dish as soon as he's gone.*

Cupcake fingered one of her curlers, causing it to come undone. He handed it to her. "Sorry."

Wendy toyed with the sticky roller. The set had belonged to Mom. There were much easier ways to get curls these days but using them made Wendy feel close to her. "I'll need to—"

A knock at the front door sent her scurrying that direction. "Who is it?" she asked in a voice too breathless for such little movement.

"Delivery for Wendy Travis."

She opened the door and frowned at the delivery guy. "You're late."

He shrugged. "It happens."

Not bothering with a scathing reply, she grabbed the food, shut the door, and dropped it on her kitchen counter before returning to her living room. She stopped in front of Cupcake and smiled. "As I was saying, I'll need to think about your offer."

"What's there to think about?"

"My other demands." Was she really considering asking him to be her booty-call contract man?

He widened his stance. "What are those?"

Do it. He'll stop thinking of you as boring.

Don't rush me. Wendy liked to think about her decisions. Make sure she hit her choices from every angle. Proofread them for errors.

Boring.

"I don't know yet. I need time to consider my options."

He blew out a minty-fresh breath. "When will I have your decision?"

"Wednesday night. I'll come upstairs and give it to you in person." She really wanted to get a peek at his bedroom. See if it looked like a room you'd find in a brothel. Mirrors on the ceiling. Black satin sheets. One of those white furry rugs.

He glanced away. Fidgeted with the watch on his wrist. "I'll come to you."

Interesting. Was he afraid she'd run into one of his gazillion women? Had him and his friend gone back to being just friends? "If you insist. Shall we say seven?"

"Deal."

6

Jackson stood on the other side of Wendy's door and scratched his head. It wasn't the fact she'd had goop all over her face that had him feeling off-center. Hell, he'd grown up with a girly-girl sister. He understood the whole facial mask thing. But hearing her ask for an Armani gown and then ask for time to think had spun him in a double upside-down loop.

Why the stall? He would've bet one of his Manhattan condos she didn't give two flips about fashion.

He had assumed she'd see the invitation as a treat. One to jump all over with enthusiasm. Not because it was him asking, his ego wasn't that big, but because it was something out of the ordinary to liven up her life. *Bingo!* The woman played weekly bingo.

And what in the hell had Mitch been doing at the apartment last night? Jackson had moved him to another apartment. One that was over the furnace room so Mitch's activities wouldn't disturb Wendy and her wayward knitters. Was he going to have to kick Mitch out altogether? Might not be a bad idea.

Jackson shoved concerns about Mitch to the back of his brain and walked to the elevators. Once inside, he pulled out his phone and called his sister. "She has to think about it."

"Who has to think about what?"

"Wendy? She has to think about what she wants out of the deal if she says yes." He wasn't sure why this threw him. Hell, he negotiated deals daily. No one ever agreed to the first offer. Why had he expected Wendy to be any different?

His sister laughed. "I like that gal. She's got spunk. I knew she wouldn't see you as husband material. If she did, she would've been all over the offer."

Her words didn't soothe the way they should have. "If she doesn't see me as husband material, it's probably because you told her I wasn't any good in bed." Damn, but he wanted to set Wendy straight on that belief.

Annie laughed. "You're welcome. When did she say she'd give you an answer?"

"Wednesday night."

"What did you offer her as an incentive since your face didn't get the job done and word is out you're a lousy lover?"

"A ball gown."

"And?"

He stepped outside and signaled a taxi. "Why does there have to be an and? Isn't a damn Armani ball gown enough?"

"Armani? Whose idea was that?" The pitch of her voice told him she was highly amused.

"Hers."

"I'll be damned. That girl's got some style hidden under those frumpy sweats. You should offer her a day spa as well. The works. Makeup, hair, mani-pedi, and shoes. You can't put a girl in an Armani without the right shoes. Oh...and accessories."

A taxi edged toward the curb. He hopped in and gave the driver his address. "Accessories?" He loosened his tie. How much was this damn auction going to cost him?

"Jewelry, purse, and a diamond tiara. Yes. That will get her to say yes. Any girl who sits around knitting in a fake tiara will love a diamond tiara. Or one in a stone that matched her eyes. That is if you remember what color they were. Do you recall?"

"Blue."

"What color are mine?"

"I don't know. Green. Brown."

His sister laughed. He realized too late that had been a test to see how much he remembered about Wendy. "Sapphires then," she enthused. "Buy her a tiara with sapphires and give it to her tomorrow night before she's had a chance to respond on Wednesday. That will tip the scales in your favor in case she's leaning toward no. Which she probably is, because I'm sure you presented your offer in the most condescending way possible."

"I didn't present it in a condescending manner." He hadn't sounded like he thought he was superior, had he?

"You wouldn't even recognize the tone if you were listening for it."

She might have a point. Shit. "Real sapphires?"

She sighed the sigh of a disappointed mentor. "You did not just ask that."

He blew out a breath. "Real it is."

"You didn't tell her who you were, did you?"

"No. You told me not to."

"Good. Whatever you do, don't."

"Why?" He should have already told her he wasn't the snake-in-the-grass that lived upstairs. Wasn't Cupcake.

God. What man wants his cock referred to as a cupcake? Now that he thought about it, why exactly hadn't he come clean? Sure, his sister had told him not to, but since when did he listen to her advice when it came to women? The obvious answer was that he enjoyed listening to 4C fake orgasms. That and his brain failed to fully function around her.

"Thinking you're a womanizer will protect her from falling in love with you while she enjoys the grand adventure of dressing up and bidding thousands of dollars on a man. Unless you're ready to search for love and you think she might be the one. In that case, tell her everything."

Hell no, he didn't want Wendy to fall in love with him. He'd have no fucking idea how to handle unwanted emotions from someone like her without breaking her in the process. His sister had a valid point. If it meant not accidentally hurting Wendy, then he'd swallow his pride and let her think he was a cad. "If Wendy says no, I'm not doing your damn auction."

She laughed in the irritating way only sisters could pull off. "Of course, you will."

7

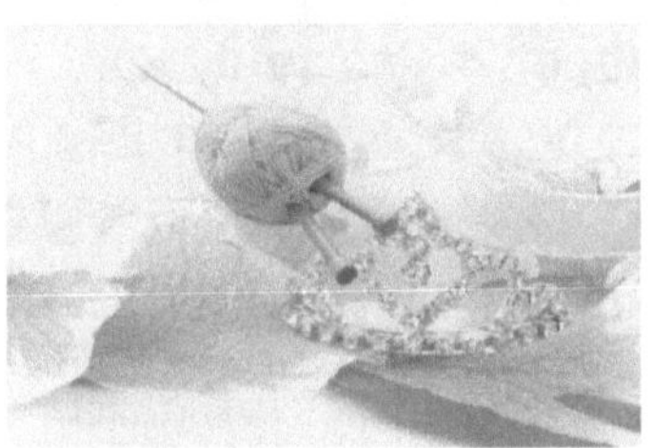

T uesday morning, Wendy poked her head through Mr. Morgenstern's open door. "You wanted to see me, sir." His secretary hadn't been at her desk.

Her boss glanced up, frowned, shoved a stack of papers in his desk drawer, and slammed it shut. "Come in."

She did. Not once in all the time she'd worked for him had she been summoned by him. "How may I help you?" His office looked like a page out of *How to Decorate a Dickweed's Workspace*. Everything shouted *I have money but no class*. The guy even had a leopard print couch. She wasn't surprised. She'd heard rumors about him bringing his lovers back to Contracts R Us after hours for a little scene-playing sex.

"Have a seat." He lit a fat cigar and blew a ring of smoke in her direction.

She coughed and waved the smoke away. Damn it. Now her outfit would need to be dry cleaned. She took a seat on the edge of the black leather chair. Tried not to wonder if any sex acts had taken place there. She placed her palms in her lap, so they didn't fidget and waited for him to speak.

He pulled at his tie. "A mistake has been uncovered."

All her calm whooshed out of her. "A mistake?" What mistake? She'd been so careful. "On a contract?" She couldn't afford to be fired or killed. Financially speaking, this was a great job. And the perks were superb. Living speaking, she had a lot of breathing left to do before cashing in her life chips.

He took out his handkerchief and mopped sweat off his brow. "In a manner of speaking."

Shit. Shit. Shit. "Which one?"

His beady eyes pinned her with disgust. "You signed an Angelino contract with your name as the proofreader. Which means you now have your first strike. Two strikes and you're history."

Holy Devil's Kiss. When? She recalled how freaking tired she'd been the prior day. "Yesterday's contract?" This was Cupcake's fault.

"I wasn't told which contract. All I know is the inconsistency in the proofreader's name came to the attention of the matriarch of the Angelino family. She's not happy. Our ability to handle her contracts under the radar is why she hired us."

Wendy's mouth opened but words didn't tumble out. Her lungs were squeezed tight, like they were in the trunk of a mother elephant who thought her baby was in danger.

Hell. It was one thing for her to glibly worry that a hit would be placed on her if she made a mistake with the contract—a whole other for her boss to be sweating like a pig in front of her while he mentioned the sensitivity of said contract. "I'm so sorry." The three words croaked out in a raspy tone. Was his secretary home sick, or had she disappeared like Pencil Thin from cubicle 33? Oh God. Had Pencil Thin made a mistake on the contracts? Was that why he'd failed to show up for work one day? Was he in hiding? Fearful for his life?

Mr. Morgenstern cleared his throat. "An associate of Ms. Angelino would like to meet with you."

Meet...with a mob boss's associate? Oh, hell no. That wasn't happening. She'd watched enough crime shows to know better than to let the bad guys know you know what they look like. If her outfit hadn't needed to go to the dry cleaner before, it certainly did now...to get the smell of fear out of it.

I bet Pencil Thin also made a mistake and was summoned to meet with an associate. I bet that's why he's in hiding. We should go into hiding.

Wendy fanned herself with her hand. "I don't think that's a good idea." She placed her hands on the arms of her chair and was about to stand when Mr. Morgenstern pounded the desk with his fist. She collapsed back into the seat.

"No isn't a fucking option. I will let you know what day and time works for the associate. Under no circumstances will you be too busy to make this meeting happen. Do you understand?"

Wendy waited for her heart to settle. It took a while because the thing was down around her toes. This was not okay. Being placed in this position was not okay. No way in hell was she going down without a fight.

As if reading her mind, he added, "Unless, of course, you want to be fired."

She bristled. Only a slimeball would place an employee in this delicate position without warning them of the danger ahead of time. "What I understand is that I am suddenly vitally important to you at the moment." Her razor-sharp retort cut his upper hand off at the wrist, causing him to bluster.

But he didn't reply.

Negotiate.

"I think now would be a good time for me to ask for a raise. Shall we say thirty percent. No, make that fifty percent. And two extra weeks of vacation. And a clothing allowance. A substantial clothing allowance. And dry-cleaning expenses. And an office. No more cubicle dwelling." She paused. Took a breath. "And you'll erase my mistake."

Is that all? Please, tell me you've got more demands than that. You're on the radar of a mob boss.

"And permission to start carrying my gun to work."

Mr. Morgenstern's eyes bulged as he took another puff of his damn cigar.

That BB pistol is not going to hurt a flea.

"You're overestimating your worth." Mr. Morgenstern stood and waddled to his door like a lopsided wind-up duck. "You're dismissed."

Wendy stood.

Don't just stand there like a loser. You have the upper hand, not him.

Wendy gave her boss a benign smile and walked to stand in front of him. She held out her hand. "Do we have an agreement, then? You'll meet my demands."

Mr. Morgenstern left her hand hanging. "Minus your own office and the erased mistake."

"Excellent." Wendy dropped her hand. She probably should have asked for double her current salary. What was the going rate for a person whose career placed them on the radar of a killer?

As she left Mr. Morgenstern's office, she racked her brain to come up with which contract she'd signed her name to. Had it been one from yesterday?

Could it have been the original booty-call one? She'd been super tired that day as well, and the whole contract had thrown her off balance.

She took a seat in her cubicle. What does one wear to meet a mob boss associate?

8

Tuesday nights were open mic at the O'Doule Comedy Club across the street from Abigail's loft. The Manhattan Knitters went every week for happy hour and stayed for the sets.

But first, they would start at Abigail's loft for pre-happy hour.

Tonight, the three of them reclined in purple lawn chairs in the bottom half of Abigail's loft, a massive space currently devoid of stuff. Renovations were underway.

"I love what you've done with the place." Wendy leaned down to set her plastic wineglass on the newly installed hardwood floor. It had taken three full glasses to unwind, forget her worries, and focus on her friends. "You bring the term *minimalist* to a whole new level."

Abigail flipped her the bird. "Come back in two weeks and you won't recognize this room. My contractor is installing the shelving soon."

Eddy sat up straight in his recliner. "Why are you blushing? Did he ask you out?"

Wendy stared at Abigail's cheeks. "Eddy's right. You're blushing. Did he?"

Abigail fanned her cheeks with her hand. "I'm not blushing. It's simply hot in here. He can't ask me out. I'm a paying customer. That would be unseemly. I don't do business with the unseemly."

Wendy scoffed silently. Abigail might not do business with the unseemly, but Contracts R Us sure did. Ugh.

"Honey, what's hot...is you...for some man," Eddy declared.

"Bless your heart, you think you're Sherlock Holmes." Abigail's Midwest twang became more pronounced when she drank. Or got nervous. It was downright adorable when she was both.

"Have you actually met a New York City man you like?" Wendy loved teasing Abigail. "Tell me, is the wicked Northeasterner who has you all aflutter cute, sexy, available?"

"Darling, you think you're being funny. As a matter of fact, he is cute and sexy and available. But he doesn't make me want to run out and catch lightnin' bugs. Those kind of men can't be found in these parts." A tiny frown marred her forehead.

"In other words, you're using him for his carpentry skills and not his *tool* skills." Eddy wiggled his eyebrows when he said *tool*.

"Exactly." The tips of Abigail's ears went bright red. "If a little flirting entices him to do his best in hopes of impressing me, then so be it."

The lofts on Wooster Street were set up to house businesses in the lower half and living facilities in the upper area. When the economy had hit rock-bottom, a lot of the companies had gone out of business and the lofts had been sold. Abigail's aunt hadn't sold but she had closed shop, bought an old-fashioned RV, and had it delivered to Abigail's driveway in Mayhem, Missouri, where she'd proceeded to live while helping Abigail run her yarn shop. Unfortunately, a tornado had taken out the town and her aunt. "Now, no more talk about my contractor." Abigail's words echoed in the empty space.

"Have you chosen a name?" After the day she'd had at work, Wendy could use a distraction. Helping Abigail pick a name for her business might just do the trick.

Abigail sighed. "Back home, my shop was called Feel Good Yarn. But I can't have a country name on a city store."

"These double-pointed needles are going to be the death of me." Eddy ripped out a row he'd just knitted.

"You and me both," Wendy responded.

For the past couple of weeks, they'd been watching YouTube videos on how to use the dang things. Abigail had taken to them with ease. Eddy and Wendy, not so much.

"How about Stitches with Bitches?" Eddy said as he ripped out a row of knitting.

"Will the city allow a business name with a curse word in it?" Abigail asked.

"I don't see why they'd object," Eddy said. "Curse words *are* the new black."

"I hope I know what I'm doing." Abigail reached for a new color of yarn. "I'd be so embarrassed if I spent my whole inheritance on something that went hog-belly-up the first year."

"You'll be fine." Eddy's voice oozed conviction. "I'll buy all of my yarn from you, and I'll tell all of my showbiz friends to buy yarn from you." According to Eddy, actors loved to sit around backstage and knit while waiting to go on. And big corporations were starting mindfulness knitting groups within the walls of their companies. *Naked Runway* and *Vogue* had made this idea all the rage. "No worries."

Wendy cleared her throat. "Speaking of worries, I have a dilemma." She needed help, and she'd prefer to get to it before Eddy finished *his* third glass of wine.

"Finally. I've been bursting for the true details." Eddy gave Wendy his full attention. "Tell us everything. Starting with why your neighbor showed up last night, and why the 911 message. Please tell me it didn't all involve him wanting to borrow a cup of boring brown sugar."

Wendy sighed. That hadn't been what she wanted to talk about, but perhaps a better topic. Why bring her friends into her pending meeting with a mob boss associate? "Eddy, you know me so well. Of course, the guy wanted more than a cup of my cabinet sweetness."

Eddy slapped his hand on his skirt-covered knee. "I knew it. I knew you had a secret. Spill. What is Hot Lips' real game?"

"He's to be auctioned off as an eligible bachelor at some upcoming charity event."

"Yummy," Eddy said. "What's the cause?"

"The money will be used to bring shelter dogs and the elderly together."

Eddy scooted his chair around so he could stare directly into Wendy's eyes. "I'm listening. Keep talking."

"Did you offer to help?" Abigail asked. "Since it's one of the missions of the Manhattan Knitters to do kind deeds, we should help. Maybe we could offer to knit sweaters for the dogs. Oh, and matching ones for their senior citizen."

Eddy gave Abigail a high five. "Oooooh, I like it. Very inclusive." Then he turned his attention back to Wendy.

"Did he invite you? Are you his date? Oh honey, please tell me you're his date."

"Not exactly." Maybe talking about Jackson's proposal with her friends wasn't a great idea. Not because she begrudged them the details. It was just that the three of them tended to get carried away when they plotted a path for one of them to take. Right now, doggy sweaters were on the table. By tomorrow morning, it would be Wendy trotting down a topsy-turvy road...possibly wearing a doggy sweater.

I am not wearing a doggy sweater.

"Honey there's only two answers to the question I asked. Yes. Or no." Eddy whipped his hand through the air, his bracelets clacking together against his wrist. "'Not exactly' isn't an option."

Wendy stuck her needles in her yarn ball and gave them her full attention. "Then no."

"Oh. My. God." Eddy gave a sharp shake of his head with each word. "He asked you to donate money. What a swindling swine. First, he keeps you awake at night, and now this. The guy's a real piggy. Eddy now hates him and invites both of you to hate him as well."

Wendy wrinkled her forehead. "We don't need to hate him. That's not what happened."

"Then what happened?" Abigail stood and refilled their wineglasses.

Wendy's head was already feeling fluffy, so she took a pretend sip of hers. "He asked me to come to the auction and buy him."

"Say what?" Eddy's falsetto voice dropped to that of a bass. His God-given voice.

"He doesn't like the idea of a strange woman buying him," Wendy explained. "So, he asked me." Did it sound weirder when she said it out loud than it had when he'd made the request?

Eddy threw his hands in the air, palms out, fingers spread. "You replied, hell to the hard no—right?"

Well, that answered that question. *Weirder* it was. Wendy didn't respond. Hell to the hard no was definitely what she should have said when her boss had demanded she meet a guy probably known for breaking kneecaps. Then again, the pay raise would come in handy. Not to mention the clothing allowance. Too bad he'd held firm on the strike one request.

"Right?" Eddy pressed.

Wendy shifted uncomfortably in her chair. "Not exactly."

"Not. Exactly." Eddy uncrossed his legs. "Dollface—"

"I asked him what was in it for me," Wendy blurted.

Eddy stared.

Wendy wasn't sure if the look in his eyes screamed good or bad. Did he find this trait a plus or a negative?

Then he threw back his head and laughed. "Da-amn, girl. You're sounding more like me every day."

"The city only needs one of you," Wendy said pertly. "Anyway, here's what Jackson offered." She spent the next five minutes laying out his proposal. "I need to know from you guys what you think I should add?" She didn't mention her *maybe plan* to ask him to be her neighbor with benefits. Not because she didn't want them to know, but because she wasn't sure if she had the necessary brass to ask a virtual stranger to sleep with her on her demand.

"That about sums it up if you ask me. Very generous on his part," Abigail said. "Is there something more you want to add but haven't found the nerve to mention?" She gave Wendy a speculative once-over.

The hair on Wendy's arms went up, and then dominoed chills over her body. Abigail had an uncanny knack for knowing when someone wasn't saying everything. "Going to this event will require dancing. I have about as much rhythm as a ball of yarn."

Abigail laughed. "I've noticed." The Manhattan Knitters, minus Eddy, had been known to put down their knitting on nights they met at Abigail's big empty loft and enjoy a dance party instead. Eddy always complained his feet were killing him and dancing would simply destroy his pedicure. So, he never joined them.

"Not helpful." The last time she and Abigail had danced, they'd been trying to learn the latest dance craze on TikTok so they could upload a video. Wendy's two left feet had hindered their quest.

"Y'all could take lessons," Abigail suggested.

Cupcake could probably dance. He'd, no doubt, find her lack of moves a flaw. And for some reason, she really didn't want to show him any more of her flaws. "That would be embarrassing."

Eddy leaned forward and plopped his big hands on top of hers. "I'll teach you how to dance."

Wendy blinked. "Are you sure you can?"

Eddy fluttered his eyelash extensions. "I have no idea why you look shocked. I earn a living working on a stage. You don't think I get up there and just look pretty, do you? I'll have you know, not only do I have to look amazing, I have to also sing and dance. And am perfectly capable of imparting my knowledge in such a way that even *you* could learn."

Wendy shrugged. She'd always wanted to learn how to ballroom dance. Guys these days always liked to meet in bars with dance floors on the first date. "What if he says no?"

Eddy stood and pulled her to her feet. He placed her left hand on his shoulder, raising her elbow to a ninety-degree angle with his elbow, and took her other hand in his. "He won't." He moved her through a few steps.

"I haven't stepped on your foot once." Wendy sounded as shocked as she felt.

Eddy beamed. "Let's do this. It'll be a hoot." He let go of Wendy, grabbed Abigail, and swung her around the room. Abigail was a natural. "Hot Lips can be your dance partner and Abigail can be mine."

Wendy wound a curl around her finger and watched. Jackson would probably say no. Then she would have to insist he said yes or else... This could be fun. "Where would we have lessons?"

"You could take them here," Abigail said from an upside-down position as Eddy dipped her.

Eddy raised her and then stepped back and bowed. "Perfecto." He turned and glanced at Wendy. "What do you say? Are you in?"

Wendy shrugged. Why not? "I'm in. You'll have to recommend someone very expensive to do my hair and makeup."

Eddy gave her a dreamy look. "Um...darling, of course I have just the guy. Did you already forget my guy who wants to join the Manhattan Knitters' Club is a magician with hair? This can be part of his initiation to see if he's suitable material."

"What's his name?" Abigail asked.

"His name is Bobby. Just Bobby."

"And how many times have you slept with him?" Wendy asked. "I really do believe we should limit new members to those we have no desire to bonk."

"Bonk? Is that a Northerner word?" Abigail asked. "Sounds painful."

"It means fuck." Eddy tossed Wendy a frown. "Darling, please tell me you're not still on your kick to exclude former, current, or future lovers from our little club?"

"It's the smart thing to do." Could she say the same about asking Jackson to be her booty-call guy?

9

Wednesday evening, Jackson stood in Wendy's living room. How in the fuck had he let his sister talk him into this?

Wendy glanced up at him from her position on the couch where'd she'd plopped to open his gift.

He held his breath.

A frown wrinkled her brows and a grimace her lips. She pinned him with a squinted-eye stare. "You bought me a tiara?"

Damn it. His sister's suggestion was shit. "I did." He'd stopped by last night to give it to Wendy, but she hadn't been home. Not home the first time he stopped by, nor the last time he stopped by at midnight. After which he'd spent the night wondering if she'd slept over at a lover's place.

Wendy returned her attention to the Tiffany box. The movement caused a zillion curls to fall over her face and mar his view. She lifted it out of the box and mumbled, "But I already have one."

He shifted his weight from one foot to the other. "It's blue...like your eyes."

Her chin jerked up. "You remembered the color of my eyes?" She sounded awed.

Why did women find that such a big deal? "It was all I could see of your face the other night."

"Oh." She blushed, running her finger over the tiny butterflies with sapphire wings that adorned the bottom row of the tiara.

"They're real sapphires," he blurted.

"How did you know I love butterflies?" A frown tightened her lips.

"I didn't."

"They remind me of my parents." She placed the tiara back in the box and closed the lid, before frowning even harder at him. Bad-cop harder. "Why would you buy me a tiara with genuine stones?"

Certainly not a girl after his money. "I want you to say yes, and my sister said this would tip the scales in my favor."

Her eyes widened, a hint of a smile in them. "Are you and your sister close?"

"Total pain in my ass." She would say the same about him. "But yeah, we're close."

His response appeared to make Wendy very happy. She patted the cushion next to her. "Younger or older?"

He took a seat, careful to leave one cushion between them. Why he felt that need, he wasn't sure. "Younger."

Wendy again took the tiara out of the box and handed him the empty container, a dreamy smile on her face. "I always wanted a sister." She placed the tiara on her head.

He studied her. One of a kind. The other night, he'd thought of her as ordinarily beautiful. Tonight changed that. Adorably beautiful was more like it. There wasn't anything ordinary about her. Beautiful in an approachable way. No doubt, too nice for a guy like him. He felt an odd pressure in his chest. "Are you an only child?"

She fiddled with the tiara. "Yes, and an orphan. Both my parents died three years ago. No other relatives. I like to believe when I see a butterfly, it's their way of communicating with me."

His heart twisted at the pain in her voice. What would it be like to have no one? "I'm so sorry. What—"

"I'd prefer not to talk about it." Her gaze met his, and her eyes were a darker blue than they'd been the other night.

"Sure."

She straightened and rolled her shoulders back. "You're here for my answer."

God help him, he was. "Does that mean your answer is yes?"

"It does not mean that." Her prissy delivery added thistles to her rejection. The kind of burrs that got in a guy's boxers and did damage.

What exactly did *not* mean? And was that disappointment he felt? Had he been looking forward to spending time with Wendy, not just having her buy him at auction? "Then your answer is no?"

Of course, he could simply ask her on a date.

A bad idea for so many reasons. Starting with she didn't look the sort who dabbled in casual relationships. She looked the sort who might start naming their children after their second dinner. And the whole butterfly story left him off kilter. He'd had no intention of picking the tiara with the butterfly, but at the last minute he'd gone with it. Like something, or someone, had whispered in his ear...*this is the one.*

"Do I have to give you the tiara back if my answer is no?"

He chuckled. "I don't know. I hadn't thought the gift through that far. But if you say yes, you can keep the tiara, and I'll throw in a makeover and accessories."

Something in her posture changed, and the temperature in the room dropped low enough to send goosebumps up his arms. "That's very generous. Do you think I'm in need of a makeover?"

Fuck. Why was it every other word out of his mouth came across as not appreciating her as she was? "Not at all." Tonight, she wore makeup, a faded T-shirt that clung mouthwateringly to her curves, and tight jeans that made her ass look incredible. Not that he could tell her any of that because then he'd go from not appreciating her appearance to being too appreciative in a creeper way. "I think you look...nice." The last thing he wanted was to be accused of sexual harassment.

She raised her eyebrows. "Nice? Not sexy?" There was an acid bite to her tone. Like his answer infuriated her. Not leaning toward a yes.

"Is your answer no?" Time to cut his losses.

"No. It's yes...*but*."

He exhaled while something like joy danced in his stomach. "I can work with yes...but. Tell me what the *but* entails." He knew all about buts. Buts were the signature of someone who knew how to negotiate.

She tapped her finger on her lip, drawing his attention to her delightful mouth. An action he was sure was meant to throw him off his game. "I have a few additions to add to your proposition."

His dick shouted in his ear that it would like to proposition her with something. "Like what?" What was it about her that had him so turned on? She wasn't his type.

"I'll take you up on your makeover and accessories. Plus, I want my hair done by the hair technician of my choice."

"I like your hair like it is but done." An amateur would follow that response with *Is that all?* He knew better. Those three little words implied you were willing to give more.

"I have two more demands." Her tone shouted professional negotiator.

He raised an eyebrow. Two? What else could there possibly be? He slid on his poker face. What was it she did for a living? "I'm listening."

"One, you have to take dance lessons with me."

"Not happening."

She gave him a take-it-or-leave-it shrug. "I assume if we're attending a formal ball, there will be dancing. I want us to take ballroom dance lessons."

Christ. He didn't have time to take dance lessons. "Don't you know how to dance?"

She wound a curl around her finger. "I can twerk with the best of them and I'm not bad at flossing."

What in the hell did flossing have to do with dancing?

"But I've never had a need to learn how to waltz or foxtrot. Thus, and therefore, and whatnot, I'm going to need for us to take lessons."

"Can't you take them without me?"

She grimaced. "I can't take lessons without a partner. That's just pathetic."

"Does that mean you don't have a boyfriend?" Why did that make him feel giddy?

"Not at the moment." She shuddered. "I discovered my last one only showered in the mornings."

He pinched the bridge of his nose to stall the oncoming headache. Didn't ask how she'd made that discovery and didn't ask her why that was a big deal.

"How about one of your friends. The guy. Can't he be your partner? I'll pay for his lessons."

"That's sweet of you. Really it is. But I have my heart set on it being you."

He raised his gaze to the ceiling. Annie owed him big time. Then again, saying yes would give him the chance to see what Wendy felt like in his arms. "Fine. I'll take five lessons with you."

"It'll take ten."

His gaze dipped down. Studied what she had on display. God, they were nice. He looked up. Maybe he should offer twenty. "Seven."

"Done."

"You're a strong negotiator." He admired that.

"I have one more thing."

Wendy dropped her arms to her sides and grabbed her confidence.

You've got this. Just spit it out.

Jackson groaned. "Dare I ask?"

Wendy inhaled a deep breath. The better question would be 'dare *she* ask.' Which the answer, at this moment, seemed to be leaning heavily toward yes. Which simultaneously scared the knit out of her and excited her.

Her sex life had shriveled up to nothing lately and...well...there were some things a girl shouldn't let shrivel. One of them being orgasms. Plus, it didn't help she was on pins and needles about her future meeting with the mob associate. A good man-given orgasm or two might relax that worry away. If only for a short time.

While Jackson's eyes were still closed, she blurted, "I wish for you to be my neighbor with benefits." That sounded so much classier than booty-call man.

"Come again?" His voice came out high-pitched like she'd given his vocal cords a wicked wedgie.

Her throat slammed shut. And there was a decent chance she was having a heart attack.

Don't panic. Yes, he's surprised. But surprise isn't a negative.

She stood, used every inch of her five-foot-six height to convey conviction. "Exactly. I want you to make me come again and again like you do the endless parade of women you bring home."

Well, that's just tacky.

He stood and straightened his tie. "I'm not a gigolo."

It was not tacky. Tacky was all the sex noises he'd made her listen to over the past month. "Of course not. Gigolos get paid. I don't plan on paying you."

He's going to tell us no.

Doubt settled into the crevices of her confidence. A whole pasty, doughy glob of doubt. Would he say no? Probably. Damn it. What had she been thinking?

She tried to not feel the hurt seeping into her conscience. Obviously, she wasn't his cup of tea. Which was fine. Hell, in the long run, he wouldn't be her cup of anything. But she wasn't looking for a cup of tea, or a forever man.

"Are you serious?" He sounded like a man talking to a woman who'd recently lost all her common sense. "You want us to be neighbors with benefits?"

Hearing him say the words caused her heart to thump and her nipples to tighten. Her desire to see this through rallied. "I never say things I don't mean." Life was too short to not speak your mind. Unless it came to her boss. Then she kept her mouth shut. Life was also too short to go hungry. Or that had been her view until yesterday. Yesterday, she'd pushed back, stood up to the tweeb, and come out on top. That was if you didn't count the fact she was now on the radar of a certain mob family.

Jackson shoved his hands in his pockets. "Then have you recently been the victim of a head injury?"

"Not recently." There'd been that—

Something flickered in his eyes and her thoughts ceased. She held her breath and waited for his answer.

"Then why?"

We've got this. He wouldn't be asking why if he wasn't at least considering saying yes. Just give him a good answer.

"You see, I find I do my job better when I'm relaxed. Orgasms relax me. And according to the hullabaloo upstairs, you're decent at giving them, other than that one time when you didn't, but hiccups happen, so I'd like for you to take care of my sexual tension. And, at the moment, I'm not interested in love. Are you?"

A hurricane of horror whipped up on his face. "Absolutely not."

"Does that mean you'll do it?"

He loosened his tie. "I didn't say that."

Neck-deep disappointment engulfed her. She reluctantly took off the tiara and handed it back to him. At least she hadn't told him the whole reason for wanting his services.

Wouldn't that have been embarrassing if she'd mentioned that the last guy she'd had sex with had told her she wasn't bad but she needed some practice, and once she'd gotten it, to give him a call. Practice or not, she'd never call the shower-only-in-the-mornings asshole, but she didn't want the next non-asshole to think she needed practice. "Then we have nothing further to discuss."

He stared at the tiara. "If I did say yes, and I'm not yet, for how long would I be your neighbor with benefits?"

That was a promising question. But also a troubling one. *Forever* probably wasn't an option. Nor *until I find a man I want to marry.* Not that she deserved to find that man.

How about until you no longer interest our orgasm parts?

And you call me tacky. "Until the night of the ball."

"And then we'd be done?"

She inhaled the sweet scent of victory and manly aftershave. "That's the plan."

His gaze came back to hers, and they stared at each other in silence. "How many nights a week?"

She swallowed. "I'm open to negotiations." She pointed to her ceiling. "But on the nights we're not together, you can't have women up there keeping me awake." Did this mean he found her attractive? He'd have to or he'd be saying hell to the not happening. Right?

He raised his brows. "We'd be exclusive."

"Exclusive bed partners. And you *must* wear a condom."

The word *must* must have made it all too real because doubt suddenly reappeared on his sexy face. "Don't you think asking me to be your sex partner is a bit extreme?"

"I love extreme hobbies," she said primly. "That's why I took up no-patterns-allowed knitting with double-pointed needles. It's like the black slopes of knitting."

For a brief second, he grinned, but the smile was quickly shoved out of sight. "Why me? Why do you want me to be your neighbor with benefits?"

This she had an answer for. She'd been practicing this part. "I've yet to meet a man who can *satisfy* me the way you seem to *satisfy* your women. Listening to all the caterwauling up there has left me curious. There's no law against two consenting adults hooking up purely for sex." Lord knew Eddy made a lifestyle out of it. As did the guy in front of her.

He stabbed his fingers through his hair. "And this isn't a joke my sister put you up to?"

"Nope." The daughter of a mob boss was to blame. If Penelope Angelino could have a booty-call man on contract, why couldn't plain, little ol' Wendy Travis do the same? "And just so I'm not guilty of making assumptions, have you and your friend from the other night gone back to being just friends?"

"Who?"

She rolled her eyes. "The one you didn't satisfy."

His eyes widened as if he'd truly forgotten about what had to have been a humiliating experience. "Oh. Her." He spoke the words casually, but his body language didn't play along.

"And?"

He scratched his ear. "I guess you could say we're back to friends."

Wendy couldn't help but admire the woman. She'd appeared to be nice and normal. Good for her that she didn't give him a second chance to prove his studliness. "I'm surprised you took the loss without demanding a do-over."

"Why's that?"

"You come across as the type of guy who wouldn't want anyone walking around talking about your lack of prowess in the bedroom."

"Your opinion of me isn't good, is it?"

She didn't have a bad opinion of him. Or a spectacular one. Sort of an in-between one. Like he was a good candidate for a fixer-upper boyfriend. Break him of his serial-sexing habit, and he'd be someone she probably wouldn't mind spending some time around. "The only opinion of mine that matters is the one in regard to your aptitude in bed."

"I'm not into love—at all. Sex for me is just sex. It's not some grand adventure that leads to happy ever afters."

She didn't ask him why he didn't do love. To do so, might require her to tell him the reason why she didn't believe she deserved love—survivor guilt. "I'll have a contract drawn up. One of the conditions will be that neither of us is allowed to fall in love. Or mention love. Or ask for more once the contract is over." Those were a few of the conditions that had been added to the latest Angelino/Travinni contract. "Nor will we engage in conversation that leads to getting to know one another better."

The leery expression was back on Jackson's face. "Are you a lawyer? Are you sure my sister didn't put you up to this?"

"I'm not. And she didn't. I proofread contracts for a living. I'm quite good at discovering loopholes and closing them. I can put together a document that protects both our interests."

He held up a hand. "Slow down. I also have a *but* to go along with my yes."

She wrinkled her brows. What *but* could he possibly want to add? "You do?"

"I need to know that we're compatible before we move forward with this insane agreement."

Wendy's heart skipped a song-full of beats. "Compatible?" The word barely squeaked past the lump in her throat. "Is this because you don't want to run the risk of another woman spreading the word you're a big fat zero in the bedroom?"

10

Jackson couldn't believe the last ten minutes of his life. Who asks a virtual stranger to be their neighbor with benefits? And then badger them about being inept in the bedroom?

While Wendy's *why* wasn't easily distinguished, his *yes* didn't take a genius. She was cute as hell. For him, it would be equivalent to taking a stranger home at closing time. God knew he'd done that a time or two. But for her...could it be as simple as orgasms were relaxing? "I think we should at least kiss and make sure that goes smoothly before we have any more negotiations about your contract."

She paled a little but grasped her hands behind her back and tilted her face up to him. "Fair enough. You may kiss me." She closed her eyes. Ridiculously long black lashes cast shadows on her cheekbones.

If it wasn't for the way her chest moved quickly from heavy breathing, he'd think her cool as an ice cube. He liked that she wasn't unflappable. That part of her captivated him. There were other parts as well, but that part especially.

He ran a finger down the side of her cheek, causing her to jump, but her eyes remained shut. "This is your idea. You have to kiss me."

Her chin came down and she opened her eyes. Studied him like he was an intriguing homework project. Was she deciding if she should start at step one or skip straight to the end? Or take a zero on the assignment? "Fine." She took his hand and led him to a wall. "Stand there. I'll be right back." He watched in bemusement as she left the room. Told his dick not to jump the gun. This was a test run. Nothing in it for him tonight.

He heard a door open and close. What was she up to? Should he be concerned? Probably. Hell, why had he started this? He glanced around at her décor. Very homey. Inherited furniture? What were the holidays like when you had no one? The image made him ache. He continued his perusal. A basket of knitting sat next to the threadbare couch. A stack of photo albums next to the television. A set of drink coasters on the scarred coffee table.

His thoughts halted when she sashayed back in the room carrying something red. She came to a stop in front of him and placed the item on the floor and unfolded the contraption. A stepstool.

He grinned. Okay. He watched as she slipped off her lime-green high heels and then stepped up on her device. She placed her hands on his shoulders and stared straight into his eyes. He felt his dick push against his zipper.

Her tongue darted out and she licked her lips. The sight of her tongue hardened him quicker than cement hardens in the summer sun.

"Perfect," she murmured, her voice soft as heated honey.

"What's perfect? My lips?" He needed to make a joke to lighten the tension growing inside of him.

She grimaced. "They're okay, but I was referring to my height on this footstool. My body is now perfectly aligned with yours."

He didn't look down. Was his cock perfectly aligned with her sex? God help him. This girl had moxie. A lot of fucking moxie. "I'm ready when you are." His words came out hoarse.

She wiped her palms on her jeans and then lightly cupped his cheeks. Tilted his head to the left. And then to the right. And then back to the left.

He swallowed a groan. Things were about to get real. He told himself to remain neutral as he stared straight into her fucking gorgeous eyes. He'd feel her lashes when they kissed. The thought turned him to mush.

She tilted her head to the right. Leaned in. Paused a whisper length from his lips.

Other than his heart thudding against his chest, he didn't move.

She swiped her lips once more with her tongue before tentatively placing her mouth on his.

The contact shouldn't have surprised him. He'd seen it coming. But damn, it made him feel weak all over. Her lips were warm. Soft. And not moving.

He waited for her to turn the touch into a kiss.

She pushed her mouth firmly against his for all of one second and then pulled back. "There. Did it." She spoke sharply. Like she was making a point he shouldn't bother to argue.

He straightened his head. "You call that a kiss?"

"Our lips touched. It's a kiss."

"No wonder you need to bargain with a man to have sex." The taunt was out before he could stop it.

"I do—" Her lips slammed back on his and moved incessantly. When he still didn't participate, she bit his bottom lip, causing him to open his mouth.

She used that opportunity to sweep her sweet tongue inside.

He raised his hands and settled them on her hips, pulled her against his body. She moved her hands to the wall behind him and dragged her tits back and forth against his chest. Left. Right. Slowly.

He moved one hand up her back to her head and took control of the kiss. She tasted like wine and chocolate. He tangled a hand in her hair and tugged her head back so he could move his lips down her throat. As he nipped and kissed her jaw and neck and earlobe, she quietly pushed into him. All her body now rubbed tantalizingly back and forth against him.

His cock crowed, and he groaned.

She, he noticed, remained silent.

Was she always quiet during passionate encounters or was this her way of making a point?

He moved his hand from her hip and cupped her ass. Firm and round.

Without warning, she pulled back and stepped down. "Do we have a deal?"

He made a low growling noise. Blinked. Nodded. *Christ.* "Why the fuck not? Take out the no-conversation clause and if you want to fuck, we can fuck."

"Conversations are Cupid's playground."

She was probably right. He'd be wise to heed her warning. "I can have a conversation with a woman without giving her my heart. Are you afraid you can't? Am I that irresistible?"

"Fine. I'll leave out the conversation clause. But don't come crying to me when your heart falls for me. I'm very lovable."

"Deal. No crying."

She tugged at her T-shirt, pulling it back into place. "Shall we make a date for sex in two nights?" The words were spoken in a casual tone. As if he was nothing but a customer in need of her services.

"What's wrong with tonight?" It was a shame to waste a perfectly good hard-on.

"I'll need to draw up the contract. You should know, I'm a stickler for rules. I'll want from you exactly what is spelled out in the contract. You'll get from me exactly what is spelled out." Her voice had turned breathy, ragged, full of heat.

He forced his brain to engage. "I'll agree to be at your sexual beck and call unless business...or family requires my attention."

She frowned. "That sounds like a loophole. Is it a loophole?"

"Why would I want a loophole? The idea of servicing your needs fascinates me. I can't wait to get started."

"Fine. I'll add that to the contract."

"And make sure you add love and marriage are not on the table." He wasn't sure if he said that to remind her or himself.

"Get over yourself. Give me your phone."

"My phone?"

"I'm going to enter my number. Text me tomorrow night, and I'll let you know what time works for me on Friday."

"Where are we meeting?"

"My place. I have no plans to do the walk of shame from your place."

He raised a brow.

She shrugged. "Besides, the whole purpose of my wanting a good orgasm is so I can sleep better and thus be better prepared to do my job. That will best happen if we have sex, you let yourself out, and I fall asleep before you hit the elevator buttons."

"There's a flaw in your plan."

"No, there's not."

"There's no need for you to get a good night's sleep on a Friday night...unless you work on Saturdays. Do you?"

She shook her head. "If you can't get the job done, I want to discover that on a Friday night and not on a Sunday night. You know what I mean?"

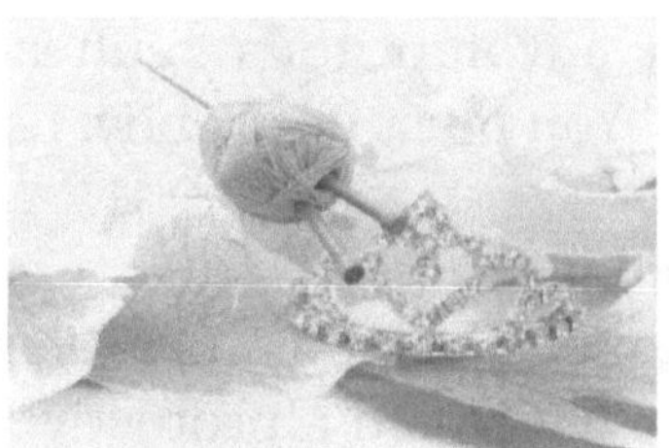

11

Filled with trepidation, self-affirmations, and a Xanax left over from the year after her parents had died—a year during which she had suffered greatly from anxiety attacks—Wendy stepped into the high-dollar, low-lit restaurant situated in the middle of Saks Fifth Avenue. She was three minutes early for her meeting with the mob associate.

Before entering, she'd stood in the shadows outside the fashionable French establishment for twenty minutes, waiting and watching for some gangster to get out of a nondescript black town car and enter ahead of her. She'd wanted to see if she saw the bulge of a gun under a suit jacket.

No one ever arrived. What did it say about her that she'd assumed they'd be meeting at an Italian restaurant? The fact they weren't reminded her this wasn't some cliché meeting. It was real, current, not a movie scene where everything always turns out okay for the heroine.

The weather wasn't even cooperating with her cliché. Although it was cold, the sun was shining. No rain. No thunder. No scary lightning strikes. As a result, she felt off balance. Were her knees about to be crushed or cracked?

The hostess, a voluptuous redhead, gave her a dazzling smile. "You must be Wendy. Let me take your coat."

Wendy handed it over.

"And your phone." The woman's smile never faltered.

"My phone?" Wendy laid a protective hand over her purse. How could she call for help if needed?

"It's one of our rules. We want our customers to stare into each other's eyes, not at their phones."

I call bullshit.

Wendy glanced around. No one had a phone out. Weird. She would have never thought you could find a New Yorker willing to give up their phone, no matter how great the meal was. She handed over her phone.

"Right this way," the hostess said.

Wendy followed. How had the woman known who she was? Had Wendy's picture been shown to her? And if so, by who? And when had they taken her picture? And was it a good one?

Concentrate. Take in the details.

Did the hostess work for the guy? And who did her hair? It was amazing. Like a quiet ocean of red velvet.

A gold-framed mirror ran along the wall. Wendy grimaced. She looked like a glob of pancake batter in comparison. Why hadn't she worn something more memorable? Murder trial witness memorable. Would any customer remember seeing her if she ended up dead in Cortlandt Alley?

Who decides to wear a Calvin Klein, two-button, white pantsuit to meet a mob boss's associate? If there was blood, it would never come out.

The hostess moved toward a table situated in the back of the room. *Which corner is this? The northeast corner?* Was this the same restaurant mentioned in that one Angelino contract she'd proofed for the family? The one where the owner agreed to always have two tables available for any Angelino, and, in return, the Angelinos agreed to spend five thousand a month at the establishment as well as provide two bouncers and pay their salary.

Ding. Ding. Ding. Ding.

The hostess stopped.

A bulky guy dressed in all black sat so his back was to the wall, and he had full view of those who came and left the establishment. Nearby, three other burly men sat in a booth. The guy before her stood. "Wendy! Thank you for joining me." He held out his hand.

Wendy shook his hand. He had nice hands. Large, but not beefy large. And no calluses. Did that mean he didn't do the actual dirty work? Did he determine a need for action, pass the information on to the boss, and then order a hit?

Maybe her pantsuit would survive this meeting after all. "And you must be—" What should she call him? She couldn't call him the knee-breaker. *Shit.* Had Mr. Morgenstern ever actually told her his name? "—the man who summoned me," she finished lamely. She tried to smile as if she was making a joke and wasn't completely brainless.

The guy smiled blandly. The kind of smile that said neither we're about to become friends, or enemies. It said nothing. Absolutely nothing. "There are many who call me Bruiser."

She jerked.

He pulled out her chair. "Please sit."

She did and wished like hell she hadn't worn heels. A quick getaway would be impeded in heels.

He took his seat across the table and poured her a glass of wine. "Shall we toast to new acquaintances?"

"To my new...acquaintance. Mr...."

"Please, call me Bruiser." He delivered the line in a spot-on *Godfather* impersonation.

It was an impersonation...right?

They clinked glasses.

What in the hell had she been thinking, agreeing to this meeting? All her hyperactive imaginings of how this might go down were playing out. She took a sip of her wine.

Yum.

"This is excellent. I'm used to cheap wine," she babbled, her nerves of steel missing in action. "I had no idea the good stuff went down so much smoother."

He settled ice-blue eyes on her. "Does Mr. Morgenstern not pay you enough? I'll tell Ms. Angelino. I'm sure he can remedy the situation."

Wendy gulped. The guy had a nice voice, but the innuendo wasn't lost on her. "That's not necessary."

"I disagree. A woman as beautiful as you should never have to drink cheap wine or wear cheap jewelry." He glanced at the ring, bought from a street seller, on her right hand.

"Oh, it's not Mr. Morgenstern's fault I drink cheap wine. In fact, I just recently received a nice raise. I'm afraid I'm one of those women who walks into a wine store, becomes overwhelmed with the choices, and settles for something in the eleven-dollar range." Still babbling.

He threw back his head and laughed. "I like you, Wendy. And because I like you, this meeting isn't going to take the turn most of my one-on-ones take."

"How's that?" In another life, she might be able to like this guy. He put off vibes of decency.

"You've managed to change my mind about something. Seldom do I change my mind."

Wendy nodded. Afraid if she spoke, she'd say the wrong thing. Say the thing that might change his mind back. And it didn't take a genius to know that wouldn't be a good thing.

He set down his drink and leaned forward. "Here's the deal. I've been watching your movements for the last month."

"You're watching me?" A queasy feeling formed in the pit of her stomach. How could someone have watched her for a month without her notice? "Why?"

"One month ago, you took over the Angelino contracts for your colleague."

"How do you know that?" Had she signed her own name to the very first contract? Did he know what had happened to Thin Guy from cubicle thirty-three? Was *he* what had happened to him?

"It's my job to know everything about every person who works on any project that concerns the Angelinos."

"Why?"

He cracked his knuckles. She noticed faded bruises on them. "Because they put a high value on their privacy."

She swallowed a fist-sized lump in her throat. "And you're afraid I'll talk about what I proof?" Oh God. She had. She had. She had.

"Initially, that's exactly what we feared. But the other night, you had the perfect opportunity to tell the Manhattan Knitters, and you didn't. I thought for certain you would."

A bead of sweat rolled down her back. "I'm a professional contract proofreader." She used her prim voice. "The minute I talk about a contract to anyone is the minute I no longer have the number one necessary credential to be hired as a proofreader." She paused to let that sink in. Then added, "Of course, I didn't tell my friends." Thank God, she hadn't told them in public.

He stared. Unimpressed.

"Employees at Contracts R Us take random lie detector tests to make sure we don't gab." This was a lie.

There was a flicker in his eye.

Oh. My. God. She'd just lied to Mr. Bruiser. "Okay. That's a lie. But I plan to recommend the idea to my boss the moment I get back to work. Not that I need the threat of a lie detector to keep my mouth shut."

Mr. Bruiser's lips twitched. "We both know there are some contracts that are so juicy that even the most honor-bound amongst us crack and leak what we know."

"Which of their contracts has you so worried? They're not that gossip worthy." A bluff. They all would make great dinner party conversation fodder.

"At the moment, Ms. Angelino is greatly concerned about the contract you proofed that concerns her daughter."

She blushed for Penelope's sake. "She knows about that one?"

"Penelope has no idea her mother knows about the contract. But, of course, she does. She knows everything."

Bruiser paused, allowing his statement time to scare the shit out of Wendy.

It didn't take long. She bobbled her head.

"Ms. Angelino wishes for you to forget the contract exists."

"I have memory problems."

Bruiser's eyes warmed up a degree. "I'm to report back to her if I think that is doable on your part. Can you forget everything you read in that contract?"

"What contract?"

Again, he laughed. "Good. Good."

He looked past her and made an upward motion with his head.

The hostess appeared at their table and handed Wendy her phone and the wrong coat. "But this—"

Mr. Bruiser held up a finger to silence her.

The hostess walked away.

"When you leave, wear that coat with the hood up. One block up is a diner. Go inside. And use their facilities. In your coat pocket are the tools necessary to tape your middle finger and your ring finger together on your left hand. If anyone asks, you caught your hand in the door of a taxi."

"Why?"

"So my boss will think I did what she sent me to do. Give you reason to fear seeing me again. You can leave this coat in the restroom."

"What about my coat? It's new."

"That's a shame." He stood. "Now, I must leave, I have other business to tend to. But please, order whatever you want from the menu. It's on Ms. Angelino. And remember, I have eyes...and ears...everywhere. If we meet again, it won't be as pleasant a conversation as our first."

And just like that, he disappeared through the kitchen exit, walking with a slight limp.

"Mitch, it's—" The voice came from the kitchen.

Wendy heard the greeting but didn't see who spoke or who they were speaking to. Mitch? Funny, some guy in the kitchen had the same name as Penelope's booty-call man. What were the odds? She listened to see if Mr. Bruiser would be addressed by his name, but that didn't happen.

She took the seat he'd been sitting in so she could see outside. Possibly see him walk by. She was so intent on watching for him that, when a black crow flew right into the sparkly clear, closed window, she jumped and yelped, causing people to look her way.

An omen.

And not a good one.

She picked up the menu to hide her face and glanced at the luncheon special. Eddy and Abigail could never know about this blip in her life. It was one thing to entertain them with the details of a booty-call contract, but she couldn't bring them further into Bruiser's world.

After all, one couldn't be too cautious when dealing with pricks and mob families.

And what did he mean he had ears everywhere? Was her apartment bugged? Thank God she'd spilled her secrets at Eddy's place.

Damn. She should have asked him how long she had to wear her fingers taped together.

12

F riday night and the Manhattan Knitters were gathered at Wendy's apartment drinking Knitters' Tears, a red wine from Missouri, and of course, knitting. She'd taken her fake splint off her fingers. No need to lie to her friends. Or to Jackson when he came over later for their first booty call.

They each sat in their favorite spot. Eddy liked the recliner even though it was broken and sat at an angle. It gave him a view outside as well as the inside. Much like Mr. Bruiser's chosen seat at the restaurant. Abigail liked to sit on a DIY, oversize floor cushion, with her back against the wall, and her legs stretched out in front of her. Wendy sat longways on the couch. The bottom of her socks read: Don't mess - with my joy. One sock had the image of a ball of yarn. The other a pair of knitting needles.

They all wore tiaras. Wendy's currently under scrutiny.

"Bless your heart," Abigail said. "I can't believe he bought you a sapphire-encrusted tiara. Did he give one thought to how the weight of this thing will give you a massive headache? Or, how you'll now have to worry about it being stolen? And don't even get me started on all the outfits you can no longer wear on knit night because they'll simply clash or lack the right class or—Lord help us—both."

Wendy glanced down at her red, threadbare sweats and white, wine-stained T-shirt that read: *Boobs and Booze for the Win*. An outfit she could remember wearing her first year in college. "I hadn't thought about any of that."

"Hell. He should've asked me to buy him," Eddy grumbled. "I'd have given him a lot more for his money." His tone clearly said he jested.

Wendy glanced at her friends. What would they say when they learned about the *whole* deal she struck with Jackson?

That you're a proper tart, that's what they'll think.

Wendy held her knitting up as if inspecting it for dropped stitches. "The guy's cost me sleep and a black mark on my impeccable performance record. I'd say he owed me a tiara."

"Before I forget," Eddy said, "I get to fill in tomorrow night. I can't make it to your company picnic."

Wendy's heart sunk for her but soared for her friend.

"That's the best news for you," Abigail gushed. "But what happened to the poor lead? Did he break a leg, bless his heart?"

Eddy sat up and leaned forward. "He says he broke the fingers on his right hand dropping a cast iron skillet on them, but anyone who knows him knows he's right-handed. He wouldn't have been holding a heavy skillet in his left hand."

Wendy lowered her knitting. "Then what do you believe happened?"

"I think a pissed-off lover smashed his knuckles when he caught him holding hands with another."

"Oh. That sounds violent." Wendy knitted a few stiches. Thank God Mr. Bruiser hadn't broken any of her fingers. She pushed thoughts of him away and focused on Eddy. "No matter how it happened, I'm happy you're realizing your lifelong dream. You've worked your sashaying butt off for this chance." Every New York actor dreamt of their Broadway debut.

Eddy preened. "I plan to be the best damn Peter Pan Broadway has ever seen."

Abigail held up her glass. "To our Eddy getting on the big stage."

"To Eddy," Wendy said. "May this be the first of many dreams coming true."

They all took a sip of their wine.

"I'm sorry my good fortune means bailing on you," Eddy said to Wendy. "I know you really wanted a date to this year's picnic."

"Don't give it another thought." And Wendy meant it. Even if it resulted in Mr. Morgenstern winning his damn bet with Julie the clerk. "I just hate that I won't get to see you."

"I'll be there to watch your Broadway debut," Abigail said. "Front row if I can score the tickets for free. Back row if I must shell out the big bucks to see you. And I'll cheer loud enough to make up for the fact Wendy isn't in the crowd."

Eddy laughed. "You're the best."

Abigail turned her attention to Wendy. "Are we on for dance lessons?"

Wendy's pulse picked up. "We are. He squawked a little but eventually said yes. Stipulation-dance-lessons is officially a part of the contract."

"Just how loud did he squawk?" Abigail didn't look up while she cast on stiches to start a new project.

"Not softly but not hard either."

Eddy paused mid-knit. "Don't say *hard* when we're talking of him. It makes me frisky."

"You're irredeemable." Wendy couldn't help but smile. "He agreed to seven lessons."

"Why do you sound breathless?" Eddy asked.

Wendy wasn't quite ready to tell her booty-call secret to her friends. "I have no idea what you're yammering about." She tried to sound ultra-casual as she kept her eyes on her project. A tiny blue hat for babies at the local women's shelter. "I sound like I always sound."

"Eddy's right. You sound different," Abigail said.

Wendy dropped a stitch and muttered a curse. She tossed them a frown. "Knock it off, you two. You're killing my joy."

She caught the look they exchanged.

"Sugar, is that because we're arguing or because Eddy's right?" Abigail teased.

"Arguing, of course."

"My erection detector is going off, and it tells me you're thinking of 5C." Eddy fluttered his false eyelashes demurely. "Of buying that big strong hunk-of-a-man at auction?"

Wendy reached for her wine and took a long sip. "Maybe." She picked up the bottle and refilled her glass to the top. She knew not to outright lie and say yes. An early capitulation during an Eddy-inquisition would alert him more than an evasive response.

Eddy put his knitting down. "Honey, some days you wear me anorexic with all of your maybes."

Hell. When Eddy smelled a secret, he became like a shopper in possession of a sale-priced Jimmy Choo. The only way to get him to let it go was to pull it out of his dead, cold hands. "Fine. I'm thinking of 5C and his being all mine at the auction."

"You're lying," Eddy said.

"What? Why do you think that?" Wendy sputtered. Her mom used to be able to read her like this. Wendy had never gotten away with anything until she left for college. In some ways, Eddy had taken the place of her parents. He protected her, much like they would if they were still alive.

"Because Eddy knows what Eddy knows. I demand you spill, and don't leave out even one delicious detail."

Wendy gave him a half-hearted, back-the-fuck-off look. "Just because you share everything doesn't mean everybody shares everything." She wanted to spill. But on her own terms.

"According to the bylaws of the Manhattan Knitters' Club—all members agree to share the interesting parts of their life, other than Wendy's work secrets," Eddy said.

"Is that true?" asked Abigail. "I don't remember seeing that in the bylaws."

Wendy nodded. "Page two. Paragraph seven. Second to last sentence." No loopholes.

Eddy bounced up and walked over to the couch. He picked up her feet, took a seat, and plopped them on his lap. "Now that we've got that settled, let's get back to the part I'm really interested in. Is it something to do with the bargain you struck with him? Did he agree to your terms?"

"I texted you both telling you he did."

"Sugar, I got the text. Didn't you?" Abigail asked Eddy.

Eddy didn't answer. His gaze zoomed on Wendy. "I want to know what wasn't in the text."

Wendy licked her lips. "I told you all the good stuff. Left out the boring stuff."

"Like what?" Abigail asked.

Like a kiss that would've straightened all my curls had it gone on any longer.

"I don't remember. It was too boring to store in my memory banks. Abigail, what new project are you starting?"

"A baby blanket—"

"Dish, you sexy bitch." Eddy interrupted Abigail, causing Wendy to jump. "And don't leave out any of the juicy details."

The three of them were best friends. They'd been there for each through many new and ending relationships. They shared the good with the bad. Details both ego-boosting and ego-bruising. So why did admitting she'd asked Jackson to be her neighbor with benefits send Wendy into a tizzy? There was absolutely nothing wrong with being a sexual creature. She sat up straight and spilled the missing details. "Let me begin with the woman who kept referring to him as Cupcake." Wendy entertained her friends with that person's choice phrases during sex and then moved on to the really good part of her story. "...and that about wraps up my booty-call story."

"Mother of Pearls, I'm going to have to buy you a tramp T-shirt of your own." Eddy pointed to the one he wore. *Real Tramps Don't Need Stamps.*

Wendy stood and paced. "Tonight's our first night. Do you think I should cancel?"

"Is retail Bergdorf for the poor?" Eddy declared.

Wendy stopped pacing. "Only if they're window-shopping."

"Then there's your answer. You can't do something as delicious and naughty as asking Cupcake to service you and then back out. What time is he coming over? You are making him come to you—right?"

"Of course." All the nerves she'd been holding back released, causing a storm of butterflies to fly amuck in her stomach. "I told him I'd text him when I'm ready to go to bed."

"Perfect. It's almost like you've done this before," Abigail said.

"What should I say when I text him?"

"Just say—come eat me, big boy," Eddy suggested, in a Marilyn Monroe impersonation. He idolized Marilyn.

"Or, come ride me, cowboy." Abigail did a lasso motion with her right hand.

Wendy groaned. "You guys aren't helping. Whatever I say, it's going to sound more awkward than saying *you too* to someone who asked, *how was your day?*"

Eddy held out his hands to Wendy. She walked to the couch, put her hands in his, and sat. "You text and simply say—it's time."

"Okay, that'll work."

"Ooooh. What are you wearing?" Eddy exclaimed. "Let's see what you bought for the occasion." He stood and made a beeline toward her bedroom.

Wendy stilled. "Bought? I didn't buy anything. We're having sex. Not starting a relationship." Hell. She'd just been on Fifth Avenue. Why hadn't she bought something?

"Very funny."

"Excuse me?"

"There's no way you're sleeping with a guy for the first time and you didn't buy a new nightie."

"I really didn't." She blamed this oversight on Mr. Morgenstern and the whole damn mob contract.

"Sugar, she won't need a nightgown. He'll come over. Take her clothes off. They'll crawl in bed. Do it. Then he'll go home. No new nightgown required."

Wendy gulped. "Oh, God. Should I take a shower before he comes, or after he gets here? If it's before, I'll *need* a nightgown to answer the door in."

"Shower in the morning," Eddy said.

"Ugh. I can't crawl into bed without being clean." Her stomach dipped. "Do you think he'll shower before he comes? I can't have sex with a dirty man." She didn't have a lot of quirks, but the cleanliness of who got into her bed was one of them.

"Have sex in the living room?" Abigail suggested. "Do you still have that blow-up mattress we all slept on last Christmas Eve next to the Christmas tree?"

"I could do that?"

"Or text him to shower first," Abigail said.

"Or cancel," Wendy responded.

"Speaking of cancelling," Eddy said, sounding unusually serious, "did you guys watch *Dateline* last night? The Boston Angelino family is muscling its way into New York City and they plan to cancel out the Montanari stranglehold on the city's black-market trade."

Wendy felt the air whoosh from her lungs. If her apartment was bugged, they'd hear this conversation. She couldn't wait for the bug detector she'd ordered to arrive. "Does anyone know if it's supposed to rain tomorrow night?"

"The show covered several reports of missing acquaintances of the Montanari family," Eddy continued.

Missing people? Pencil Thin was missing? "I'd love for the picnic to be cancelled."

"I heard that in Boston, the Angelinos were notorious for hiring people to work for them and then killing them when they were no longer of use."

"You look nervous." Jackson sat on the edge of Wendy's king-size bed and waited for her to establish the pace. Her bedroom didn't meet any of his preconceived notions. He'd expected thrifty and comfy, like the rest of her house. That's not what he'd discovered.

Three of the walls were painted a dramatic black. The other, the one with a double-wide window, stood out with its crisp coat of white. Her all-white bed rested against the wall that faced her bedroom door. White pillows. White comforter. White sheets. Above it hung a picture frame, holding an imageless poster with the words *Just another thing hanging over your head.* The words were in a small font and located about three fourths of the way down. A lamp and a tiny crystal butterfly, bathed in moonlight, sat on top of the nightstand nearest the window.

He'd like to comment on the butterfly, but the contract she'd handed him when he'd gotten here had been sterile and specific. Conversation, while allowed, was to be kept at a minimum.

"I'm not at all nervous. I've been looking forward to this all day." Her words rushed out like a faucet turned full blast. "If you don't mind, I'm going to take a quick shower, and then I'll be ready for an orgasm and sleep." She stood in the doorway of her bathroom clutching a nightgown.

"I don't mind," he said. "I'm certain you will be worth the wait."

"Yes...well..." Her teeth tugged at the corner of her lip. "In the cabinet above the microwave, you'll find a variety of liquors. Feel free to pour yourself a drink. There are drink coasters on the coffee table. I'll only take three minutes."

"Three minutes? That sounds exact."

"I've timed myself." The words were spoken with no hint of a smile.

As with everything she said, he was intrigued. "Why did you time yourself?"

She cocked her head, her pale red curls falling over her shoulder, and gave him a that's-a-dumb-question look. "To *know* how much time I need to allow myself in the mornings to prepare for work." The *well duh*, though not spoken, rung out clearly. "Don't you know how long it takes you to shower?"

"I don't." She was a breath of fresh air. A refreshing mixture of sexy and unpretentious. "What else have you timed?"

She picked at the material of her nightgown. Something silky. Something he couldn't wait to feel against his skin. "The usual. Makeup, eating breakfast, getting dressed. How long it takes me to put BBs in my pistol. Falling back to sleep after the idiot upstairs wakes me up with sex noises."

He grunted. He hated she still thought he was that guy. A lie allowed to live for a couple of reasons. One, to keep from breaking Wendy's heart. Two, because Annie thought it would be good for him to have a woman in his life he had to work to impress without the benefits of his bank account or notoriety. Truth be told, though, he was looking forward to the opportunity as well. "You won't have to worry about that anymore." *She owns a BB gun.* A perfect form of protection for someone who owned two tiaras.

Her lips lifted into a smile radiating happiness. "Excellent." She glanced at her watch, stepped into the bathroom, and firmly shut the door.

For a moment, he simply stared, resisting an urge to join her. He shook off the thought, pulled out his phone and placed it on *do not disturb*. He reread the text she'd sent him and chuckled. *Take a shower and come on down.*

He glanced at the clock. Eleven fifty-seven. How many minutes had passed while he'd fantasized? Probably all she'd allotted.

He pulled back the covers, stripped down to his boxers, and climbed into her bed. The nerves in his stomach left him rattled, but not surprised. Hell, she'd made it very clear her expectations were high. This might be the most important performance of his life.

##

Wendy got undressed and stepped under the shower head. Dear God, what in the hell had she been thinking inviting a virtual stranger into her bedroom to service her?

You were thinking he can give you orgasms that'll make you scream inane phrases.

And protect me from a hitman, should one come calling. She quickly went through her nightly routine all the while reminding herself no matter how good the orgasm, she wouldn't make a peep. Out loud that was. She'd make all the peeps she wanted in her head. But none raucously infused with sound. She didn't want the neighbors in 3C mimicking her moments of joy over coffee with their best friends the way she did with Eddy and Abigail over knitting.

And, just in case there were multiple mechanical ears in her apartment, she didn't want Mr. Bruiser listening to her carnal activities. After meeting with him, she'd come home and done a thorough search of her apartment but hadn't found anything.

She'd even done a Google search on the best places to hide a listening device. The list had been three-freaking-pages long. Those tiny little suckers could be anywhere. She'd gone to the library and, using one of their computers, ordered a bug detector. If her apartment had a bug problem, she didn't want Mr. Bruiser to know she had found them. The handy gadget should arrive tomorrow.

Wendy wiped down the shower door, dried off, and slipped on a pink, silk nightshirt with matching panties. Not new but pretty. Taking a deep breath, she opened the bathroom door with an Eddy-taught flare. The pithy comment she had on the tip of her tongue—*ready or not here I cum*—didn't happen.

How could it when her breath whooshed out? Jackson, mostly naked, lying on her bed on his side, propped up on one elbow, and watching her under hooded eyes.

She inhaled and wiped her damp palms down the length of her nightshirt. They weren't the only thing the sight of him made wet.

"You look beautiful." He patted the spot next to him. "Come. I've got plans for you. Plans that will take a hell of a lot longer than three minutes." The guy had a romance-worthy chest and voice and eyes and, from the look of the tent in his pants, a have-your-way-with-me-worthy cock.

She pointed at him. "And you look..." She struggled to find the words she wanted. *Good* would be an understatement. Sexy slightly better but not nearly descriptive enough. "Better than the best cream-filled cupcake I've ever eaten."

He tossed back his head and laughed. "Fuck. You're going to destroy my ego." He sat up and scooted to the edge of the bed, his gaze taking on a serious glint. "Is this still what you want? It's not too late to change your mind. I'm willing to leave."

She blinked.

Leave? Nobody mentioned leaving.

God. Could he not tell the level of heat consuming her? Hell's furnace heat. And her lungs, normally a well-oiled machine, had stopped working the moment she'd opened the door and saw him spread out on her bed like a bachelor-of-the-month calendar pinup. "I don't want you to leave." This might be the first time she'd ever entered into a sex-only relationship, but that didn't mean she planned on regretting the decision. Men had been doing this for years. Eddy swore by it.

Operation Booty-Call-Neighbor was a go.

She reached for the hem of her night shirt and lifted it over her head. She kept her eyes on his chest as she folded it and carefully laid it over the reading chair next to her dresser. His clothes, nicely folded, were there as well. Not strewn across the floor. *My kind of man.*

She took a breath, and somehow doubt snuck in with the oxygen. Did he like what he saw? How did she compare to the other ladies he'd been servicing lately? Her curves couldn't compete with the curvy woman the Manhattan Knitters had seen him leave with Friday night. Did the size of her breasts disappoint? She blew out the backstabbing breath and shook away the comparisons. Her body wasn't perfect, but it was good.

She looked him in the eyes. Stood proudly in a pair of pink-lace panties and waited for him to say something. His gaze lefts hers as it slid down her body.

He didn't speak.

She refused to ask him if he liked what he saw. She'd be damned if she'd be the girl who wasn't proud of her body. She had curves. She had muscles. She had cellulite. She had it all. Like a normal woman.

When it became apparent he didn't feel the need to speak, she took a step toward him. Moving didn't take nearly as much effort as she'd thought it would. Obviously, her body liked this latest episode in the ongoing life of Wendy Travis.

He raised his face and their gazes locked. His intense. She tore her gaze away and noticed he clutched the mattress like a man trying hard not to make a move. She told herself it wasn't because he wanted to leave. It was because he wanted her. Wanted her badly.

Two more steps and she stood in front of him. Close enough she could feel his warm breath caressing her bare breasts. Her nipples pebbled in response.

She reached out and placed her palm on his shoulder. "Have you changed your mind? Do you want to leave? It's not too late if you'd rather be bowling."

14

Jackson came out of his desire stupor. "Bowling?" He laughed. "Why in the hell would I rather be bowling?" Her fucking body was the hottest thing he'd ever seen. So hot he expected a fire truck to show up at any moment.

"You don't bowl?" she asked, in a husky voice. "I just assumed you did ever since that one night when I heard so much thumping upstairs. Thought maybe you kept dropping your bowling ball."

"Never." He'd suspected she had a glorious body beneath all her sweats and T-shirts but seeing her naked blew his fucking mind. Her tits were the size of baseballs, equipped with pale pink nipples. The perfect size for a man's mouth.

She raised her hands and skimmed her fingertips across his chest, stopping when they were flush with his pecs. There she wrapped her hands around his arms and squeezed. "Weight lift?"

"Wendy?" His eyes moved down, over her slightly rounded belly to her panties. Sexy, pink lace. Sheer enough he could see her waxed mound. Completely waxed. That little detail had the heat, already building in him, coming close to exploding.

"What?"

He groaned and ripped his attention back to her beautiful eyes, which were currently the color of a stormy sea. "I haven't changed my mind."

She widened her legs so that his were now between hers. "Good. This is going to be fun."

"Damn straight it is." He unfisted the mattress and raised his hands to settle them on her ass. *Bare ass.* Sexy, princess-pink, lace thong. Fuck. If she wanted a couple weeks of a wild ride with a player, then he'd damn well give her the experience.

She moved her hands to his shoulders and pushed.

He didn't resist and fell back into the mattress. She crawled up on the bed until she straddled him. Her hair was tousled, still slightly damp from the shower.

"You should know, I'm not a screamer. If that turns you on, prepare to be disappointed."

He liked how her chest rose and fell with each word. "How will I know if you're enjoying yourself?"

"Ask me." She wiggled until his cock was cushioned against her.

Somehow, he managed to put words together. "You're wet." He could feel it through her panties and through his boxers.

She placed a smooth hand on his dick. Ran her hand up and down the covered length. "You're hard."

He tried to breathe through the effect of her hands on him. "I'd like to be naked. I'd like for you to be naked." He reached out and slipped his finger under the lace edge of her panties, slid it slowly over her slit.

She jerked.

"Did you like that, Wendy?" Saying her name felt very right even though it caused his heart to thump hard in his ears.

She nodded, her eyes heavy. Her lashes fluttering downward.

He did it again.

She closed her eyes and pushed back, leaving the bed, and standing. He sat up on his elbows and watched as she slid her panties down her curvy legs.

He puts his hands into the band of his boxers, preparing to rid himself of their encumbrance.

She knocked his hands away and took over the job. When she had them off, she laid them on her chair and then came back to him. Her eyes locked onto his cock. Her mouth formed an O. "I'm beginning to understand what all the brouhaha has been about upstairs."

Someday he'd tell her the truth. But not tonight. Not until this relationship was over. Would he, stripped of his money and his fame and his moral compass, be enough in the eyes of this woman who enthralled and charmed him like no woman before her? Not that it would matter in the end. But damn, right at this moment, he wanted to be enough. "Come back up here."

She met his gaze. A line between her brows. "All joking aside, I'm a little intimidated by that thing."

His chest puffed out like a warrior who'd won a hard-fought battle. "I won't hurt you. I'll take it as slow as you like until you're comfortable." He stood. Took her hand. Turned her around so that the back of her knees were at the edge of the bed. "My turn to give the orders."

She scooted back until she could place her feet on the mattress. Then she lay back, bent her legs. "I like a man in charge." She slowly opened her legs to him. "As long as he knows what he's doing."

He loved how comfortable Wendy was with her body. Chasity had constantly needed reassurance from him that he found her beautiful.

He slid his hands under Wendy's ass and enjoyed the weight of her cheeks in his palms for a moment. Perfect round globes made to be held during sex.

He settled between her legs and softly ran his tongue along her slit. She bucked against him. He did it again. Why didn't she like to scream during sex? Was it a personal preference or had she not met the right man?

He moved his mouth to her inner thigh and kissed the pale skin there. Then he slowly slid his mouth back over her mound and to the other thigh, where he spent time nibbling the sensitive skin.

She grabbed his head and tugged. "Not there."

"Where, babe? Where do you want my mouth?" He scraped his teeth along her inner thigh.

She pushed at his head.

"Say it. Where do you want my lips?"

"On my sex."

"Your pussy?" He ran his tongue up and down where his teeth had been.

"Yes."

"Yes what?"

She made a low, growling noise. "Yes, that's where I want your mouth."

"Say the word. Talk dirty to me."

For a moment she didn't respond. Her hips came off the bed as she tried to force his mouth where she wanted it.

He resisted. "Say it." Was he a greedy pig for starting down here? He should have started at the top and made his way down. But how could he have resisted when she spread her legs for him? Surely, that meant she didn't need all the other bells and whistles.

"Fine. Eat my pussy," she hissed.

He groaned. Brought his mouth back to her mound and sucked, hard.

She bucked like an unbroken filly.

He paused long enough to say, "Hold still, darling."

She obeyed.

He opened her slit and was given an unfiltered view of her clit. He leaned forward and ran his tongue around that tiny bud of nerves.

Her knees crashed against his head.

For a moment, his ears rang. When he could hear again, he said, "Open your legs. Give me full access."

She did. Still not making any loud sounds. Sounds he normally heard during sex.

He tasted her. Sweet. He found her opening, rolled his tongue and stuck it inside of her.

He used one hand to play with her clit while tongue-fucking her.

Her hips jerked, but she kept her legs open. She grabbed his head. Pulled on his hair.

"Stop," she panted.

"Not yet. I want to make you come."

"Not this way. I want to come with you inside of me. Did you bring condoms?"

"I did. Reach under the pillow and pull it out."

"Which pillow?"

"I put one under each."

She chuckled, reached for a condom and made quick work unwrapping it. She sat up on the edge of the bed.

This time he widened his legs and straddled her as he stood.

She touched him and he hissed. Watching her slowly roll the condom down his length was pure torture.

"I ate you. Have the taste of you on my tongue. Now, what do you want me to do to you?"

A blush stained her cheeks and travelled down her neck and over her chest. "Give me an orgasm." She scrambled back on the bed and lay down.

"I think I can manage that." He crawled up on the bed, straddled her, and settled the weight of his cock between her legs. Nudging, he found her opening.

##

Wendy stilled. She was ready for him. For this. More than ready. But she'd never been with a man quite so big. Would it hurt? "What are you waiting on?" she teased, not wanting him to know about the nerves somersaulting in her stomach. She should have known Cupcake had Mr. Wonderful in his pants. Women didn't howl to the moon over penis-runts.

Jackson leaned forward and captured her lips. The kiss wasn't soft. It was hard like him, tasted like her, and distracting as hell as he slowly pushed inside of her. Then he braked.

"Okay?" he husked into her ear.

Words stumbled all over themselves in her head, tried to escape her throat, but nothing emerged. So, she nodded.

He slowly began stroking her. She held her breath until her size fears subsided. Then she breathed. As if feeling her breath of relief, he changed his rhythm. His rhythm became faster, his strokes harder.

Pleasure built inside of her. She moved her head from side to side, trying to not scream, not moan, not be like every other woman he'd ever known. She wanted to be different.

"Open your eyes," he ordered.

She tried. They were too heavy.

"Open them. I want to see what color they are when you come."

She forced them open. Stared into moody gray eyes.

With their gazes locked as one, they fucked. Wild fucking. Their bodies slick from sweat. When she could stand it no longer, she wrapped her legs around his waist and squeezed. She bucked against him and forced her eyes to stay open as she fell apart. The orgasm so intense she might have lost consciousness.

"Starry night blue," he said, then threw back his head and jerked into her.

When she was sure he was done, she released her legs.

He collapsed beside her, wrapping one arm around her waist and pulling her into him.

The desire to snuggle and fall asleep in his arms made her think things she shouldn't. Things that weren't part of their iron-clad agreement. He'd given her an orgasm. Now she'd give him his freedom. "That wasn't bad for our first time," she said, going for lighthearted.

He slowly leaned up on his elbow. Nothing lighthearted about the storm in his eyes. "Wasn't bad?"

She forced a nonchalant shrug. "You can go now. Thank you."

His breathing stilled. "You're done?" Disbelief rang loud in his tone.

Why? Did he want to go for round two? Or had she startled him with the ease in which he could take care of her needs, and he was secretly thrilled he could escape so quickly? "I have yoga at eight in the morning." She glanced at the clock. "It takes me four minutes to fall asleep after an orgasm. If you leave now, I'll get seven hours of sleep."

He frowned but stood and pulled on his boxers. "Same time tomorrow night?"

She gave a dreamy sigh. His ass was almost as glorious as his cock. "I have a company picnic tomorrow. I already know I won't be in the mood by the time it's over so you're off the hook."

"A picnic that takes away your sex drive? That sounds like a drag." He turned and faced her while he slipped on his jeans and pulled on his shirt.

She refused to let thoughts of the picnic ruin her current mood. "Pay no attention to me." She sat up and pulled the sheet up to cover herself. "I'm sure this year, it will be a hoot."

He took a seat on the bed and put on his socks and shoes. "What aren't you telling me about the picnic?"

She scooted upward until she could lean against the wall. "I overheard my boss making a crass comment to another employee about me." The words rattled out of her like he'd given her some type of truth serum.

"And?"

"They have a bet—" She broke off. Blinked. "Never mind." If Mr. Bruiser was listening, what would he surmise if she told Jackson about the workplace bet? That she couldn't keep a secret?

"What kind of bet?" He tugged at the sheet she held clutched to her chest like a lifeline.

She refused to let go. Then again, this had nothing to do with a contract. No reason she had to keep what she'd heard a secret. "The kind that humiliates a girl."

A fierce glint appeared in Jackson's eyes. "What?"

She dropped the sheet to nibble on her thumbnail.

"Better," he murmured gazing at her naked body. "Tell me about the bet."

She huffed. "He bet her I wouldn't have a date. He's under the impression I'm quite boring."

"Are you kidding me? Does he not know you at all? You're the most fascinating woman I've ever met."

She gave him a bemused smile. "I know...right?"

He shook his head. "Don't go. Make an excuse to miss?"

She lifted a shoulder. "It's unofficially mandatory. One of those unspoken threats."

"Fuck. I don't know this guy, and I already hate him. Where are you having your picnic? I'll come and give him a piece of my mind."

The sweetness of the offer crumbled half of her bad opinion of him. "Not necessary. We're not a couple. That's not part of our contract. Besides, I can handle the men in my life. But you're a sweetie for offering."

As she watched Jackson leave, it dawned on her that Mr. Bruiser had also seemed the type to come to a woman's defense. If he knew Mr. Morgenstern had called her boring, would he be like Jackson and want to seek revenge on "her" behalf?

Holy Devil's Kiss. What had she done?

15

Saturday early evening arrived before Wendy's inner-voice pep talk could get her in the right frame of mind to enjoy the company picnic. Thus, she stepped into the event with a snarl in her craw. Or at least, that's how Abigail would describe her snippy mood. It didn't help that the first person she encountered was her boss. Ugh.

"Wendy, so happy you made it." Mr. Morgenstern had paired his company-branded baby-blue T-shirt, mandatory for all to wear to the event, with yellow dress shorts that failed to cover his bony knees. Knees, which Wendy noted, were very much intact. Not broken by Mr. Bruiser. To finish off the look, he wore white socks, brown sandals, and a company ball cap. "Even if you are late. We started five minutes ago. I was worried you didn't plan to show."

She'd been late because her bug detector had arrived this morning. And she'd gotten sidetracked with learning how to use the contraption. Once she'd mastered the device, she'd carefully searched her apartment for listening devices. She'd uncovered squat. Nada. Zilch. The outcome made her feel both better and foolish. She'd clearly read way too much into her whole conversation with Mr. Bruiser. Either that, or his equipment was way more sophisticated.

"I wouldn't miss it for the world." Wendy also wore the ugly-as-hell mandatory company shirt. She glanced around for someone to talk to. Anyone else would do. Even a homeless person waiting for the picnic to be over so Central Park could go to sleep.

Julie walked up to them and gave Wendy a pinched look. "Hi, Wendy. Where's that date we've all been hearing so much about?"

Wendy flushed. She'd mentioned one time while standing at the copy machine that she had a date for the picnic. One time. Why was Julie making it out to be more than that? "He had to cancel."

Julie's pinched look grew layers of disdain.

"What is it he does?" Mr. Morgenstern asked.

Damn the luck that Eddy had to cancel. "He works—" Wendy's phone rang, cutting off her sentence. She didn't care who was calling. She loved them. They were her savior. She glanced at the caller's name right as a butterfly landed on the face of her phone. The call was from *Jackson*. Was the butterfly a coincidence? Or a sign from her parents? What kind of sign could they possibly want to give her regarding Jackson? Probably...beware.

She glanced at her boss and Julie. "I need to take this. One moment." She walked several feet away and clicked the receive button. "Hello."

"Hey, gorgeous. I see you're at your picnic. Nice legs. Of course, I prefer them causing hearing damage wrapped around my face."

His sexy tone and flirty words did delightful things to her thoughts. "Where are you?" She turned in circles but didn't see him.

"Across the street. I'm attending a gala at the Metropolitan."

"Oh." She turned toward the street and saw him. Sex in a tuxedo. Her stomach fluttered. The pleasurable sensation caused other parts of her to wake up.

He waved. "Is the boss behaving?"

How lovely. He'd remembered their discussion. "He was quizzing me on Eddy's occupation when you called."

"Eddy?" Jackson's tone lost a bit of its easygoing charm.

If she didn't know better, she'd think he sounded jealous. However, that couldn't be the case. "My date who backed out at the last minute."

"I thought we weren't dating others while we did what we're doing?"

"Eddy's my best friend. Not a real date. You met him the other night. Tall, tiara, women's clothing."

"You were going to present him to your boss as your date?" His voice echoed with horror.

She frowned. "Beggars can't be choosers."

There was a short pause. "How about I come over and put in an appearance as your date?"

The offer swam in sweetness. Reeked of consideration. And thumbed its nose at the terms of their contract. "Not necessary. I can—"

"Think about how much fun it would be to handle your boss as a team."

Wendy glanced toward Mr. Morgenstern and Julie. They'd moved off to the side. Julie had handed him money. Damn it. She'd taken him up on his bet. No wonder she had been looking pissy. "Actually, that sounds delightful." Just this once, she'd allow her and Jackson to deviate from their contractual agreement.

Just. This. Once.

##

Jackson crossed the street. He hadn't planned on attending tonight's gala. But when he discovered, after some snooping, that Wendy's picnic would take place across the street from the Metropolitan, he'd decided to go so he could fortuitously bump into her. Juvenile stunt? Maybe. But he didn't care.

He wanted to meet the man who thought her boring. Wanted to do physical harm to him, but would settle for meeting him and setting the record straight.

"Hey." He dropped his arm around Wendy's shoulder and inhaled her scent. Honeysuckle. Sweet and sexy at the same time. "Let's go chat with your boss."

Wendy glanced up at him and gave him a cute grin. One that highlighted the freckles hanging out on her button nose. One that made his brain freeze and his breath hitch. "I'll owe you."

He pulled her in close. "I'll collect." The words were for her ears only.

They walked to where a man and woman were deep in discussion.

"Mr. Morgenstern, I'd like for you to meet Jackson." Wendy's voice had the appropriate amount of respect and deference one gives a boss you want to keep happy. "And this is Julie. She works in the mailroom."

Julie blinked.

Jackson inwardly groaned. He knew that look. It was recognition. He'd been pleasantly surprised that Wendy hadn't recognized him, nor her posse. But his luck had just run out. It had been asinine to think he could keep his identity from Wendy. What had he and his sister been thinking when they cooked up their scheme to keep Wendy in the dark?

"Is this your date?" Julie asked. "The one that couldn't make it?"

Jackson gritted his teeth. Yep. He'd nailed it. Julie recognized him. Or at least, she thought she recognized him, only she couldn't reconcile him with Wendy.

"He surprised me." Wendy cast a happy smile toward him. "He can't stay, but he knew how much I wanted him to meet those I work with, so he dropped by on his way to a work event." She looped her hands through his arm and leaned against him as if they were indeed a couple.

He dropped a kiss on the top of her head, enjoying the heat of her body despite the temperature outside.

"What kind of work is it you do?" Mr. Morgenstern asked.

Julie squinted, obviously still trying to believe what she knew to be true.

"I'm in project management."

"I knew it," Julie said.

"What exactly does a person in project management do?" Mr. Morgenstern asked.

"I buy up property in rundown communities and revive the area. Bring in new business."

"Mr. Morgenstern, this is *the* Jackson Adler. Tell me I'm wrong?" Julie demanded of Jackson.

Wendy glanced up at him. For a brief second their eyes met, confusion clearly in hers. How would this affect the way she was around him?

"Guilty," Jackson said.

Julie grabbed Wendy's hand. "Why didn't you tell us you were his newest girl?" She turned back to Jackson. "Didn't you like *just* break up with Chasity Kennedy?"

Wendy's grip on his arm intensified, but she didn't say a word.

He should have gone into the gala and left well enough alone. "I'm sure Wendy doesn't want to stand here and listen to us chat about an old acquaintance."

"Not that old. Only like last week old. Wendy, how did *you* snatch him off the market so quickly?"

He untangled his arm from Wendy's death grip and dropped it around her shoulders, pulling her in tight. Damn it.

She wrapped her arms around his waist, glanced up at him, and smiled. Not a shock and awe smile. It didn't make it to her eyes. Wasn't in her body language. And sure as hell wasn't in the death grip she had on his side. "Honey, why don't *you* tell Julie how I snatched you up off the market so quickly."

Fuck. What was the rule of thumb about lying? Something about keeping it as close to the truth as possible. Let's see... "We both joined the same dance class, and since neither of us had a partner, the teacher paired us."

"Yes. Yes, tha—that's exactly how it happened," Wendy stammered.

"How fun," Julie enthused. "I don't see the Wendy I know as a dancer."

Jackson gave a knowing chuckle. One meant to imply so much more than his next words. "This girl has moves that would make a Kardashian blush." That much he knew to be true. Sex with her had blown his mind into a million shattered pieces.

"You don't say?" Mr. Morgenstern gave Wendy an assessing glance. "It's the quiet ones that always surprise you."

Jackson kicked himself for drawing Mr. Morgenstern's attention to Wendy in a sexual way. Damn it, he'd just meant to get under Julie's skin. "I couldn't agree with you more. My life hasn't been the same since I met Wendy."

Several people gathered a few feet away, preparing to participate in some sort of relay game. "Are you going to join us, Mr. Morgenstern?"

"We'll be there in a minute." He turned his attention back to Wendy. "Wendy—"

"Enough talk about me." Wendy's voice came out high and tight. She tilted her head to look at Jackson. "You're going to be late to your event." She reached up on tiptoes and kissed his cheek. "Thanks for dropping by. You're the best." She put her hands on his chest and pushed. Hard. As in, *I'm-pissed* hard.

He hoped she could read the apology in his eyes. "Anything for my girl. Just wish I could stay and get to know more of your work family." How would she handle all the questions Julie would no doubt toss out the moment he exited the scene?

Mr. Morgenstern handed him a business card. "If Wendy hasn't already hit you up, I hope you'll consider doing business with Contracts R Us. Your little perfectionist can sniff out a contract error like nobody's business. I don't know what we'd do without her."

Jackson took the card. Studied the simple design: *Contracts R Us - Where Perfection and Discretion Are Guaranteed.* That's a big promise. Was Wendy their Golden Goose? More valuable than she knew? "I might take you up on that offer if you'll do me a huge favor."

"What would that be?" Mr. Morgenstern took a handkerchief out of his back pocket and mopped his brow.

"Allow me to steal Wendy away from your picnic. I want to show her off at my work function."

A small sound of surprise came from Wendy. Did that mean she didn't want him to whisk her away? Or was it a happy sort of surprise?

"Oh, I...I..." her boss stuttered. "I believe companies that play together stay together."

"Wendy did tell me about your motto, and how she'd hate to miss out on the epic fun."

Mr. Morgenstern puffed up. "It *is* the event of the year."

Jackson went in for the kill. "You know what, never mind. I'll show her off some other time."

"Nonsense. Wendy, go with Jackson. I insist."

16

Wendy's brain flashed a tilt error over and over and over as she and Jackson strolled casually away from her company picnic. Cupcake wasn't the sexy nobody she had assumed. No freaking wonder he had a different woman every night in his bed. He could. So he did.

Once they stood in front of the museum, she pulled her hand out of his and took several steps away. "You were two-timing a movie star?"

"It's complicated." He sounded pissed that he had to admit to the relationship.

"And you didn't think to mention this complication?"

"It wasn't in the contract."

He has a point.

"Is she at the gala?" Damn it. Why had she asked him that? It was none of her business.

He sighed. A deep, frustrated sigh. "Maybe. Probably. I don't know."

She glanced at her watch and walked a couple of feet to the bus stop sign. The next bus would be here at any minute.

He followed her. "What are you doing?"

Wasn't that obvious? "Going home. It's not like I can go with you. I'm not dressed to go to a gala."

"That's okay. We're not going to the gala." He grabbed her hand and tugged until she fell into step with him.

His admission hurt. Shouldn't. But it did. "You lied about wanting to introduce me to your friends."

He stopped walking, turned her, and lifted her chin with his palm. "If you want to meet my friends, I'm more than happy to take you to the gala."

Good Lord, no, she didn't want to meet his friends. That wasn't in the contract. She jerked away from his touch. "I told you, I'm not dressed for it."

He chuckled. "I know and that's why we're not going." He grabbed her hand and laced their fingers together.

"Oh." She willed him to add that he wanted to someday introduce her to his friends. He didn't. "Where are we going?"

He hailed a taxi. "Someplace we can talk in private."

Private? Like he didn't want to be seen with her private? That kind of private? "We could've talked at the gala." She liked the way holding his hand felt. Warm. Secure. Perfect. "Besides, if I get in a taxi with you, what will Mr. Morgenstern think?"

Cupcake let go of her hand and pinched the bridge of his nose. "If he mentions it, tell him I took you home so you could change."

So, he *did* want her to go. This perked her up. "I thought we weren't going to the gala. I don't have a dress." She didn't want to go—she simply wanted him to want to take her.

His lips twitched. "I told you. We're not going to the gala. We're going someplace we can talk."

Ugh. Why didn't he want to take her? "Talking isn't in our contract." Neither were galas. What was wrong with her?

"Does that mean you don't want to talk? You don't have any follow-up questions to what Julie said?"

"None that are any of my business." But, *hell yes.*

"Then let's go buy you a dress and go to the gala."

Would he really... This was so not in their contract. "I thought you said we weren't going."

"We weren't." Frustration darkened his voice. "But you said you want to, so we will."

How sweet. A womanizer with a heart. She wrinkled her nose...the closest thing he was going to get to an apology from her. "I don't want to go to the gala."

He hailed a taxi.

Fifteen minutes and no discussion later, Wendy and Jackson sat in the back booth of a hole-in-the-wall coffee shop sipping on a strong cup of coffee. The only other patron in the place had pink hair, granny glasses, and a dime-store tiara missing its tip and half of its fake jewels. The unexpected sight of another tiara wearer surprised Wendy. It seemed like an odd coincidence.

That'll be us in thirty years.

Wendy swallowed. It really could be. Especially if she had to go into hiding from Mr. Bruiser. She glanced surreptitiously at Jackson. He didn't appear to have noticed the woman. Had the universe placed the sad woman here at this moment for a reason? Was the sight of her supposed to be Wendy's wake-up call?

Or Jackson's.

Was she supposed to be Jackson's peekaboo into the future? Like the universe was telling him: *Look what Wendy is on the road to becoming. Abort now.*

Eddy would say that's exactly what the broken tiara wearer was. A sign.

While Wendy scrambled with her woo-woo thoughts, Jackson simply stared at her. She blocked her theories of what the universe was up to, raised her lashes, eyeballed Cupcake, and waited for him to comment…on anything.

After a few seconds, she realized they were trapped in a game of who-will-end-the-silence-first.

Talk already. I'm bored.

"Have you priced a ball of yarn lately? It's crazy how expensive it's gotten."

Really. That's the best you could come up with?

Jackson sighed. "Wendy, is there something else you wanted to ask?"

"Why didn't I recognize you? I read *Naked Runway* and *Page Six*. I should have recognized you." The words spilled from her lips like marbles from a broken glass jar.

I didn't think we planned to get to know him on this level.

We didn't; you pressured me.

"Because in the scheme of things," Jackson said. "I'm a nobody. Obviously, Julie is a huge fan of Chasity." A half-smile raised his lips.

That makes sense.

"Did Chasity learn about all the other women you've been screwing? Is that why you guys broke things off?"

A pulse jumped to life in his jaw. "Chasity decided I should propose."

Wendy frowned. "Why would she want to marry someone who wouldn't even give her an exclusive relationship?" Had the actress been in it for the sex, too?

"You'd have to ask her."

The urge to pry further was strong, but in the scheme of things what did it matter? What mattered was what they decided to do now. Continue with their contract or not. "Am I your rebound woman?"

He reached out and grasped her hands. "Technically, you could be called that...if you were my woman. But since we're not dating, I don't think the tag fits you." He rubbed the inside of her wrist with his thumbs, making it hard to concentrate.

He has a point.

She pulled her hands back and forced herself to think about what mattered. "How long did you date?" Translation, how many times did you have sex? The answer was irrelevant. One time was too many to follow. But follow she had. Last night.

He cocked his head and studied her like an art exhibit. "Six months."

"Was it an open relationship for the entire six months?" She wished she would have paid more attention to all of Eddy's gossip about the star. The only thing she remembered him mentioning was that he had a crush on Chasity's hairdresser and wanted him to join the Manhattan Knitters' Club. Was that a coincidence or the universe once again putting people where they needed to be for life to happen according to its grand plan?

"I have a confession," he said.

Oh for the love. Nothing ever good followed when those words were uttered. She sighed. "I'm not a priest, but let's hear it."

As if afraid she might bolt if left untethered, he grabbed her hands.

She braced herself. "Just spit it out."

"I'm not your upstairs neighbor."

She opened her mouth to laugh, but a grunt emerged. "Nice try. Not buying." She leaned forward and waited for him to convince her of his bullshit story. She blamed the action on his touch. It's like his hands on hers caused her common sense to take a vacation.

"What I'm saying is true. My tenant lives in the apartment above yours. Or he used to. I moved him to a different one in the building. One in which he's not as likely to disturb the other residents."

Her ears picked up the hard-to-manufacture sound of truth in his voice. She tugged her hands out of his and sat back. "Your tenant?"

"I am the new owner of the building you live in." The words were spoken calmly. Truthfully. And most importantly with honest eyes.

He's not lying.

Which meant he *had* been lying all this time. A ball of indignant fire ignited in her brain. "You're not… the crex-sazed, I mean sex-crazed neighbor…I thought you were?" What had she done? Why had he allowed her to do it?

"I'm not the guy who kept you awake. I was in 5C that evening doing a favor for the guy who had really been keeping you awake."

The desire to crawl under the table and die from humiliation was strong. "Then who was the woman in the apartment with you? The one who said you're lousy in the sack?"

He sighed. "My sister, Annie. She has a warped sense of humor. It's because of her that I'm in the bachelor auction."

The mention of *family* hit Wendy in the gooey part of her heart and threw her off her mad. She focused on the waitress refilling coffee cups at the counter. An old man now sat on one of the tattered barstools. Next to him, was a child playing on an iPad. She forced her gaze back to Jackson. "You're not Cupcake?"

He grunted. "Thank God, no."

"Then why in the hell did you agree to my proposition?"

A devilishly disarming grin slid onto his face. "Isn't that obvious?"

"Not even a little." She refused to be beguiled by his brand of charisma. "Spill."

"Because you wanted to have sex with me, and I wanted to have sex with you."

She resisted an urge to scream. The last thing she wanted was to draw attention to her and Jackson. For all she knew, the man at the counter was a spy for Mr. Bruiser. "I wouldn't have *asked* if I'd known you weren't my upstairs neighbor." The fact she had thought Jackson to be a man-slut had been what had made him the perfect guy for the contract. Someone who wouldn't blink an eye at having a woman ask him to service her.

"Then I'm glad I didn't tell you."

Kick him. No one will notice that.

Good point. Wendy made solid contact with his shin.

He jerked and looked at her like she'd lost her mind.

She raised her brows daring him to reprimand her.

"Feel better now?"

"Not even a little. Why would you let me believe you were a cad? You could have just asked me out and hoped it led to sex."

He scraped a hand through his hair. "I liked the idea of you not knowing my identity. I liked knowing you didn't choose me for sex because you were after fifteen minutes of fame."

Flaw. Flaw. Flaw in your story. "Try again. As you admitted yourself, you're not famous. Your ex-girlfriend is."

"I couldn't agree with you more. There's nothing spectacular about me. But I've discovered sometimes you become famous for nothing."

She resisted an urge to kick him again. "What's that supposed to mean?"

He studied her for what seemed like a century. "Just so there's no more secrets, once upon a time a reporter from *Naked Runway* decided to dub me and five other guys as the Elusive Six. A moniker given to us because of our career success combined with our lack of desire to get married. That fame lasted for thirty seconds. The only time it gets mentioned now is when I'm photographed with someone who is truly famous or in a bachelor auction."

She groaned. That must have been before she'd read the magazine. Eddy had introduced her to it a few years ago to help her up her wardrobe game. What exactly had the criteria been back then to make that list? She would Google it when she got home. "And *that's* why you wanted me to buy you? Because you're still considered a hot commodity on the local marriage market."

"Something like that." A smile didn't lift his lips, but she caught a twinkle in his eyes. Did he find her blunder after blunder after blunder amusing?

He's seen Chasity Kennedy naked, and he's seen you naked. One of those things does not look like the other.

Holy die-of-embarrassment Hell. They needed to get things back on track. "Ask me a question. Anything."

A line formed between his eyes. "Tell me about your friends."

Wendy took a breath. "Abigail's a proper Midwestern Lady from Knotty, Missouri, which is now called Mayhem. And by proper, I mean she knows how to put you in your place without leaving a visible scar. She inherited this great loft and is turning it into a knitting store. Eddy's bisexual. He cross-dresses because he enjoys it. He's a hoot." She kept rambling and somehow found herself telling him a lot more details than she'd planned.

"Ask me a question?" he said, once she quit talking.

"Why are you against marriage?"

His eyes clouded to a putty gray. "Mom's been divorced more times than I care to share. I don't trust myself to be any better at love than she has been."

"Sounds like a classic case of commitment phobia."

He studied her for a minute. "What are your views on marriage?"

She exhaled a long breath and then inhaled another. They were getting in too deep. She should steer them back to the shallow end of the get-to-know-you pool.

Oh, get over yourself. Just tell him.

"That I don't deserve it."

He frowned. "Why in the hell would you think that?"

"I was supposed to come home one weekend from college and didn't because I thought my boyfriend planned to propose."

"And?"

"As a result of my decision, my parents decided to go on a last-minute ski trip. They died in a freak avalanche. Had I come home, they wouldn't have gone skiing, and they'd still be alive. I don't deserve a happy ever after." She surprised herself by getting through the story without tears, but not without pain. Every muscle squeezed and every bone ached. "My therapist calls it survivor's guilt."

"I'm so sorry. That's a horrible burden to carry. I have a friend who survived a bombing while in the Marines. Several of his friends died that day. He also suffers from survivor's guilt. It's really messed with him. What happen to your fiancé?"

"He never proposed."

"Fuck."

She tried to smile but ended up blinking back tears.

"I'm not a shrink, but I'm pretty sure your parents wouldn't want you to blame yourself. Who's to say if you'd gone home, you wouldn't have all gone skiing that weekend, and you'd be dead as well?"

She wrapped her palms around her coffee cup. Maybe. Maybe not.

"Tell me more about your butterfly fascination."

"Dad bought Mom a butterfly figurine on their honeymoon. He bought me one on my first birthday. Over the years, since their death, whenever I see butterflies, I get this sense that they are with me. I think butterflies are their way of telling me to pay attention to that moment in my life."

"What do you think they were trying to tell you when I showed up with a butterfly tiara?"

"I don't know. Maybe that just like a butterfly tiara was too good to be true, so were you."

He didn't respond. Did that mean he agreed?

She gave a deep sigh and grabbed a new topic of conversation. "Tell me something you would never do...besides get married."

"Get a tattoo," he said without a second of hesitation.

She cocked her head. "Why?" What was wrong with body art?

He shrugged. "Don't laugh, but I suffer from trypanophobia—the irrational fear of needles."

That is an absolutely adorable admission.

Did he really think she'd laugh? Kind people don't laugh when you share a fear. Shared fears are more intimate than sexual relations.

"What is something you'd never do?"

"Trade in my knitting needles for a crochet hook."

His raised eyebrow told her what he thought of her response. While he'd dived to the bottom, she'd swam on the surface.

Before he could call her out on it, she put the brakes on their get-to-know-you gab session. "I think now would be a good time for you to go to your gala and for me to go home." The moment the words were out there, a sense of sadness swept through her. Getting to know him hadn't been an awful way to spend the last hour.

He ran a hand through his lovely thick hair. "You're probably right. Are we still on for our dance lessons tomorrow?"

She cocked her head. Did she want to continue with their contract knowing what she knew now?

If you say no, I'm never going to talk to you again.

"Are Jimmy Choo stilettos expensive?"

17

Dance lesson day was here.

Wendy and Jackson currently stood on the corner of Wooster and Bleecker, where they had agreed to meet, and were eyeballing each other like opponents about to go several rounds of boxing. Only instead of boxing, it was ballroom dancing. Neither of them spoke. She knew her reason but had no idea his. She felt awkward after last night's chitchat.

Today, he wore dark sunglasses, black trousers, and a white dress shirt with its sleeves rolled up on his forearms. She preferred this look to the tuxedo. The tuxedo made him feel out of her league. This combo made him look like a guy she could lick and he wouldn't complain.

"Hi," she said.

"Fancy meeting you here." He removed his glasses and the heat in his eyes made her knees wobble. "You look good enough to eat."

She laughed. "Funnily enough, I was just thinking about licking you." Jackson had wanted to pick her up at her place, but she'd squelched his idea. The act would have felt too much like a date. This was most certainly not a date. They were not a couple.

"Feel free to lick me anytime the mood strikes."

"Oh. That would be inappropriate. Unless it's during a booty-call session." She turned in the direction of Abigail's loft. "Just so you know, I've told Eddy and Abigail who you are."

Falling into step next to her, he said, "I wish you hadn't."

"I'm not a great secret keeper unless it's a boring secret. Like the kind I deal with at work." She'd FaceTimed with them last night and told them Jackson wasn't who he'd led them to believe he was, and the why behind his deceit.

"Did I mention how lovely you look in your dance clothes?" His voice had a rumbly warmth that she liked…a lot.

"You're not looking too bad yourself." Not for the first time, or even the fiftieth time, she wondered if he'd gone home last night after he dropped her off at her door, or if he'd gone back to the gala. She hadn't invited him in or even asked him to come back for a booty call. She'd been too wound up with everything she'd discovered. She had needed alone time to think.

What if he and Chasity were to get back together before their contract ended? The question made Wendy's stomach twist. It had been doing a hell of a lot of that lately, and she sighed.

"Is everything o—"

"We're here." She glanced at the new heart-shaped chalkboard hanging from a hook on the colorful door. Its greeting was written in Eddy's handwriting. Wendy laughed. She'd bet money Abigail had no idea what had been written on her shop sign.

Jackson turned to see what caused Wendy to laugh. It was the sign hanging from a hook on a purple door.

Opening soon: Stitches with Bitches & Britches. Where stilettos and dicks coexist.

Jackson chuckled. That sign would bring customers through the door. Even those who didn't know one end of a ball of yarn from the other. "Here as in at the dance studio?"

Wendy nodded. "That is exactly the kind of here I meant when I said here."

A warning bell went off in his head. "Did you trick me into taking knitting lessons?" Why would she do that?

She tucked a curl behind her ear. "That's the thing with a well-written contract—there's no room for tricking. Or not much, anyway."

"Not much?" He made a mental note to reread their contract. Had he read all the fine print?

"Correct." She opened the door and hurried inside.

Against his better judgment, he followed and discovered a mostly empty room. The part that wasn't empty made him anxious.

It was the part where a very large man, wearing a tutu, twirled a sweet-looking woman around the floor in a swing move to Elton John's "Crocodile Rock." Not just any man and woman. They were Wendy's tribe of misfits.

"Are they taking dance lessons as well?" he asked Wendy.

"Not that."

"Then what?"

She laid a hand on his bicep as if to keep him from bolting. "Mom once told me you could tell a lot about a man by placing him in an uncomfortable situation and watch how he handles himself."

"We've already established I have no character. Why are they here?" Jackson glanced back at the door. How much of an asshole would he be if he left?

"Eddy, the perfection that he is, offered to teach us. For free. And nothing in our contract spelled out who the lessons would be given by. But don't worry. He's quite good."

Dance lessons given by a drag queen weren't what he'd had in mind when he'd agreed to the stipulation in their contract. "I would have preferred to have taken lessons by an expert. I don't believe in wasting my time on good when excellent is available."

"Is it that or is it that Eddy is too much for you?"

"He is more than I'm used to."

Her lips tightened. "Does that mean you're going to bail on this part of our contract? And before you answer, you should know, if you do, I'll bail on the part that means the most to you."

Jackson rubbed the back of his neck. He would be lying to himself if he didn't admit he admired her ability to twist situations into her favor. She was no man's doormat. "Nothing against Eddy, but if you hired him because he's free, let me make it clear, I'll pay for a real teacher."

She laid a hand on his chest. "To be honest, I asked Eddy about our hiring his private dance instructor—who also happens to be Eddy's ex-lover from last year—to teach us." She paused and took a breath.

He also liked how she tended to ramble when nerves had her by the throat. Or at least, he thought it was nerves that caused her to ramble.

"But anyway," she continued, "according to Eddy, his ex charges an arm and a leg and a *look* at the guy's junk."

Jackson shook his head. "He was kidding, right?"

"Quite possibly, but one never knows with Eddy." Wendy swept her gaze down Jackson's body, *to his junk*, and then quickly back up. "I could try and get him for next week's lesson, and we could discover the truth."

"Eddy will do."

Eddy turned and noticed Wendy and Jackson standing in the doorway. He stopped his dance partner mid-twirl. "Alexa, turn the music off."

"Okay, I'll turn the music off."

The room went silent. Then, with his arms outstretched, Eddy glided with a right-hip-bump, left-hip-bump move across the wooden floor toward them. When he stopped, he lifted the sides of his pink, scratchy-looking skirt and executed a deep curtsy.

"Welcome to Eddy's Dance Studio." He stayed deep in curtsy pose. When he straightened, he winked at Jackson. "Where dancing and prancing are not only taught but like encouraged...as a way of life."

Jackson scowled at Eddy. "I don't plan on doing any damn prancing."

Eddy tittered. "I also teach sashaying, shimmying, and, for hunks like you, swaggering."

"Behave yourself," Wendy said to her friend.

The woman, who'd walked normally across the floor, held out her hand to Jackson. "I'm Abigail. Welcome to my home."

He recalled some of what Wendy had told him about her. "So, this is the loft you inherited?" Jackson glanced around. The room held three lawn chairs and nothing else. "I see you're into minimalism."

"Bless your heart. You're quite the charmer. I live upstairs. The yarn shop will be down here."

"Let me know when you open for business. My sister, Annie, mentioned the other day she wanted to learn to knit. I'll send her your way." Annie worked too hard. It would do her good to get a hobby. Make some friends who knew how to have fun and not just network for the sake of the corporation. Last night when he called Annie and told her that Wendy now knew everything, she'd been amused and asked if the three of them could get together for coffee someday. She wanted to get to know Wendy. She also warned him not to break her heart...which, according to her, was a real possibility now that Wendy knew he wasn't a loser.

Wendy slipped out of her pink jacket and draped it over the back of a lawn chair. "The Manhattan Knitters are about to hold auditions. Do be sure and let her know. But be warned, we only have one available spot."

Eddy clapped his hands three times. "Time is money. Shall we get started?"

"I thought the lessons were free," Jackson whispered to Wendy.

"Me too," she whispered back.

"Did you have something to say?" Eddy asked.

Jackson lowered his shoulders and tried to relax. He would survive this. "I take it you're capable of teaching something other than cabaret moves or Wendy wouldn't have chosen you." Jackson eyeballed Eddy's ballet shoes.

Eddy swatted at him, his fake nails flitting across his arm. "Mr. Jackson, are you trying to seduce me?"

Wendy laughed.

Jackson liked the sound of her laughter. It made his chest tighten. Every. Damn. Time.

"Eddy, knock it off," she said. "Teach us to dance like Ginger and Fred Astaire."

"Honey, with a hottie like him, I'm going to teach you to dance like Baby and Johnny."

"Who?" Jackson asked.

Eddy plopped his hands over his cheeks and gave Jackson a wide-eyed stare. "Baby and Johnny are just the sexiest couple this side of me and my future guy." He threw his hands out in front of him and then opened his arms out wide. "Haven't you watched the classic...*Dirty Dancing*?"

Jackson shook his head.

Wendy placed her hand on his. "Next time it's on, I'll give you a call, you can come d—you can come over, and we'll watch it together."

"Showtime," Eddy announced. "Alexa, play the first song in my Waltz collection."

The sound of a banjo being strummed and a quirky, familiar voice from childhood asking why there are so many songs about rainbows filled the room.

Wendy laughed again.

Jackson didn't. "What the fuck kind of dance music is that?" Son of a bitch. He'd been played. This was all one huge joke on their part. "Very funny. I lied about being your upstairs neighbor, and now this is an elaborate ruse on your part to get even."

"The Manhattan Knitters are not into childish retaliation," Wendy said. "If we ever feel the need to get even, trust me, you won't describe our revenge with words like *antics* or *ruse*."

Eddy fluttered his false lashes. "This happens to be 'Rainbow Connection' by Kermit the Frog. One of today's best modern songs to waltz to. Listen to the beat. One, two, three. One, two, three."

Jackson listened. Sure enough, it did have a one, two, three beat. "My apologies. I guess I'm tenser than I thought about showing Wendy my lack of dance skills." He grabbed Wendy, placed both her hands on his waist, and then placed his on hers. "Let's do this."

Eddy shook his head in a woeful fashion. "You're doing it all wrong. *This* is how it's done." He demonstrated with Abigail how to hold your partner during a waltz.

With a little effort, Jackson and Wendy managed to mimic Eddy and Abigail.

"I won't judge if you don't," Wendy whispered to him.

"Deal."

Eddy let go of Abigail and did a circle around Jackson and Wendy. "Jackson, you're going to step forward with your left foot, out with your right and then together. Wendy, you're going to do the opposite. He'll lead. You *can* lead, big boy, right?"

"I can lead."

"Fabuloumento." Eddy pulled Abigail back into his arms. "Watch us. Join in when you're willing to step out of your comfort zone. Forward out together. Backward out together. Forward out together."

Jackson stared into Wendy's eyes. "How many dance lessons did I agree to?"

"Seven."

"Fuck. We might need ten."

"Mr. Not Cupcake," Eddy said in a cheery voice, "if you keep saying fuck, I'm never going to be able to get through this lesson."

Wendy giggled. "He doesn't have a polite-company filter."

Jackson put his lips next to her ear. "You told him? About Cupcake?"

She zigged when he zagged and stepped on his foot, causing him to grunt. "He knows everything."

Jackson had no idea how to handle Eddy. The guy looked and acted like Cupid on crack. Only instead of a diaper, he wore a tutu. And a tiara. So, instead, Jackson focused on Wendy.

She'd been blushing all night. He wasn't sure why. He couldn't wait to get this lesson over so he could take her back to her apartment and make love to her. Fuck. Where had the word *love* come from? And why didn't it sound a strident musical note in his brain like the theme song in *Jaws*? Duuun Dun...Duuun Dun.

"You feel great in my arms." *Sex* was the word he needed to focus on when around her. He pulled her in closer.

"Your elbow is drooping, Jackson," Eddy said, from across the room. "A drooping elbow is a sign of other manly parts being droopy."

Wendy grinned up at him. "I believe the two of you will be best buds by the time our lessons are over."

"Either that, or I'll be sitting in jail for punching him in the nose for inferring I have a limp dick."

"Let him have his thoughts. Besides, if he believes you're not as perfect under your clothes as you are with all visible body parts, it helps him to keep his heart."

"Do you believe I'm perfect?"

She tilted her nose into the air. "I wouldn't ask just *any* man to be my neighbor with benefits when I have a perfectly perfect vibrator at my disposal."

Thoughts of her and a vibrator did things to him. To his dick. "Hmmm. It goes both ways."

She widened her eyes. "You have a vibrator?"

He had walked right into that one. "I wouldn't have said yes if I didn't think you were perfect." He pushed against her so she could feel his arousal.

Once again, she stumbled, and stepped on his toes. "If you don't want me stepping on your toes, stop startling me with your lies."

He studied her face. Tonight, she wasn't wearing makeup, which suited him just fine. Wendy had the kind of pretty you couldn't buy at a makeup counter. "What did I lie about?"

"My having a perfect body."

Fascinating. He'd meant the whole of her was perfect. Not just her body. Her misinterpretation revealed she had a layer of insecurity beneath her thick layer of bravado. A layer she'd hidden well up until this point. "That wasn't a lie. You do."

She stepped on his toe again. This time he was certain she'd done it on purpose. "Whatever. I've got a mirror. My body doesn't look anything like Chasity's."

What did Chasity have to do with this conversation? "I thought you liked your body."

"I do. Mostly. But Chasity has the kind of body that would make even a runway model green with self-doubt."

The way a woman's brain worked was mesmerizing. "I didn't find Chasity to be perfect."

"Lie."

"Time to switch partners." Eddy stopped beside them. "Abigail will work with Wendy on the girl parts, and I will work with Mr. Jackson on the man parts."

Jackson cursed under his breath. He wanted to finish this line of conversation with Wendy. "Is that neces—"

"Honey, loosen up. Honestly, it's sooooo needed. You've got a droopy table and your palm-to-palm leaves something to be desired. I'm telling you, a woman longs for a man with a good hand." Before Jackson or Wendy could resist, he whisked Jackson out of Wendy's arms and began moving him around the floor like a man holding a stiff mop.

Jackson didn't speak.

"So, you see, Mr. Not Cupcake, a woman knows to go back when you put pressure on her palm, like this." Eddy pushed his hand against Jackson's hand.

Jackson took a step back followed by a side together and refrained from commenting.

"Now, you guide me."

Jackson bit back the retort stuck behind his gritted teeth. Instead, he put pressure on Eddy's palm. This was a load of crap. He didn't need to learn how to lead. And he damn well knew how to use his hands with a woman.

"Yes. Yes. Fuck yeeeesss." Eddy's squeal caused Wendy and Abigail to glance their way.

Jackson narrowed his eyes.

"Behave yourself, Eddy," Wendy said.

"Sorry, darling." Eddy giggled. "Sometimes I forget I'm in polished company."

"Only sometimes?" Wendy countered.

Eddy gave her a limp hand motion. "Look at you, being sassy."

Jackson almost laughed. The guy really was an acquired taste. But not a bad one. Just a little more flamboyant than Jackson was comfortable dancing with.

"Okay, darling. Playtime is over. Back to work. When you want your partner to turn, you put pressure on her back." Eddy demonstrated the move as he spoke.

Jackson stumbled and stepped on Eddy's toe. "Sorry." His tone might have implied the opposite.

Eddy shot him a pissy look. He leaned in and whispered in Jackson's ear, "Not Cupcake, if you break, you buy."

Jackson knew better but couldn't stop himself. "How exactly would I break your shoes?"

Eddy stopped and took a lace handkerchief out of the waistband of his tutu. "By leaving your manly scuff all over their unspoiled surface." He bent at the knees and wiped at the footprint on his pink ballet slippers.

Jackson watched in befuddlement. Eddy should be wearing black shoes. Dark-colored shoes wouldn't show marks when beginners accidentally stepped on them. Luckily, the footprint wiped off. "See, no mark."

"Not from lack of effort on your part. I'll have you know I am not a tree for you to mark your territory upon."

Jackson had no idea how to respond but that didn't stop him from trying. After all, he was a guy. Guys liked to have the last word. "No harm. No foul."

Movement out the window drew his attention. Two guys were talking. Or arguing. He could only see one of their faces. The bald one. Even from this distance, Jackson could see a scar running down the side of his face. The type of guy who reminded you why it wasn't safe to roam uninhabited streets after dark. Scarface pulled something out of his pocket and handed it to the other guy. Jackson really wanted to get a glimpse of the other guy's face. For some odd reason, the way he stood reminded him of the real Cupcake.

"There will be plenty of fouls and harm if your hurt my Wendy." Eddy stepped into Jackson's space, blocking his view of the sidewalk.

"Your Wendy?"

"Correct. She's my friend," Eddy said. "I protect my friends in any way necessary."

Jackson glanced at Wendy. She and Abigail appeared to be in deep conversation. Jackson tried to be perturbed by Eddy but couldn't. "And you think I will hurt her?" Why in the hell would he do that? She was doing him a favor.

"I think you're capable of hurting her. Especially now that she knows you're not a man-whore."

"It's not my plan." Then again, it hadn't been his plan to hurt Chasity either, but he had. But that's because he and Chasity had been in a real relationship that hadn't worked out. He and Wendy weren't in a real relationship. They had a precisely worded contract that didn't leave room for hurt.

Eddy pursed his red lips and shook one fist at him. "Your plan is of no concern of mine. All I'm saying is if you hurt her, I will kick your fine ass."

Jackson tried not to laugh. Not because he thought the subject was funny but because Eddy didn't look like a fighter. "If I hurt her, then you'd be right to try and kick my ass."

Eddy smiled. "There'd be no try. Just do. With rules attached...of course."

"Rules?"

"If an ass kicking is necessary, you have to agree to no punches to the face." Eddy framed his face with his hands, fingers wide open. "This is my moneymaker."

Since when did guys enter into agreements on how an ass kicking would go down? "Yeah, sure. Whatever."

"Then we're done here," Eddy said tartly. "Wendy, your man awaits."

Wendy hurried over to them. "You're already finished?"

Eddy plopped his hands out, elbows tight at his waist. "I've done what I can to turn him into a leader and not a bumbler."

Wendy hugged Eddy and kissed him on the cheek. "You're the best."

Eddy blushed. "Oh, don't thank me." He tossed Jackson a look that Wendy didn't see. "Honey, I did what I could."

"Which, if I know you, means you have accomplished a miracle."

Eddy tittered. "I wouldn't go that far. He's rough around the edges. Even sweet Jesus would be hard-put to create fine wine from what I had to work with."

"Hey. I'm standing right here," Jackson said.

"You gave me nothing," Eddy stage-whispered toward Wendy.

"Sorry about that," Wendy said to Eddy. "I didn't know he would have two left feet on the dance floor."

"Well, Eddy did what Eddy could do."

"And Eddy's do is always full of awesomeness."

"Girlfriend, you know I don't do anything halfway. But even when Eddy gives it his all, there's still no way he can turn a JC Penney beige wedge into a Jimmy Choo red stiletto."

"If you guys are done making fun of me, maybe we can get back to dancing. I have some new moves I want to try out on Wendy," Jackson said.

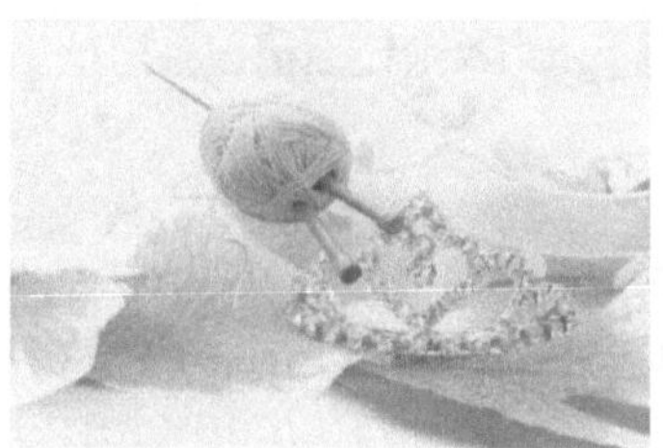

18

Two hours later, Wendy and Jackson stood in her doorway. A strong, undeniable buzz of awareness had consumed her from the moment they'd met on the street corner for lessons. Spending two hours dancing so closely together had only made the need more potent. "Do you want to come back in a couple of hours?" Too late, she realized she shouldn't have formed it as a question. She had control of their booty-call nights.

He tilted her chin and kissed her softly on the lips. "Now works for me."

She took a step back, causing his hand to drop. "What's wrong with two hours?"

He gave her a large smile that made her body tingle. "That's two hours we could be enjoying each other's company."

She crossed her arms under her breasts. "Go home. Shower."

He laughed.

She didn't. Call her a freak, but cleanliness was important. Besides, she needed some time to make sure her heart wasn't getting the wrong idea about what was going on between them.

"Fuck. You're serious."

She tilted her head and studied him intently. "Is that a problem?"

"I could shower here. With you."

Her body jumped immediately on board with the idea which was probably why her words came out sounding breathless. "You don't have clean clothes."

"I'll crawl into your bed naked."

She put her hand on his chest and pushed. "I'll see you in two hours. You can let yourself in when you come back. I'll be in bed."

He leaned against the doorframe, ran a finger down the side of her face. "Or you could stay up, and we could talk. Unwind with a drink. I'll bring the wine." He leaned down and nipped her earlobe.

She swallowed. "Not necessary." Was it her imagination, or was he trying to treat them like a real couple?

"What's not necessary?"

"Foreplay." Now that she knew he was a decent guy, it was imperative she didn't allow him to get close to her heart. Because decent or not, he'd made it clear he didn't do love. And deserve it or not, her heart wanted love and marriage and family.

He raised an eyebrow. "You don't need foreplay?"

"Seeing you naked is all the pre-game I need. Besides, we're not a couple. Foreplay is for sweethearts. It's for when two people fall in love with one another."

"Invite me in."

"I did invite you in. Once you go home, shower and change, that is."

He straightened and frowned. "At some point we need to talk."

She raised her eyebrows. "We talked last night. What's left to discuss?"

His eyes took on a stubborn stain of gray. "The charity ball. Our dance lessons. Your makeover."

Did he want her to get a makeover right away? "I guess you're not wrong." Of course, he did. If he, one of the Elusive Six, was going to be seen in public with her, he'd want her to fit his image. She realized a little part of her had wanted him to think she was perfect as is. Not a dull diamond in the rough awaiting a spit shine and buff. "Come in."

"If you insist."

She ignored his tone, mostly because she couldn't decipher it. Was he amused at her expense, or what? "Have a seat. I'll be right back." Wendy retreated to her bedroom where she took a couple of deep gulps of emotionally stabilizing air. It was perfectly reasonable for Jackson to want her to go ahead and get her makeover. Getting the makeover sooner rather than later would help him to get the most bang for his buck.

She took off her new dance shoes and placed them on the special-made shoe rack in her closet. She slipped out of her tights and put them in the hamper, leaving on the flouncy dance skirt and T-shirt. She walked into the bathroom, washed her face, and pulled her hair back in a messy bun. Later, she'd take a shower. But for now, she was semi-comfortable.

Time to go back into the living room and keep him at a distance. She reached to turn off the bedside lamp and knocked her crystal butterfly off the nightstand. She picked it up.

What were her parents trying to tell her? Something about the lamp being left on? It was odd she hadn't turned it off this morning when she got up. She always did.

Or maybe they wanted to tell her something about Jackson.

She padded back into the living room and found Jackson sitting on her couch, thumbing through her picture album. For a second, she stood in the doorway and watched him invade her privacy as if he had every right. Nice guy or not, he didn't. "What are you doing?"

He glanced up. "You were cute when you were little."

She stepped closer to him and glanced over his shoulder.

He ran him thumb over a picture of her and her parents on Christmas morning. She'd been about five.

A familiar pain stabbed at her chest. "That's a private family album." She missed them so much. Wished with all her heart she had gone home that weekend, instead of out with a guy who not only hadn't proposed but had also cheated on Wendy the same weekend. A guy who wouldn't know the truth if it slept with him.

Jackson set the album down on the coffee table. "Sorry. I didn't realize you would care if I glanced through it while I waited."

"I do care. It's personal. It's…" She paused and took a breath. *It's not his fault.* "Sorry," she said stiffly. "Now more than ever, I think it's important for us to keep our personal lives off-limits for discussion. It's less messy that way."

He gave her a searching look, one that made her want to hide. "Of course, you're right, but some of the best things in life are messy."

She blanched. "I prefer neat, orderly, and structured." She didn't used to be that way. She used to love to wing it. But flying by the seat of her pants was the reason she'd cancelled on her parents that weekend.

"Great sex isn't neat, orderly, or structured." He stretched his legs out in front of him and folded his hands behind his head. His shirt now had several buttons undone, giving a view of his chest.

She tried to keep her gaze at chin level and above. "I disagree."

His nostrils flared ever so slightly, like they had when he'd come the other night. "Is that how you prefer sex?"

Normally, her answer was an easy yes. But two nights ago, their sex had not been any of those things. Definitely not orderly. Instead of starting at the top and working his way down, he'd started down and worked his way up. And the structure she preferred hadn't happened either. She liked sex on the left side of the bed because she slept on the right side. Their first night of sex had happened all over the bed. "Yes."

"Then what you're saying is you didn't enjoy our hookup? It wasn't any of those descriptors."

She pushed the fact he was right out of the way. "Not true. Our joining of bodies wasn't messy. You wore a condom. So, things stayed neat between us. I showered before sex, so orderly came into play. And we were done in time for me to get enough sleep to do my job. I call that following structure."

"We should add quiet. I've never known a woman to be so quiet during sex."

She bristled. Was he a man who needed his ego propped up by the sound of a woman screaming during orgasm? "I simply don't see a need to bore the rest of the building with what I'm feeling during sex."

He raised an eyebrow. "I wouldn't be bored. I'd love to hear what you're feeling during sex."

Heat pooled between her legs, and she gulped. "That's not part of the bargain we made. It's too late now to try and make changes to the contract. You've signed it. I've signed it. It's been put to bed."

"Hmmm. Speaking of bed." He glanced toward her bedroom.

"I've changed my mind about tonight. I'm tired. I think I'll sleep fine without an orgasm. You may go." For some reason, she had a sudden desire to retreat. Maybe it was because of the butterfly falling. Maybe it was because he had looked through her picture album. Probably it was simply because she wanted to say yes to messy.

He sat up straight. Looked confused. "But we haven't talked about the rest of the contract."

She sighed in exasperation. "What about it?"

"When do you plan on buying your new dress? When will you have your makeover?"

"I haven't decided yet."

"Best you get right on those things. I don't want anything left to chance."

She leaned her head from right to left, popping her neck. "Noted."

He didn't move. He picked up a magazine. It was opened to the crossword puzzle she'd been working. "At least you don't do your puzzles in ink."

Should she tell him she'd only used a pencil because her Bic had decided not to work? "What would be wrong with it if I did?"

"I've found the types who do are too uptight."

"What does using a nonerasable instrument have to do with being uptight?"

"Those who use ink don't think they ever make mistakes. And when they make mistakes, they either blame someone for the problem or they come unhinged. When they become undone, they make unwise choices."

Had she come unhinged when her boss had disciplined her for making a mistake on the job? Did asking Jackson to be her lover constitute an unhinged decision? "It's a good thing we don't plan on falling in love. I make a living off not making mistakes. If that makes me too uptight for someone like you, oh well."

He ran his hand through his hair. "I didn't mean to insult you."

"You didn't. You pointed out I'm not your type. I already knew that. Which is why our contract is still doable."

He stood and took his wallet from his back pocket. "Here. It's my personal credit card. Use it to buy the gown, the accessories, and all the services I promised."

She took the card. Gold American Express. "Aren't you afraid I'll overspend?"

A genuine smile lit up his eyes. "Not at all. I don't know a lot about you, but I trust you."

"I *am* very trustworthy." Why did he trust her? What had she done to warrant such an honor? "And in the spirit of giving each other the benefit of the doubt, I trust you, too."

The words were supposed to be a little white lie. So why did they feel like the truth?

"Are we on for tomorrow night?" he asked.

"I'll text you."

Wendy's sterile dismissal caused something inside of Jackson to snap. Not *something*—something was too vague. He knew exactly what had snapped. It was the part of him that wanted to keep everything between them superficial. The snap caused a lesion in his iron control. A lesion large enough for that sterile need to leak out and a new need to filter in. A need for something with substance. Not a relationship of substance, but a moment of substance. Something real and not contractual. He reached for her hands and pulled her to him.

Her eyes widened, but they weren't filled with fear. More like desire. He kept his voice gentle, not wanting to break the moment and cause her to change her mind about what she surely knew he intended. "I'm going to kiss you. And it's going to be on my terms. Not yours."

She licked her lips and nodded.

He let go of her and slid a hand around her back. His mind and body warred over what he should do next.

She tilted her head up and leaned in.

He captured her chin with his other hand. The impatient beat of his heart urged him to go faster. He didn't. And was rewarded with the sensation of the ghost-like whisper of her breath on his mouth. He slowly brushed his lips against hers. Tonight, she smelled of lilacs and tasted of wine. Wine they'd drunk during their dance lessons. According to Eddy, even pros need a nip of the grapes before they can dance like Johnny.

She moved restlessly in his hands and took a step forward until their bodies touched.

God, she was all woman. He rubbed his erection against her belly, letting her know what kissing her did to him.

She didn't moan, but her hands came up and gripped his shirt as if hanging on for dear life.

He nipped her bottom lip and a tiny gasp escaped her. Nothing noisy. A sound for their ears only. He soothed the pain with his tongue. Was he an ass for wanting her to scream his name for all to hear?

Her lips parted to allow him in. He didn't take her up on the invitation. Instead, he kept the kiss light and playful. Nowhere near the I'm-going-to-fuck-your-brains-out kiss he wanted to give her. After a few minutes of slow exploration, he dragged his lips away from hers and took a step back. His voice dropped to a low growl. "That was a neat, orderly, functional kiss. It's not the kind of kiss a passionate woman like yourself should ever ask for from a man. So tomorrow night when you text me a request to come and fuck you, just know, it won't be neat, orderly, or functional...unless you specifically tell me that's what you still want."

Wendy raised a finger to her lips, her blue eyes bemused. "Okay."

He turned and walked toward her door.

"Stay," Wendy whispered.

Jackson stilled but didn't turn around. "Why?"

An eternity passed, then he heard her say, "I want a messy orgasm."

He still forced himself not to move. "On my terms?"

"Yes."

19

Before Wendy could second-guess her request, Jackson turned, walked back, grabbed her, pressed their bodies together, and stepped her backward until her tush bounced against the wall.

A brief second flicked between them as if he were giving her a chance to say no. She didn't.

He raised her chin and took her mouth. The breath-grabbing kiss forewarned of the type of sex he had in mind. It wouldn't be neat, orderly, or functional. It would be aggressive, magnificent, and quite possibly—

His tongue flitted over her lips and into her mouth, robbing her of all common sense. It was as if he was sampling the potency of what she had to offer. Was she a fine brandy or a two-dollar bottle of wine?

God help her, she wanted him to find her finer than the finest. Yet also down and dirty like the cheapest. When his tongue touched hers, she countered with everything she possessed. He didn't give an inch, proving himself an excellent kisser.

Delicious sensations surged through her body. Starting in her throat, lingering in her private parts, and curling her freshly pedicured toes. He tasted of her favorite wine and smelled a tad dangerous.

His hands were suddenly under the skirt she'd worn to dance lessons and tangled in her panties. Before she could gasp her surprise, he yanked. The material ripped and her panties dropped away. They pooled at her feet.

Still, he didn't stop to allow her time to process. His fingers opened her, and one clever digit slid inside while his lips continued their ravaging of hers.

Sweet baby Yoda, touch him already.

She grabbed at his shirt and pulled it out of his slacks and ran her hands underneath so she could palm his pecs. This guy should never wear a shirt.

His lips slid across her jaw to nibble at her earlobe. He nudged her legs wider with his knee. Then a second finger joined the first. She bit down on her tongue, a cry of pleasure ready to sing soprano.

As if aware her voice wanted to be heard, he bit her ear. The sharp pain, tangled with the pleasure of his fingers ruthlessly pushing her toward orgasm, shoved her toward the edge where good-girl silence met wild-girl verbal screams of ecstasy.

Courtesy of a miracle, she managed not to be a screamer.

Her hips on the other hand, were all in. They pressed into him, enthralled and thrilled at the hardness of his cock. Her hands went to his belt buckle.

He placed his free hand on hers. "Not tonight. Tonight, is simply me giving you an orgasm."

"You're not in charge. I—"

"We're doing things my way." His thumb found her clit and did a delicious circle of the sensitive nub.

Her body tightened. Every ounce of her wanted his touch. Wanted it harder, faster, more. Her brain tried to remind her there was a problem. No other part of her body gave a rat's ass. She pushed into his fingers. "I want—"

"An orgasm. I know." He slid down her body, lifted her skirt with one hand, and then with the other he opened her to him. His tongue found her sweet bundle of nerves.

She reached down and held her skirt up for him. She wanted both of his hands free to do more of their magical tricks.

Once again, he slid a finger inside of her and bent it at an angle that caused her knees to turn to jelly. His tongue ravaged her clit with long hard strokes, while he tapped, tapped, tapped against her G-spot.

She whimpered and then slapped a hand over her mouth to keep any more noises from escaping. She glanced down to see if he'd heard.

His eyes were on her. His white teeth flashed in a cocky grin. Then he sucked her into his mouth, and her world exploded. The orgasm came in waves. Starting small and building to one pleasure-packed punch that had her holding his shoulders to stay upright. Only when the waves died down did she find the ability to form a series of thoughts.

One: Her panties were unrepairable. Two: The picture on the floor must have fallen off the wall. Three: Her skirt was a crumpled mess. Only a dry cleaner could save it. Four: His shirt was a mass of hand-created wrinkles. Five: Holy fucking phenomenon, the guy had superpowers.

"I've never had someone perform oral sex on me up against a wall." Her voice sounded like it had gone through the eye of a tornado.

He stood. Brushed his lips softly against hers, which were now tender. "I've never enjoyed giving oral sex to a woman, up against a wall, quite so much."

She sucked in a breath. "I'm sure if you've done one, you've done them all." That would have been a great place to stop talking. She didn't. "They have to be basically the same experience from your standpoint." *Ugh. I sound like I'm fishing for a…*

He laughed.

She wasn't sure if it was because her words surprised him or amused him.

He kissed her forehead. "Not true. Your taste. Your smell. The tiny whimper as you came against my mouth. Those I've not experienced with any other woman. They were all uniquely you. And uniquely you leaves your booty-call man in awe of the lady his…he's beholden to."

She resisted the urge to smile like a besotted woman. "Okay then." She reached down, picked up her panties, and walked to the door. "It's time for you to leave, so I can shower, get into bed, and fall asleep before the effect of that orgasm wears off."

"Honey, if it wears off too quickly, I didn't do it right. But never fear, I aim to please. If later tonight, you decide you're not satisfied with any part of what happened, give me a call, and I'll come back and try again."

"Good night, Jackson."

Jackson removed his dark shades as he arrived at his office the next day. He'd donned them when he left his condo to save his tired eyes from the sunshine. After leaving Wendy's apartment last night, he'd been wound too tight to sleep.

Hazel glanced up from where she sat behind her desk and held out his empty coffee cup. "You look like hell."

"And you look as beautiful as ever. I have a fun task for you." A task he'd conjured around four a.m.

Hazel stood and walked to the hot pot where she proceeded to make herself a cup of tea. "I'm all ears."

He gave her his million-watt grin. The one he'd learned in high school made females swoon. "Have apartment 5C in Uptown Apartments furnished to fit my standards. Put a rush on everything. I plan to stay there for the foreseeable future."

Hazel gave him the hairy-eyeball look over the rim of her teacup as she took a sip. "The one you kicked Mitch out of?"

"I relocated him to an apartment better situated to his needs."

"Annie said you evicted him."

"Annie doesn't know all of my business."

"If that's what you want to believe."

He'd have a word with his sister about discussing his business with his assistant. Hazel was difficult enough without his sister giving her more reasons to be contrary. "Be sure and purchase a king-size bed and a memory foam mattress. The sheets should be at least five-hundred thread count."

She harrumphed. "I thought you said you wanted it to meet your standards."

"What does that mean?"

"Five hundred thread count is for people...like me." She stomped over to her desk and took a seat. "You sleep on at least double that."

He leaned a hip against her desk. Why couldn't she just be impressed he had a working knowledge of thread count? "I knew you would be the right person for this job."

"Creating a love shack for you is not in my job description."

He blinked but didn't bother to deny her assumption. He was a grown man and the boss. "It falls under other duties as assigned."

"I'm pretty sure it doesn't fall under that." She plopped down her tea and some of the liquid sloshed over its side.

He handed her his handkerchief. The one he always carried in his shirt pocket in case of tears...or spilt tea. Something he'd learned from watching Dad deal with Mom when they'd still been an intact family. "I'm sorry. You're right. It doesn't fall under other duties, but it is something I would like for you to take care of for me. If you do, I will owe you a favor."

She studied him. "I thought all those apartments came furnished. Did Mitch's rotating bedroom door result in him breaking the bed, or are you too good for secondhand furniture?" Her tone was sharp, but then it was always sharp when it came to wasting money.

"What's the use of having money if you don't spend it?"

She gave him the look that said he'd disappointed her. He hated that look. "Why do you want apartment 5C? It's one of the smaller floor plans in that building."

"Why do you know that?"

"It's my business to know your business. Why 5C?"

He walked over to a picture on the wall and straightened it. He smiled, remembering the picture he and Wendy had caused to fall off her wall last night. "I could tell you why, but then you'd be disgusted with me, and I prefer not to give you the satisfaction."

She picked up his stained handkerchief and held it out to him. "That building doesn't even have a doorman."

"Hire one for every shift, plus a relief one for days off." He took the handkerchief and shoved it in his jacket pocket. "Arrange for them to have apartments in the building as part of their benefits. And let's fast forward my plans to upgrade the building. I want it done much sooner than originally planned."

She handed him a piece of paper and an ink pen. "Sign this."

"What is it?" he asked even as he signed.

She took it and laid it on a pile of papers in an outgoing file. "Your release of liability should something happen while on a date with the woman who purchases you at your sister's charity."

"I don't know why I let her get me into these kinds of things."

"The same reason you're setting up a tiny apartment in a building you bought to flip. You're a sucker when it comes to women."

"What makes you think it has anything to do with a woman?"

"The only time you do stupid shit is when a female is involved." She handed him another piece of paper and pointed to a sticky note. "Sign here."

He handed the signed paper back. "If you know the answer, why do you ask?"

"I hope she's not another gold digger."

"She's not after my bank account."

"Says who? Your gut, or the brain in your pants?" Though her words were crass, the concern in her tone was real. Hazel was sensitive when it came to scammers. The company where she had spent twenty-eight years had folded and her boss had skipped town with everyone's pension. Who could blame her for being bitter and suspicious?

"Hazel, just do what I've asked you to do."

"On it. Is there anything else I can do for you to make your life easier?" Hazel's tone was full-on frostbite.

He hesitated. His next words would put her over the edge. "There is. I gave my American Express to a young lady named Wendy Travis. If the company calls to see if she's legit, you're to give my approval." He braced himself for the unleashing of Hazel's form of hell.

She smacked her palms on her desk. "For the love of all things safe, have you lost your mind? You gave a stranger your credit card? Your no-limit credit card? It's like the brain in your head has shrunk to the size of a shriveled pea."

Part of him wanted to laugh. Hazel rarely came unglued. But when she did, he knew better than to laugh. "What I do with my money shouldn't concern you."

Her posture stiffened. "Don't take that tone with me, and of course it concerns me." She wagged a finger at him. "You hired me to handle your office and your life. I'm simply doing my best."

The next time he hired an office manager, it would be someone mild mannered. Not pushy. Someone not against fetching him a damn cup of coffee. And he would do the hiring himself. Wouldn't let his sister talk him into bringing in a stray. Annie had found out about Hazel's predicament while she'd been doing some pro bono work for the state and had insisted Jackson hire her. "I won't take my tone if you don't take your tone."

"So, she's free to buy anything she wants?" Hazel asked sharply.

"Anything that is to prepare her for Annie's charity ball is approved."

"The least you can do is respect me enough to tell me what's going on."

She was right. And knowing Hazel, she wouldn't drop the conversation until he spilled the facts, anyway. He briefly explained about Wendy, about the dance lessons with Eddy and Abigail, and how they tied into the upcoming bachelor auction.

When he stopped talking, there was the sound of a throat clearing behind them. They both turned.

Son of a bitch.

"Chasity?" How long had she been standing there? How much had she heard? "What brings you to my office?"

Chasity gave him a too-bright smile. "Sorry to drop by unannounced. Could we talk?"

21

Tuesday afternoon, Wendy's nerves were playing hard rock along her spine and sweat beaded between her boobs. Why? Because it was a workday, and she wasn't at work. She was playing hooky. A decision she didn't make lightly. She would have taken a vacation day, but Mr. Morgenstern required a two-week notice when requesting vacation.

Wendy hadn't been given a two-week notice of a need for this day off, so hooky had been her only option. The Manhattan Knitters, not just her, were having fancy-ass makeovers, courtesy of Jackson's generosity.

According to Hazel, whom Wendy had met when she'd gone upstairs to complain about the commotion coming from 5C, Jackson had asked Hazel to tell Wendy that he wanted to not only buy her everything she needed for the ball, but he also wanted to buy Eddy and Abigail the works. Whatever Wendy needed for the occasion, he wanted her friends to have as well.

Which meant tickets to the ball. A one-thousand-dollar value.

They had started their day by meeting, before opening hours, with a personal shopper at a fancy boutique. The woman had assisted them with the picking out of their ball gowns and then a tailor fitted them. No *Rent the Runway* for the Manhattan Knitters.

Wendy had chosen a simple black silk Armani. The plunging neckline and low cut back shouted body confidence. And she did like her body. Sure, it wasn't thin like Chasity's, but it had its own plusses.

It helped that Eddy, upon seeing her in the gown, had enthused with much gusto and hand gesturing as he'd exclaimed she'd be able to stop hearts and traffic.

Eddy had chosen a unique dress with a slit up the front that showed off his tan killer legs and new Louboutins.

Abigail had fallen in love with a strapless gold Versace dress. The form-fitting bodice bedazzled with colorful shards of glass that were glued onto the silky fabric. The skirt flared and had lots of lacy ruffles. The split up the front would show off her choice of footwear—blinged-out Tony Lama cowboy boots.

Now they were having their hair cut, colored, and styled as well as their makeup done. Which was what had brought about the last-minute day off.

Last night, Bobby had called Eddy and told him he had a rare cancellation, and he invited the Manhattan Knitters to his shop for cuts, colors and pre-makeovers. Which were test runs for the day of a big event just in case things went sideways and adjustments had to be made. Like when you get married, you don't wait until the day of your wedding to try out sex to see if you're compatible.

"Darling, are you ready?" Bobby asked Wendy.

Wendy took a deep breath and released. This was why her nerves were singing and her boobs were sweating. The last time she had done anything drastic with her appearance had been one month before Mom and Dad had died. They'd seen her new look via FaceTime and loved it. After their deaths, Wendy couldn't bring herself to change her style. She wanted her parents to recognize her when they looked down on their daughter from heaven.

"I'm ready." This would be the only time she could afford someone of Bobby's quality to style her hair, so she'd given him permission to do what he thought best. Besides, according to Eddy, those that didn't give Bobby carte blanche lived to regret the decision.

"Ta-da." Bobby swirled her chair around so she faced the mirror.

Wendy blinked. Who the hell was the blonde in the mirror? Not her. Surely not her. How could it be her?

Her below-the-shoulder curly hair was now a notice-me-on-street-corners, above-the-chin, white blonde, the unruly locks tamed into a 1920s style. The person staring back at her looked like someone out of a fashion magazine. A very specific someone.

She took a breath, but it couldn't wiggle past the lump in her throat. She coughed so hard tears sprung to her eyes. Bobby had made her over to look like Chasity. Did he do this to all his non-celebrity clients? Transform them into celebrity lookalikes?

Bobby fussily handed her a bottle of water. She took a sip without taking her gaze off herself in the mirror. *Dear Lord, what have I done?* Her makeup had been kept low key except for her lips. Those lips. Were they hers? Or had Bobby stolen them off the face of Angelina Jolie? They were made to look even larger by lipstick in stop-the-traffic red.

"Do you like it?" Bobby's expression was one of supreme confidence.

"Eddy...I need Eddy." She blinked rapidly and took another sip of water.

"Eddy's being waxed," Bobby informed her with a delicate shudder. "If you listen closely, you'll hear him crying for *mercy*."

"Abigail." She massaged her chest. Was she having a heart attack?

Bobby's expression of world domination stilled. "Abigail's holding drama-baby's hand. Don't you like my exquisite vision?"

"Get them." Tears weren't going to be denied much longer.

Bobby fanned his face as if he too might cry. "Darling, please don't cry. Tears will ruin my masterpiece."

Wendy sniffed. "Okay." What would Jackson say? Would he hate it? Why did she care? All that was important was if she hated it. Did she?

"Give me but a *momento*. I'll bring our Eddy to you."

Two minutes later, Eddy and Abigail rushed to Wendy.

"Darling, Bobby says—"

Abigail gasped. Her eyes widened. "Bless your Manhattan heart."

That bad? Oh God. "Eddy, please tell me it's going to be okay."

Eddy grabbed both of her hands. "Honey—you make me want to be straight-up straight."

22

Thursday, Jackson stood inside apartment 5C and gave a low whistle. Hazel might be temperamental—which he would be, too, if someone robbed him of his pension—but she'd done a damn fine job of pulling off his request.

Clean lines. Windows without frills. An L-shaped couch with square throw pillows in a beautiful shade of blue. The blue of Wendy's eyes. A plush ottoman. A leather chair sitting atop a sleek stainless-steel base. All the furniture white. A multi-color, geometric rug added warmth.

A circular, gray marble coffee table anchored the furniture. The kitchen, visible from the living room, appeared to be equipped with things he knew how to use. Keurig, griddle, electric Rabbit wine opener, et cetera. The dining nook held a sleek black table for two. Sitting in the middle of the table a beautiful bouquet of lilacs. No wonder he had Wendy on the brain. The room smelled like her.

How had Hazel known Wendy smelled of lilacs and had eyes the color of sunset blue? God, had the two of them met? He shook away the worry. Better Wendy meet Hazel than Chasity.

Chasity had sworn she didn't hear any of his and Hazel's discussion Monday morning, but his gut told him she'd heard plenty. Especially when she'd pushed to stop by his apartment and pick up her passport that she'd left at his place. Much to her frustration, he'd told her he'd have a messenger take it, and all the rest of her things, to her apartment. Too which she'd had a meltdown.

Shaking off thoughts of Chasity's temper-tantrum, he strolled into the bedroom. Sunset-blue satin sheets on a California king bed conjured up tantalizing images of Wendy spread out naked in the middle. Or on all fours. Waiting for him to enter her. Fuck, yes. That thought had his dick ready for action.

Call him a wuss, but he liked the idea that Wendy would be the first female to share this bed with him.

He walked to the nightstand and spilled out the contents of the oversized shopping bag his sister had handed him when she'd come to see him right before he got off work. Having been brought into the loop by Hazel, Annie had been filled with invasive questions about Wendy.

The contents amused him. Toothbrush, toothpaste, makeup remover, mascara, deodorant, glow-in-the-dark condoms. A *night before and a morning-after bag.* He grunted. Partially in appreciation, partially in embarrassment. Sisters were a strange sort.

Down below, he heard a noise. He glanced at his watch. Did Wendy always get home this late from work? He shrugged. Her work schedule didn't concern him.

What she did off the clock, on the other hand, definitely concerned him and his cock.

"Let the good times roll." He walked back into the living room and jumped up and down on the floor. Within seconds, he heard her knocking against her ceiling. He chuckled. Jumped some more. This time doing his best to land hard.

More broom-knocking.

He rubbed his hands together and turned his television up loudly.

Muffled thumps made it to his ears.

He jumped some more. The distinct slam of a door set him into action.

He turned down his television. Walked to his door. And leaned casually against the frame and waited. How long would it take for the elevator to get her up here?

"What an ass. Tell me he's going to be faithful and then pulls this shit." Her voice reached his ears on the other side of the door, right before she knocked.

He swung the door open, and his breathing came to a screeching halt. This wasn't Wendy. Well...it was. But it wasn't. This Wendy reminded him of Chasity. Slick. Elegant. Worldly. "What did you do?"

She raised a hand to her short, blonde hair. "Do you like?" Her voice came out high pitched. Like she wasn't sure. Completely at odds with her normal self-assurance.

"Why?" It wasn't that he didn't like what he saw. After all, beautiful was beautiful. But New York City was full of perfectly styled women. He didn't want a perfect woman—he wanted a real woman. One that walked around the city in sweats and sneakers all while rocking a crooked ponytail. One who swiped on a little lip gloss, added a tiara, and called it good.

Her lips quivered. "You hate it?"

Damn it. He was being insensitive. "Not at all. I'm shocked. I didn't think you were the type who'd want to look like"—*his ex-girlfriend*—"someone else."

Her expression remained neutral. "It's okay if you don't like it. I'm still getting used to it."

He chose his words carefully. "I think you look beautiful."

She touched her hair. "Thank you. I gave Bobby the freedom to do as he saw fit."

Jackson jerked. "Bobby? You have a stylist name Bobby?" Damn it.

Wendy blanched. "Eddy does. Why?"

Shit. That couldn't be a coincidence. "An odd name for a stylist." Had she gone to Chasity's stylist? He'd heard her rave about him on more than one occasion. "You have beautiful eyes. And I've never noticed what lovely cheekbones you have. What's the occasion?"

She blinked. "Trial run for the ball. Make sure we liked the vision Bobby and his team had for us."

"We?"

"Me, Abigail, and Eddy. Thanks, by the way, for including them in the makeover and gown shopping. And tickets to the ball."

He masked his surprise. No wonder Hazel had seemed gleeful when he'd asked how the decorating had gone. "I take it you met my office manager?"

"I came to see what all the noise was about. It was Hazel directing the movers." Wendy's smile faltered. "She's precious. We really hit it off. She said I was a breath of fresh air. She reminded me of Mom."

His fingers itched to touch her hair. See if the hooker-blonde strands felt different. "I bet you miss her." It must have been hard on her to lose her parents at such a young age. And both at the same time.

Wendy's face lost its flush. "More than I would miss oxygen."

"I can't im—"

"Are you alone?" She glanced past him and into the apartment.

Did she still meet with her therapist? Talk to him or her about her parents? "I am."

Her nose wrinkled in a cute little way. "Then you weren't having sex with someone just now?"

He stiffened. What kind of guy did she think he was? He hadn't been making sex noises. He had simply been being noisy. "We have a contract."

She gave him a searching glance. "Then why all the commotion?"

When was the last time he'd done something so playful? "Me trying to get you up here." No matter what transpired between the two of them over the next couple of weeks, all they ultimately were to each other was a contractual arrangement. The fact he was enjoying himself, just a bonus.

"Why?"

He reached out and trailed a finger down her cheek. "Why do you think?"

She shook her head. "That's not how our contract works. I text you, and *you* come to *me*."

She was right. The contract gave her all the power. Which left him wanting to say fuck the damn contract. He wouldn't. He was a man of his word. "It's been eons since you summoned me." Since Sunday night.

She nibbled her bottom lip. A lip ripe for kissing. "I didn't want to inconvenience you, since you don't live above me."

Of all the inane reasons to deny them one another's bodies. "I adore inconvenience." He took a step back and motioned her to enter. "Welcome to my home away from home. Come in. I'll fix us a drink. We can chat. Get to know one another. Schedule some booty-call texts."

Wendy didn't budge as she contemplated him from beneath her thick lashes. "Casual conversations are Cupid's playground," she said, sounding like a Catholic nun.

A very sexy nun.

23

Wendy wrapped her arms under her chest and eyed Jackson. She hadn't meant to step inside the door.

Jackson waved her toward the living room. "Will you walk into my parlor." The sound of his sexy voice—or perhaps it was his reciting the opening to a famous poem in which a fly was caught in the silky web of a smooth-talking spider—caused her to shiver.

She waved a finger at him. "Just because I'm in your web doesn't mean we're chitchatting." Conversation led to knowing one another led to emotions led to—

Jackson lifted a sexy eyebrow. A movement her body construed as an invitation to play with the devil. "Then that only leaves us with sex on the buffet table."

Temptation trotted hussy-like through her veins. "-*That's* not currently on the table either." As much as Wendy wanted to have sex with him every single night between now and the end of their contract, she didn't want to become a Jackson groupie in the process. Thus, she had decided to limit herself to twice weekly.

He hooked his thumbs in his jean pockets. "Then why did you come inside?"

She ripped her gaze away from his splayed fingers and back up to his face. "To see what Hazel did with the place." Liar.

A grin twinkled in his eyes. "And what's your opinion?"

She glanced away. Focused on the décor. "Impressive if you like the crisp, clean, corporate feel. I personally would want some touches of love."

"Like what?"

Good question. "Everybody defines love differently. What makes me feel loved might make you want to pull your hair out."

He nodded as if he perfectly understood and agreed.

Damn it. They were chitchatting. Now would be a good time to leave. Go back to her apartment. "I thought you lived in a different building."

"I do."

I do. An image of a bride and groom standing in front of a minister saying those two little words popped into her brain. She zoomed in closer to the image. *Dear God, Jackson's the groom.*

She quickly zoomed out, but not before she realized a blonde stood under the veil. Who was the bride? Herself? Chasity? The barista at Wendy's favorite coffee bar? Before she could zoom in again, the image evaporated.

Get a grip. In what universe do you visualize weddings?

"Then why did you have Hazel decorate this apartment for you? I asked her but she said she wasn't at liberty to say."

A boyish grin lit up his face, causing his so freaking expressive eyes to spark with mischief and her sex drive to shift gears.

Vroom. Vroom.

Three nights a week wouldn't be a disaster.

"I told you," he said, "I have a hankering to get you in my apartment on my terms."

Had any woman ever turned him down when he put his pearly whites to the test?

Not many. If any.

"And I told you, that's not what our contract says." Some days it was easier to be a rule stickler than others. Today wasn't one of those days so she had to force the words.

"Can't we take a night off from our agreement?" Now it wasn't only the boyish grin he deployed. He also used the sexy voice. The voice that made her want to drop her panties.

Damn his superpowers. "I'm not saying yes. But if I did, are you implying you went to all this trouble for one night of maybe sex?"

"What trouble?" The way he said the words made her heart thump.

So freaking smooth.

He motioned for her to have a seat on the couch. "I own the place. It was a simple matter of having new furnishings delivered."

"Speaking of owning the building, do you plan to raise the rent? Turn it into luxury apartments?"

"For new tenants, the rent will go up. But if you've been here at least a year, your rent won't go up for five years."

"Not that it matters to me, my rent is part of my benefits package." Unless, of course, he raised the rent and Mr. Morgenstern decided to no longer offer rent to his top proofreaders.

"Killer perk. I should offer that to Hazel. I don't know why I didn't think of that. Thank you for the idea."

"I'd love it if she lived in this building." Wendy walked toward his couch but didn't take a seat. Sitting felt like capitulation. "Sooooo, this is your new love nest."

He chuckled. "You say that like it's a bad thing. What's wrong with wanting a love nest for afternoon quickies with the current...blonde...in my life."

She ignored the prick of jealousy his words caused. Who would be the next blonde in his life? "If you're going to have a place in this building, why not one of the larger ones?"

He walked over to a portable bar and poured them both a glass of wine, handing her one. "Because they don't sit above your apartment."

She cocked her head and took a seat.

Capitulate much?

"I'm not following." She took a sip. Damn. Smooth man. Smooth wine. Smooth leather couch.

He took a seat across from her.

She was thankful for the distance. Every time she got a whiff of his cologne, she wanted to strip.

He gave her a gotcha-wink. "You're the only tenant who heard the sex noises coming from this apartment."

"I find that hard to believe. But even if it's true, still not following."

"If you're up here, then there's no one in your apartment to hear us. And none of our other neighbors will hear us. So, you're free to be as loud as you like."

Should she tell him she didn't do loud? "How do you *know* none of the other neighbors heard?" Did she turn him on less because she didn't crank up the volume? Was he the type who needed his manhood praised? Was that her problem with men in general? Did they have sex with her and find *her* meh?

"Two of the walls have no neighbors. They are being renovated. I had management check with the other neighbor to see if she'd been disturbed by the last tenant and his harem."

"And?"

"She's eighty and can't hear a thing without her hearing aid. Only puts them in when she's leaving her apartment. She's blissfully ignorant of Mitch's lack of manners."

"Mitch?"

"The guy who lived here."

"I see." The guy had the same name as Penelope Angelino's boy toy. What were the odds? Weird—it had been a few days since she'd stressed about Mr. Bruiser and his intimidation tactics.

"Now, can we get back to why I got you up here?"

She picked at the hem of her T-shirt. "Remind me again why that was."

He placed an arm along the back of the couch and stretched his legs out in front of him. "I want to have sex with you on my terms." His body language, so languid and self-assured, said he expected a yes.

She stood and yanked up her commonsense panties. "That's *not* what the contract says."

He undid a couple of buttons on his shirt. "I know."

She glanced away from the chest hair display. The guy had the perfect amount of chest-hair. The kind that veers into an arrow aimed toward his package. She shook her head. Reminded herself contracts were created to keep individuals thinking with their brains, not any other part of their bodies. Especially their hearts. "I'm going to—"

"Wait. Kiss me first." He stood. "If you still want to leave after the kiss, I won't stop you." Now his voice wasn't all cocky confidence.

Contracts are made to be broken.

Despite having her commonsense panties in place, Wendy looked Jackson in the eyes and took a step toward him. "Okay." She lifted her chin and closed her eyes.

"Not here," he said gruffly.

Before she could open her eyes to ask what was wrong with here, he picked her up.

Her breath hitched. No man had ever swept her off her feet. Literally or figuratively.

He sat her on the edge of his bed and stepped between her legs.

"Is bringing me into your bedroom a tactical move? Like, I'll cave easier from here than I would have in the living room?"

"You've got the sexiest brain I've ever met."

"Why thank you. I exercise it daily."

"I'd like permission to exercise your lips daily." He cupped her cheeks and leaned down. "To be their personal trainer."

Her eyes fluttered shut. "They're not in the market—"

His lips on hers cut off her words.

She opened her mouth, and his tongue slid in.

What's a broken contract between booty-call friends? There are more heinous acts.

She gripped Jackson's head and groaned against his mouth. The sound startled her.

He drew away and for a weird moment she felt less whole. *Damn it.* What was that about? He picked her up and sat her farther back in the middle of the bed before roughly pushing her down. She smiled.

Whole? Half? Who cares?

She lost her smile when he straddled her and seared his lips to hers in a kiss that short-circuited what little circuitry was still operating in her brain.

The kiss went on for minutes, hours. Hell, Wendy lost count of time. A century might have come and gone. Or an eternity. It was everything a kiss should be. Hypnotizing. Persuasive. And so much it shouldn't be. Addictive. Very, very addictive.

When the kiss ended, she breathed in his earthy masculine scent and shivered. Hot, tangy desire uncoiled deep inside of her, enticing her to jump off a ledge because surely she could now fly.

But then he pulled back and stood.

Her whole being protested.

"Tell me you want this," he ordered. "Tell me you don't want me to stop."

Yes. Stop. That's what she wanted him to don't. "Don't stop." Her breathing was too heavy for the words to come out articulate. For all she knew he heard her say *Dot snot.*

"Tell me you'll be mine tonight. No contract. Just mine."

Why was he talking? Talking allowed time for her sexy brain to think. "Why are you against the contract? Against our terms." Damn him for talking. For making her struggle with her line in the sand.

He ran his hand through his hair. "Tomorrow, we'll go back to the contract. But tonight is off the books. In my bed."

When you step over the line in the sand, it shifts. Your world rocks. Bad decisions are made. "Doesn't my bed do it for you?" Then again, you can stand perfectly still on your side of the line and the sand still shifts and you face-plant.

"I want to see you naked on silk sheets." The hunger in his eyes was potent.

If you're going to face-plant anyway, why not have fun on the way down?

"How exactly do you want me on your sheets?"

He grinned. "Naked."

"Just naked?"

"That's for starters." He studied her. As if imagining his favorite fantasy in which she was the star actress. "On your hands and knees."

She pulled her T-shirt over her head and tossed it toward him. Shimmied and struggled out of her sweats before sending them flying. Reached behind her to unsnap her bra.

"Leave it on. And your panties."

She smiled saucily and rolled onto her stomach. She went up on all fours and with her back to him, took a moment to take in the room. The king-size bed dominated the small space. Matched in size by a picture hanging above the bed. *I have neither the time nor the crayons to explain this to you.* The word *crayons* was done in multiple colors. The rest of the words in white on a black background.

Wendy giggled. It was like her base desires talking to her brain. Brains were way overrated.

"Fuck, your body is amazing." Jackson reached out and ran a finger down the crease of Wendy's ass. The silk of her thong kept him from touching skin.

A small groan came from her. Nothing loud. Almost inaudible. But there. "Do that again."

"I don't make noises during sex."

He slapped her bottom, and she jolted. Fell onto her stomach, rolled over and sat up. Her eyes held a storm.

He lifted a brow. "My bedroom. My rules. Rule number one: a sassy mouth has consequences." It wasn't that he was into kink, but he was into getting a verbal reaction out of her in the bedroom. Anything that would unleash the emotions she didn't express during sex.

A flush crept along her cheeks and down her neck. Her tongue darted out and moistened her lips. "Do that again and I break your arm."

He choked back a laugh. Her spunk turned him on. Fuck. Everything about her turned him on. "Then don't hold back your enjoyment. I told you, no one can hear you."

She reached behind her and unsnapped her bra. The view of her slowly peeling it off caused all thoughts to flee. She tossed the bra at him. He let it fall to the floor. Then she hooked her thumbs into the elastic of her panties and pushed them down her legs and kicked out of them. "Your turn."

He undressed while she watched. He liked the way her breathing intensified with each small action that got him closer to being naked. He fucking loved the way her nipples pebbled. "On your hands and knees."

She obeyed.

This time when he ran a finger down her crease, he was rewarded with the wetness of her juices. He ran his other hand along his length and his thumb over his head. He wiped his pre-cum on her clit. She arched her back and pushed back like a cat stretching.

Her ivory skin on his silk sheets far bypassed his visions. He covered her body with his and nibbled at her earlobe. "I'm not sure I have the patience to give you foreplay. You look too fucking ready."

"I am ready."

He grabbed a condom, rolled it on, and positioned himself at her entry. He sank in about an inch. "Do you like?" Fuck. Did he just ask that? God, he hadn't asked a girl that since he was in high school.

"Very much."

He slid in further. She squeezed her muscles around him, and he cursed. His need to be all the way in was too consuming to ignore. "Careful. You don't want me losing control before you're ready."

"You're so big."

He grinned. "What did you say? I couldn't hear you."

She shook her head as if telling him no.

He pumped in and out of her a couple of times. "Talk to me."

"Fuck me," she said in a voice slightly louder than normal.

He pulled out and rolled her onto her back. She opened her legs and guided him back inside of her. He captured her mouth with a hard kiss. All the while giving the lady what she asked for. A good fuck.

Her hands came around his back and clutched. Her nails digging into his skin.

"Fucking you is like winning the lottery," he heard himself admit. "I'm never going to want to stop playing. I'm always going to want that next win."

"You can play this lottery all you want...until you can't."

He closed his eyes. A finite number of days until the ball. A finite number of nights to get her out of his system. Was that even possible?

He slid his lips along her cheek to her earlobe and bit down.

"Ouch."

He lathered the spot with his tongue before reaching between them and finding her clit. There, he languidly rubbed up and down.

A tiny moan escaped her lips. He rubbed harder as a reward. When no more moans were forthcoming, he let up on the pressure.

"Harder," she hissed.

"Keep moaning if you want harder."

"I don't."

He rubbed harder.

"Oh God, I love your thumb."

He chuckled. "Is that the only thing you love?"

He placed his hands on the bed on either side of her face. Pumped in and out of her.

"I love your cock," she groaned. "Don't fucking stop." Her legs came up and wrapped around him. "I love—"

He placed his lips on hers, swallowing any other declaration. They both came at the same time, their emotions lost in the kiss that took them over the edge. He shifted to his side so his weight didn't crush her. He stroked a hand through her short hair, cursed Bobby for cutting it off and dying it blonde. Chasity had to be behind the ambush. He'd listened to her tell stories of more outrageous schemes she'd pulled off. She had heard his and Hazel's conversation. It was the only explanation. But how had she arranged it so quickly, and why?

Wendy opened her eyes. Gave him a smile so tender it got past all his barriers and touched his heart. "I hope you know what you've done, opening Pandora's box." Her expression revealed so much more than her words.

Her expression revealed thoughts of possible love in their future. Which was bad. She was the sort to believe in forever love. He'd only ever be able to offer her a season of love. Forever wasn't in his damn DNA.

Too late, he understood the reason chitchat was the devil's playground. He'd asked for it *all* not knowing what it *all* would contain. Shit. They'd not only played with fire—they were charred.

The walls of the room closed in on him. His large, king-size bed suddenly not nearly big enough. He gave her what he hoped was a natural smile. "Good thing we have a contract to deal with these minor glitches."

The comedy club bouncer gave Wendy a friendly wink. "What brings you to the club on a Friday night?"

"One of those weeks where I need a dose of laughter twice." It hadn't been hard to talk the Manhattan Knitters into meeting there for their weekly meeting. She wasn't sure if that was because their weeks had been as roller-coasterish as hers, or if they'd simply heard the panic in her voice.

Panic because she didn't want to be home when Jackson arrived at his new love nest. That was if he planned on spending the night at his new digs. Which, considering his cool dismissal of her this morning—yes, this morning—he might not.

Okay, cool dismissal was a bit harsh. More like business dismissal. As in phone in one hand, computer up and running, coffee in the other hand. A jerk of his head in acknowledgment as she came into the kitchen.

Then another when she walked to the front door and mouthed goodbye.

She blamed herself. She never should have spent the night. But really, he could have at least put the damn coffee down and one-arm hugged her.

"Wine?" the bartender asked when Wendy stopped at the bar.

"Make it a Devil's Kiss."

"Shaking things up?"

"Time to stop being a creature of habit." The first habit she needed to break was not following her own rules. And it wasn't even like her rules were complicated. Follow the damn contract. *Easy peasy, Jackson squeezy.* And rule number one of sex. No loud moaning. Since when did she shout, *Oh God, this is better than a yarngasm,* while climaxing? No wonder Jackson didn't want to talk to her this morning. That would teach him not to push her to be loud during sex.

"I like your new 'do," the bartender said. "Very sexy."

"Thanks." She glanced in the mirror behind the bar. A night with Jackson's hands passionately running through her hair had left it a mess this morning. She'd done her best to restyle it the way Bobby had, but to no avail. Ugh.

Jackson had been sweet to pretend he liked her new look. Of course, she hadn't believed him. The eyes don't lie. She'd seen his briefly fill with horror. Not that she blamed him.

"You'll have to let me know if it's true that blondes have more fun," the bartender said.

"Make that a double, and I will." She made her way to the back table in the corner. *The Knitters' Table.* On Tuesday nights, a reserved-for-knitters sign occupied it. The brawny bar owner had the sign made when he realized the knitters were going to be a permanent fixture. Wendy was pretty sure he had a crush on Eddy, but Eddy wouldn't give him the time of day. Said the guy was too much man for Eddy.

She took out her knitting and listened to the first comedian. She'd missed the joke, but the audience groaned. She peered closer at the guy on stage to see if it bothered him to have a joke flop. It would her. In fact, if she owned a comedy club, she'd make the audience sign an agreement promising to laugh at all jokes. And the comedians would sign one promising to be funny.

Contracts were so beneficial. Took all the messiness out of trying new things. Like having a booty-call man.

Nope. Not going to think about Jackson.

"Have any of you ever been guilty of being a fake pooper scooper?" the comedian asked.

This generated some self-conscious laughter. Wendy glanced around. Having never been a pet owner, she had no concept of the likelihood of the answer being yes. She knitted a row.

"It's a thing." The guy was cute in a non-cute sort of way. He pretended to walk a dog. "You carry the little bag and get props from all that see you because you're a responsible pet owner. But when your dog does his business, you don't actually pick up the poop. You make a production of getting your bag ready, you bend over, and you pick up... nothing."

Wendy chuckled, imagining Jackson walking a small poodle and doing this.

"This is a skill employers don't even know to ask for." The comedian pointed to a man sitting in the front row. "Could you use a fake pooper scooper at your business?"

The guy sat at a table with three other guys.

"He *is* the fake pooper scooper," one of them bellowed.

More laughter.

The comedian took a sip of water. "And don't even get me started on how useful a person with this skill would be in politics. I mean, every fucking president could use one of these guys. *Hey, I shit over there, go trick the country into thinking it's been cleaned up.* Oh wait, every president already has one of these on staff—the press secretary. Politics invented the fake pooper scooper."

"What did we miss?" Abigail asked, startling Wendy, who'd become engrossed with the act.

Tonight, Abigail wore jeans with boots, a T-shirt that said, *Y'all, I'm a Knitter and I Like Balls,* and her hair was pulled up in a high ponytail. Eddy had on a pink T-shirt, with a short-sleeve button-up shirt over it. The button-up was left unbuttoned. On the bottom, he'd donned gray linen slacks, and sparkly loafers. They both wore their tiaras. As did Wendy. The regulars were used to them.

Seeing Eddy dressed as a man always startled Wendy. As a cross-dresser, he was flamboyant. As a man, he was sexy and serious. He never did *serious* unless upset.

"This guy bombed until the end. You're looking nice tonight," Wendy told Eddy. She couldn't just ask him what was wrong. When it came to the important stuff, he didn't easily share.

Eddy shrugged. "I simply don't have the energy to be divine tonight."

"Why's that, sugar?"

"Bobby refuses to tell me why he turned you blonde without your permission. These things are simply not done."

Abigail leaned back so that Eddy couldn't see what she was doing and shook her head at Wendy. Sign for don't ask any more questions.

"Oh Eddy, I'm sorry. I didn't want you and Bobby to fight because of me."

Eddy gave her a stare. "I don't know a Bobby. All Bobs are dead to me."

Wendy bit her lip. "He can't be dead. At least not until he's fixed my hair before the ball."

Eddy smiled. A sad smile painted in broken-heart blue. "Honey, I know you hate your hair, but you look lovely. In fact, you need to text your booty-call tonight. He needs to see your new look."

Wendy grimaced. "He did see me. Last night. And he doesn't like it."

Abigail made a noise of displeasure "He's such a man. They all—"

"Oh. My. God." Eddy slapped his palms on the table. "Girlfriends, do you see who just walked in with her clique?"

Wendy turned. Whoever the woman was, she now had her back to them. "Who is she?" Built like a brick house. Short...blonde hair.

"That's Not Cupcake's *ex*-girlfriend." Eddy used a lot of hand motion to emphasize his words.

Wendy sat up straighter and sucked in her stomach. Focused her eyes on Eddy so she wouldn't turn and gawk.

"What is *she* doing *here*?" Abigail leaned out on her barstool in an apparent attempt to catch a better glimpse of the movie star. "I loved her in her last movie."

"You'd better get your sass on, and I don't mean sasquatch, because she's headed our way," Eddy said to Wendy.

Her heart rate grinded into overdrive. She stuffed her knitting into her satchel. "Why is she coming this way?"

"I don't know," Abigail whispered while waving.

"Are you waving at her?" Wendy asked. Unbelievable.

Abigail dropped her hand to her side. "Umm. She's like a movie star."

Eddy reached out and grabbed Wendy's arm. "Brace yourself."

"No way—" The rest of the words were lost in a whirlwind of belly flutters as Chasity Kennedy glided to a stop at their table.

"You must be Wendy. I thought maybe we should talk. You know...woman-to-woman." The blonde goddess held out her hand. "I'm Jackson's girlfriend."

Wendy shook her hand. What could they possibly have to talk about? "You mean ex-girlfriend."

The actress gave her a closed-lipped smile. "Is that what he told you, too?"

"Too?" What the hell did *too* mean?

Chasity leaned forward and whispered, "I assumed he would tell you the truth."

"What truth is that?"

Chasity stepped closer. "That you and Jackson are a temporary cast. One meant to keep the press from figuring out he and I are only pretending to be broken up."

Wendy shivered. Could one be hot and cold at the same time? "Pretending?" She spoke too loudly.

Chasity shushed Wendy. "A necessary detail which allows him the freedom to raise a lot of money for his sister's little charity."

Wendy ground her back teeth. "You do know we're having sex."

If the statement surprised Chasity, she hid it well, other than maybe paling a fraction. "I'm afraid that's my fault. When men get their feelings hurt, they have to go play in someone else's sandbox to make themselves feel better."

"*You* hurt *his* feelings?" Just who exactly had broken up with whom?

"He wasn't pleased with the write-up on *Page Six*."

"Thank you."

"Excuse me?" Lines formed around Chasity's lips. "Did you misunderstand what I said?"

Wendy licked at the sugar on the rim of her glass and took a sip. "Not at all. If it's your fault I'm having sex with Jackson, thank you." When you have a contract with someone, the rebound tag is of no consequence.

Chasity squared her shoulders. "I see. You're not quite the mouse he said you were." She pulled out her phone and placed a call.

Had Jackson called her a mouse? Why?

"Jackson, darling, I've had the most delightful conversation with Wendy." There was a pause.

She'd called Jackson!

Chasity tossed Wendy a throwaway smile but didn't walk away. It was as if she wanted Wendy to hear their conversation. "I couldn't agree more. It's adorable how she tried to have her hair styled to look like mine, don't you think?"

Wendy blinked. Were they making fun of her?

"Why did I call?" An underling handed Chasity a glass of wine. "Forgive me for breaking our rules not to talk until after the charity, but your poor little mouse is falling in love with you."

Wendy gasped. That absolutely wasn't true. Was it? No. Of course it wasn't true. That would be against the rules. She didn't break rules.

"It's written all over her face." Chasity mouthed goodbye.

Wendy stood. By God, she was going to rip the phone out of Chasity's hand and tell Jackson the truth.

Eddy placed a hand on Wendy's arm. "Let her go. That's between them. All you need to worry about is the contract."

It took a moment for Wendy to relax. "How do you think she found me?"

"I'm afraid this is all my fault," Eddy said. "During pillow talk, I mentioned to Bobby you were going to the ball with Chasity's ex-boyfriend. The swine must have called her, as you know she's one of his clients, and told her everything I told him. Thus, his death in my eyes."

Wendy patted him on the arm. "You told Bobby about the contract I have with Jackson to buy him at auction?"

"Honey, I talk about so much right after sex, and I never remember half of what I've said."

Wendy pulled out her phone and sent a text to Jackson. *Let's have sex. My place. Say 10:00 p.m.* She didn't really want sex, but that would get him to her place. Once he was there, she could tell him to his face she wasn't in love with him.

Eddy leaned forward and adjusted her tiara and read her text. "You go, girlfriend."

Ten minutes later, Jackson texted back. Had he been on the phone all this time with Chasity?

Sorry. Tonight's not good.

Saturday morning, wearing an Armani suit, Jackson rode the elevator to his office. He scowled at his reflection in the mirror. He refused to believe his subconscious chose the seldom-worn suit as a salute to Wendy.

When the doors slid open, Hazel glanced up from her computer screen. "Good morning." The unexpected cheerfulness in her tone confused him. He'd asked her to work on yet another Saturday.

"Next time I ask you to prepare a love nest, tell me to go fuck myself."

"Trouble in paradise?" she asked.

He ignored the question and walked to her desk. "Stop buying for my lover's friends whatever I'm buying her."

She handed him his empty cup.

Damn it. For once, he'd like her to surprise him with actual coffee.

"I was helping you garner points with the flavor of the week. Plus, I like Wendy."

"Since when do you like any woman I date?"

His office manager peered closely at him. "Are you and Wendy dating?"

"Women are impossible."

"Says a man who never sticks around long enough to actually get to know one beyond their bra size and favorite jewel."

Not a damn thing wrong with his approach. "Get my sister on the phone."

Hazel gave him a speculative look as if she'd seen something on his face he hadn't meant to show.

What in the hell did she think she saw? Before he could ask, his cell buzzed. He pulled it out of his pocket and glanced at the screen. *Chasity.* What did she want now? Last night's bizarre phone call had left him rattled and confused. He hit speakerphone, not caring that Hazel would hear. "What?" His tone had the same snap his insides felt.

"Why did you hang up on me last night?"

"I said goodbye."

"I wasn't done talking."

He sat in the chair across from Hazel's desk. "You were drunk and talking crazy shit. I did you a favor cutting the call short."

"You know that's not true, because you know I've got people who keep me from drunk texting or calling."

She had a point. Her posse followed her like groupies. Hell, they would have come along on their dates if Jackson hadn't said their presence was a deal breaker. "You were seriously with my...with Wendy last night?"

"I can send you a picture as proof."

Before he could say yes or no, a picture popped onto his screen. Wendy was scowling at someone. "Why did you take a picture of her?"

"That was taken by one of my friends when your mouse told me to stay away from you. That I had my chance and now it was hers."

No one who knew anything about Wendy would ever call her a mouse. She'd been a lion since the day they'd met. "That doesn't sound like something she'd say." But why would Chasity lie? What was in it for her? "Besides, Wendy's made it quite clear she's not looking for love."

"Honey, no one's ever looking for love. I can assure you, the mouse is falling hard for you."

"Stop calling her that, and I can assure you she isn't."

"How?"

"We have a damn contract."

Hazel groaned and made windshield wiper motions with her hands.

Chasity laughed liked a woman who'd just stumbled upon the motherload of gossip. "You have a contract that will prevent her from falling in love with you?"

Damn it. He needed coffee. His brain didn't function until it had two cups. "This conversation is over. Don't call again." He hung up.

Hazel groaned. "You don't have a brain in your head."

"My personal life is none of your damn business either," he snapped.

A long moment of thick silence passed between him and Hazel and then she grinned. A grin that said *I know something you haven't figured out.*

"What?"

"I can't say if Wendy has fallen in love with you, but you've fallen in love with the *mouse.*"

"Don't be ridiculous." Jackson stood. "Wendy has more personality than anyone I've ever met." A woman who scared him so much he'd turned down the chance to hook up with her last night.

"Are you in love with her?"

Of course, he wasn't. "Didn't you hear? Our contract forbids the falling in love with the other."

"Does your mother know she raised an idiot?"

He scowled. While he wasn't worried about giving away his own heart, two women had now laughed at the idea that hearts could be overruled by a contract. And while he didn't give much credence to Chasity's view on the matter, he did Hazel's. "I need you to pull the files on the Hartley project. See if you can find out from our contact how many are bidding on the project?"

Not waiting on a reply, he walked into his office and shut the door. He quickly sent Wendy a message.

Last minute business trip has come up. I'll be gone a week. Will text you when I get back.- Jackson

Damn. He'd just denied himself a whole week of being in her bed. But, if women's hearts didn't respect the rules of a contract the way a man's did, then it was for the best. Better safe than sorry with Wendy's heart.

He waited for her to respond.

She didn't.

26

A knock at Wendy's door caused her heart to jump and hope to ignite. It could be Jackson. He could be back from his trip. It had been a week and a day since she'd last seen him. Not that she was counting.

Earth to Wendy. It's Friday night. It's Eddy and Abigail.

Right. Knit night. Wendy pasted on a smile and swung open the door. "What's up knit bitches?"

Eddy and Abigail immediately started talking. At the same time.

"Darling, you're not going to believe—"

"I'm sure it's nothing—"

"Of course, it's something—"

"Total speculation that's going to hurt—"

Wendy placed her fingers between her lips and whistled.

They gaped.

"Well, that was rude," Eddy said.

"I know," responded Abigail.

Wendy stepped back and motioned for them to come inside. "One at a time, tell me what has the two of you rattled."

"Darling, as we were dallying in the foyer—because someone couldn't find her phone and thought she'd left it in the taxi—we saw Jackson and Chasity get on the elevator." Instead of walking into the living room, Eddy stood next to Wendy and rubbed her arm in a comforting way.

"Sugar, he *thinks* it was Chasity and Jackson," Abigail corrected, rubbing Wendy's other arm. "I think they looked more like the couple we saw coming out of your building the night we heard the thumping upstairs and investigated."

"Umm." Wendy adjusted her tiara. The one Jackson had given her. She stepped away from her friends and pointed to the living room.

Her friends poured in there and settled into their favorite spots.

Once everyone was settled, Wendy said, "How could you confuse the two couples?"

"Exactly," Abigail said. "The couple we saw leave that eventful night was more...shall we say, earthy. Their bodies melted into one another's like chocolate into hot coffee. Which is what the couple we saw tonight were doing. That kind of body language is rare."

"How far away were you when you saw them?"

"We were settling up with the taxi driver when they flitted right by us and through the doors," Eddy said. "They went inside *your* building."

"By the time Eddy took care of his share of the bill," Abigail explained, "the couple had already escaped inside the elevator and the doors—"

The sound of footsteps above their heads paused Abigail's explanation.

"I'm telling you," Eddy said, "that was Jackson's fine ass I saw outside my taxi window. I never forget an ass."

Abigail shook her head. "I'm telling you it wasn't them. If it were Jackson and Chasity, they'd been behaving in a more top-shelf manner. They were never a couple who went for public displays of affection."

Eddy plopped his hands on his hips. "Why would her old upstairs neighbor be back in the building? He got the boot. He doesn't live up there anymore."

"To be fair," Wendy said, "I think Jackson just reassigned him to a different apartment. It could have been them."

Eddy wagged a finger at her. "When did the noise up there begin?"

"Just now." Then again, she'd been preoccupied. "I think."

"There's only one solution to this dilemma. We sashay up there and check out the situation." Eddy stood, popped out a hip, and plopped his hand on it. "I want a reasonable explanation of why Jackson is cheating on our Wendy."

Wendy felt her cheeks heat. "He's not cheating. You have to be a couple to cheat."

"Couple or not, it is tacky, tacky, tacky of him to bring someone to the love nest he built for you all," Abigail said.

"I don't care. Let's just drop this whole conversation." Wendy's heart vehemently disagreed.

"What...ever," Eddy said.

Once again, Eddy wore men's clothing. His falling out with Bobby had really taken the steam out of Eddy's dress-up sails. Wendy couldn't help but wonder if part of his views of what might be going on in her building were tainted as a result of his broken heart. The if-one-man-can't-be-trusted, they-all-must-be-untrustworthy mentality.

But what if Eddy did know one ass from another? It wasn't like she and Jackson were dating. Worst-case scenario, Jackson had broken their contract. That's not the same as cheating. Her heart needed to get its shit together and stop trying to hurt. Her ego could hurt but not her heart. "I'm not going up there. He can see who he wants to see, as long as he doesn't have sex."

"I say we open the wine and get our knit on," Abigail said.

"I agree," Wendy said. "What are we drinking?"

"Tonight, we're drinking"—Abigail read the label on the bottle of wine she held—"Promis-Qous."

"It's pronounced, promiscuous," Eddy said.

Wendy forced a laugh. "Perfect. We might need to make that our new mascot wine."

Eddy, still standing, struck a boobs-on-display pose. Then he held out his arm and flopped his hand. "I told the clerk I needed the *perfect* pick-me-up wine." He paused and fanned himself. "And asked for his recommendation."

Abigail scrunched her face. "The clerks are never cute when I buy wine."

"Anyway," Eddy said, "the clerk said, Pro-mis-Q-ous. I said, I'm listening. He said, a blend for those who enjoy casual dalliances. I said, preach it baby. He said, with more than one partner." Again, Eddy paused.

"And?" Wendy asked when the pause turned into a stop.

Eddy fluttered his enhanced eyelashes. "I handed him my private card."

"Sugar," Abigail said, "you actually got yourself picked up at a wine store."

"I did, and I would squeal, but I simply can't be happy until my Wendy is happy." He took Wendy's hand. "Honey, have you talked to *him* this week?"

"I'm going to text *him* tonight." Or not. She couldn't text him if he'd brought Chasity home. Or could she?

Eddy dropped her hand. "For. A. *Hookup?*" Alarm on his face and in his voice.

"That's what one does when they have a booty-call neighbor." Why the agitation? It wasn't a bad idea. Was it? "We only have one more week before our contract expires."

"Sugar, maybe you should amend the contract," Abigail said sweetly. "Ask him for another kind of compensation for your time."

"I'll think about it," Wendy said.

"Not to beat a dead horse, but it's above-the-normal quiet up there. If that were your old upstairs neighbor, there'd be loud fucking happening," Eddy said.

"If it were my old upstairs neighbor, they would be in his new apartment, not his old apartment," Wendy reminded him.

"Oh. You're right."

Eddy took a seat and they all settled into their knitting.

"Did you all hear about the body they fished from the Hudson?" Abigail said. "The guy had been shot once in the back of the head."

Wendy took a sip of her wine. "Do they know who he was?"

"They do. Bless his heart. No one reported him missing. Poor guy didn't have any family, and the place where he worked just thought he'd up and quit when he didn't show up one day. Poor dude."

Wendy's stomach churned. Would anyone report her missing? Of course, they would. The Manhattan

Knitters would report it. Had anyone ever reported Pencil Thin missing?

For the next thirty minutes, they refocused on their needles. Occasional comments punctured the lengthy silence that had fallen like a warm blanket. Each was apparently deep in their thought. Technically, Wendy was listening for movement upstairs.

"Sugars, I'm thinking about going to a conference this summer in New Orleans," Abigail said. "I think it'll be a great way to meet...potential online customers."

Eddy lowered his knitting. "I've always wanted to go to New Orleans."

"Have either of you ever been to a knitting conference?" Wendy asked.

"They are wicked fun, heavy on the wicked." Eddy stretched.

"Wicked how?" Wendy asked.

"Let's just say the non-knitting activities planned by the organizers of the one I went to were naughty, naughty, fabulous."

"What kind of activities will they have at this year's conference?" Wendy asked Abigail.

Abigail blushed. "Coaching by a real-life Madam."

Wendy lowered her needles. "Like a brothel type of Madam?"

Abigail nodded. "Only she has guys who work for her—not females. Do you guys want to go? Please say yes."

Eddy and Wendy glanced at one another.

Eddy shrugged. "Bitch, you know I'm not turning down the chance to party with a gigolo."

Wendy was about to reply when she heard the upstairs door shut. They all jumped and ran to the window.

Fifty seconds later, they watched a couple get into a town car. The guy had a pronounced limp.

"We were both wrong," Eddy said to Abigail.

Wendy didn't respond.

What had Mr. Bruiser been doing in her building? Had that been him upstairs in Jackson's apartment? Or had it been Jackson, and he had left to visit his friend Mitch in the building at the same time Mr. Bruiser was exiting? Both scenarios were viable. Which one was accurate?

27

J ackson sat in a booth at John's Pizza with Mom and Annie. Friday night and the place had more patrons than available seating. Those waiting were eyeballing their table. "Mom, you said you had some news you wanted to share." He was in a mood because Mitch had dropped by, asked to talk, and then changed his mind and left, managing to make Jackson late in the process.

Mom dabbed at her lips. "Ted and I are divorcing."

"Christ. This is five." Jackson liked Ted. The guy had a good head on his shoulders and handled Mom well. At least, that's what he'd thought.

"I'm so sorry." As usual, Annie did a better impersonation of empathy.

Mom laid her napkin back on her lap. "That's the last time you'll have to say that. I've learned my lesson. Love isn't forever. It's for a season. From now on, I plan to live in sin."

Jackson tossed his napkin on his plate. He'd heard this spiel before. A season of love made a hell of a lot more sense than forever love. Hell, seasonal love had all kinds of supporting data, whereas supportive data for forever love seemed few and far between. The only problem was Mom had never stuck to that belief for long.

"I also have an announcement," Annie said.

He glanced at his sister. Beautiful. Smart. Soft hearted. Open book. His heart sank and his big brother instincts tightened his fists. Her announcement wasn't going to make him happy. He braced.

"Honey, is it happy news?" Mom asked.

"Mitch asked me on a non-date, and I said maybe."

Jackson's brain and brotherly instincts warred. Is that what Mitch wanted to talk about? "What the hell is a non-date?" Whatever it was, it was asinine.

"Two adults spending time together in a non-date way."

"It's good to take things slow." Mom turned her attention back to Jackson and gave him a questioning look. "What's new with you? Is it my imagination or are you glowing beneath your surly mood?"

He took a bite of the pizza still on his plate. Not because he had an appetite left, but because he needed to fill his mouth before he spoke words that would hurt.

Mom waited patiently for him to swallow.

"You can't glow and be surly at the same time." He glanced at Annie. "Non-date is just a fancy way of saying 'let's split the cost but still have sex.'"

Annie flipped him the bird. "In that case, when he calls to get my answer, I think I'll tell him yes. And Mom's right. You do have a glowiness about you. One you're trying to hide with surliness."

Women were impossible. "It's a sheen of sweat caused by the peppers on the pizza." They'd ordered a half Margherita and half Italian pork sausage with hot cherry peppers. "Definitely not a glow. Besides, women glow. Men don't."

Mom glanced at her daughter. "Darling, definitely say yes to a non-date. Enjoy the relationship until the fun ends and then move on."

Annie smiled at Mom and then bumped shoulders with Jackson. "You're in love...aren't you?"

He coughed into his hand and said, "Bullshit."

"Language," Mom reprimanded.

"It's not bullshit if you do it right. Sure, love is complicated, but it's worth sticking around for. Look at Dad and Shelly. They've been married twenty years, and they are still happy."

Mom pursed her lips. She didn't enjoy it when her former husbands found happiness after she left them.

"And, for what it's worth," Annie said, her gaze still on Jackson, "I approve of the girl. And her tiara."

How in the hell had he found himself in this conversation? "You met her once, for about five seconds."

"Who are we talking about?" Mom asked.

"Her name is Wendy. She's in a non-date relationship with Jackson."

"Is that true, son?"

"In a roundabout way."

"I don't need to know Wendy," his sister said. "I know you. You've been different since you met her. Hazel agrees with me."

He groaned. "Have you been discussing my sex life with my secretary?"

"She's your office manager, not secretary. And we weren't talking about your sex life. We were talking about your love life."

"I hate to disappoint you, but the only thing going on between Wendy and me is sex."

"Hmmm. I think you protest too much," Annie said. "Did I tell you I plan to steal Wendy from Contracts R Us? I've hired a headhunter to approach her. Unless you'd like to approach her on my behalf?"

The knot in his gut doubled in size. "That's a bad idea. When she and I split, and we will, you'll be stuck working with one of my exes." And he'd be stuck seeing Wendy and her adorable ass every day in the office building.

"Speaking of working with exes, Mitch told me he sold the franchise rights to his food truck and is in the market for a new job. I told him First Defense Security was expanding."

"Who?" he asked.

His sister frowned. "You know, the company made of former Marines in the Adler building. They rent from you."

"Oh. Them? Really? Mitch?"

"Why did you say it like that? Why not Mitch? Did you know he has a black belt in Tae Kwon Do?"

"I didn't."

"Perhaps you could put in a good word for him with the guys. They all like you."

"Not happening. I don't know the guy in a reference capacity. Other than he sleeps with married women. How can someone as smart as you choose to ignore that vital piece of information?"

"He swears he didn't know she was married until she called and told him she'd lost her wedding ring. When they met, she'd told him she was a widow and hadn't been able to bring herself to remove her ring."

"And you, a brilliant lawyer, believed him?"

"I'm giving him the benefit of the doubt."

His phone vibrated in his pocket. He pulled it out.

Sex tonight. My place. 10:30 p.m. – Wendy

28

Ten thirty p.m., Friday night, Wendy opened the door to her apartment. She wore a tank top and shorts. She'd scrubbed her face clean of makeup and allowed her hair to dry naturally, which translated into a riot of short curls. "Hi, stranger. You're very punctual." Her heart hammered. A lot had happened since they'd last seen each other. Things she couldn't quiz him over.

He reached out and touched one of her curls. "Hi, blondie. You're the best-looking thing I've seen all day."

He could pretend he liked the blonde all he wanted, but she knew better. Wendy rolled her eyes and led him into the living room.

"You're not taking me straight to bed?" He sounded leery.

"If you don't mind, I wanted to talk to you about something."

He sighed as if already weary from a conversation they hadn't yet started. "Is it about Chasity?"

"Why would I want to talk to you about Chasity?" she lied.

His eyes narrowed. "I can't think of one reason why you would."

She sat on the couch, and he took a seat at the opposite end. "I wanted to ask you for a slight change to our agreement."

"I'm listening." He looked like someone tensing for a jury verdict.

"You and I are temporary," she said, airily. Truth. "And I'm okay with that." Truthish. "We're not right for each other." Probably true. "But spending time with you has made me realize that Mom and Dad wouldn't want me to deny myself of love. You were right when you said that." Absolute truth. "And now I find myself wanting to someday be in a relationship with the right guy. After our contract is over, of course."

He stretched out and crossed one foot over his knee. "What are the qualities of your future right guy?"

She conjured up Mr. Right. "One who's not an idiot. Not afraid of relationships. Knows how to be faithful. Those kinds of things." Imaginary Mr. Right looked a hell of a lot like Jackson.

He straightened, loosened his tie, took it off, and slouched back into the cushion. "And how do I come into play?"

She ignored the desire to help him get more comfortable by unbuttoning his shirt. "When I pick out guys for myself, I suck. I pick losers. Or I attract losers. Or something. Anyway, I wanted to know if you'd teach me how to flirt. The kind of flirting that would capture the interest of a man like...say...you."

He jerked as if truly startled. "Like me?"

Okay, that made it sound like she was falling in love with him. "Like you. But not you." Did that even make sense?

He unbuttoned his top two buttons. "How would these flirting lessons work?"

Translation...he's all for me falling for someone else. Not him. Even though it shouldn't, the realization stung. "Instead of being my booty-call man for the next week, we'd go out, and you could teach me how to flirt."

He unbuttoned his cuffs and rolled them up, showing off his strong forearms. "What's in this for me? I like the sex we're having."

Her boobs perked up. More accurately, her nipples sprung to life. Good to know she had the sex thing perfected. "I like it too. There's nothing for you. Just the knowledge you did a nice thing for someone."

He leaned back and studied her. "My good deed for the year?"

"More like good deed for the week." His good deed for the year more than likely would be the money he helped raised for his sister's charity, but this was still a good deed.

"I'll think about it." He stood and walked to her window. "I do love this view."

She stared at his backside. "Me too."

He turned, gave her a wicked grin. "Now, can we take this to the bedroom?"

She didn't budge. "When will you give me an answer?" They should probably hold off on sex now that she'd asked to change the rules of their contract.

He studied her for a long time. "How about at our next dance lesson?"

Then again, she had invited him over for sex. It would be poor manners not to put out now.

On Sunday, exhilaration swirled through Wendy as Jackson twirled her around the dance floor. When they finally did an entire string of newly taught moves by Eddy without her stepping all over Jackson's feet, laughter bubbled out of her.

Unfortunately, Jackson's stoic expression did not mirror her level of excitement...even slightly. Like not at all. Wendy sighed. He'd been quiet all afternoon. The only time he hadn't been quiet was when he'd been grumpy because he hadn't gotten the moves right.

Eddy sharply clapped his hands twice to get everyone's attention. "Come. It's time to learn to salsa."

"Salsa." Jackson protested like a school kid who'd just heard the teacher say it was time to take their math books out.

"That's what the guy said." He could have his bad mood, but she wasn't borrowing it. She much preferred the sensation of wanting to laugh, giggle, and squeal because for once, she could dance. And maybe, just maybe, her mood had something to do with the sex they'd had Friday night. It had taken on a whole other level of unbelievable. Of course, that phenomenon was probably because of the very real possibility it would be their last time. But damn, if last-time sex was that good, everyone should go around having last-time sex.

"Tell me this is the last lesson," Jackson bellyached.

Wendy bit her lip and counted to three. Why did he have to say it like that? It wasn't like she was a horrible person to hang out with a couple of times a week. Nor had she constantly trampled his toes today. "You say that like you don't find my company at dance lessons delightfully refreshing."

He had the grace to look abashed. "You are delightful, it's just that I have other..." His cell buzzed.

Other what? Other places to be? Other people to be with? What?

"I know that's not a phone I hear," Eddy declared. "Phones are prohibited at Eddy's dance studio."

Jackson pulled his cell out. Glanced at the screen. Frowned. He swiped to accept the call and placed the phone to his ear. "This better be important." As he listened, he strode out of earshot of the Manhattan Knitters.

"Time is money," Eddy said to Jackson's back.

Wendy refrained from pointing out to Eddy that he wasn't getting paid. "Jackson will make it quick. He values your time."

Resisting an urge to follow Jackson, Wendy walked to the window that overlooked Wooster Street and stared out. Her friends joined her.

"I can't imagine what is so important on a Sunday afternoon that Jackson has to take a phone call." Today, Eddy wore a muscle-hugging white T-shirt, black tights, and white ballet slippers. And his tiara.

"Maybe it was family." Wendy would stop whatever she was doing to answer a call from family. If she had family.

Abigail reached out and played with one of Wendy's curls. "Are you beginning to like the blonde?"

Wendy shook her head. "Not even a—"

"Men are the blight of my existence," Eddy said.

Wendy and Abigail gave each other a look but didn't speak. He and Bobby had yet to make up.

The seconds turned into minutes.

"If he doesn't return soon, I plan to charge for my time spent waiting on him," Eddy said. "And Eddy does not wait cheaply."

Wendy had no doubt he'd invoice Jackson for time spent waiting. "I'll go hurry him along." She rushed toward the staircase and heard Jackson before he spotted her approach.

"There's nothing going on. She's more boring than vanilla yogurt."

The words hit Wendy like hail from a violent thunderstorm. Her hand flew to her mouth, trapping a sound of pain. Shock glued her in place, though everything inside of her told her to hide. To not be seen. Was he talking to Chasity?

But I like you. We were having fun.

She should go back to her friends. No way could she let him know she'd heard the insult.

Did you hear him? More boring than vanilla yogurt.

Maybe he was talking about someone else.

Of course, he was talking about you.

A morsel of anger found a foothold in Wendy's heart. The right man would find her a delicious combination of quirky and reliable. Who in the hell—

"I haven't decided what I'll tell her." Jackson's tone was disdainful.

Oh God. It had to be Chasity.

Jackson cursed. "Stay out of it. You've done enough damage. I don't want to see her hurt."

Wendy's chest squeezed tight. Yep. Chasity. They must be reuniting. Anger bubbled inside of Wendy. Even if he and Chasity were getting back together, it didn't give him the right to go around referring to Wendy as more boring than vanilla yogurt.

She'd thought they at least shared friendship. How could she have been so wrong? She took several steps backward as traitorous tears plopped on her cheeks.

Scrubbing them away, she turned and walked back to Eddy and Abigail. To her friends. To two people who thought Wendy Travis entertaining. To the Manhattan Knitters. "Jackson's almost done." She hoped the amped-up smile she gave them concealed how raw those three words sounded as a result of the internal cuts and bruises.

My heart hurts.

Wendy rubbed at the spot where her heart lay underneath her skin. It had a weird tightness to it. Fuck. It did hurt. Only one thing could explain that sensation. Somewhere between Friday night and *she's more boring than vanilla yogurt,* she'd fallen in hard like with Jackson Adler. An emotion most certainly not allowed according to their contract.

Are you sure it's not love?

Of course, it wasn't love. That would be beyond foolish. And while foolish might describe Wendy's earlier years, it certainly had no place in her current way of living.

##

Jackson took a deep breath before strolling back to Wendy and the others. The trio stood at the window, looking as if someone's pet had died. Why? What had happened? They'd been happy before he left the room. Were they mad at him? "Eddy, I know how you hate to have your teaching time interrupted, and I wouldn't have taken the call if it wasn't from someone I really needed to talk to. Please forgive me."

Eddy didn't respond.

Wendy turned and gave him a strained smile. Jackson glanced into her eyes. Damn. The sparkle of minutes ago had vanished. A sparkle he'd never gotten around to telling her looked good on her. And now, what he had to say would prevent that sparkle from returning anytime soon. "Something has come up and I must leave."

A menacing growl came from Eddy. "Would her name be Chasity?"

Jackson had no idea where that accusation had come from. "No offense, but where I'm off to is none of your business." Mitch had called to ask Jackson for his blessing to see Annie.

When Jackson told him to stay the hell away from her, Mitch had the audacity to ask Jackson if he and Wendy were serious. Jackson hadn't bothered to ask Mitch how he knew of Wendy. His sister had no doubt mentioned her during their conversation about a future non-date.

"So, you're not denying it?" Eddy persisted.

"Eddy," Wendy snapped. "It doesn't matter who or why. His business is his business."

Jackson gladly returned his attention to Wendy. "Thank you for understanding."

She took a step toward him and looked him straight in the eyes. "Of course, I understand. Just like my business is my business. I'm the one, after all, who included those phrases in our contract."

He stilled. Fuck. Please, let his senses be deceiving him. Only they weren't. He'd seen this look, heard this tone, witnessed this body language on a lady before.

They were indicators of a woman in love with a man who didn't reciprocate.

He'd been an idiot to believe Wendy could keep her emotions out of a relationship. You couldn't be that cute and adorable on the outside and on the inside possess a heart that bowed to a stone-cold brain. The contract had been a mistake.

He pushed away a desire to whisk his dance partner away and let her down gently. Right now, family was his priority. Protecting Annie was his priority. "I need to deal with a family matter."

He only hoped he could reach Annie and set her straight on Mitch before it was too late.

"Family's important," Wendy said tightly.

He blew out a breath. Was he any better than Mitch? If Wendy's expression was anything to go by, not much. The longer he allowed her feelings to grow, the bigger the dick he was. The kindest thing he could do was kill her emotions this moment. "I know you want me to stay and dance, but we're not a couple, and my real-life calls."

"Of course, we're not a couple. Leave. I'm fine and dandy."

She wasn't. "Are we still on for the auction?" He expected her to say no. In fact, the only reason he asked was so she could muster some indignation and tell him to go fuck himself. He deserved that.

"I wouldn't miss it for all the yarn in Switzerland."

"Bite your tongue," Eddy said. "Yarn is sacred. Men like him are a dime a dozen."

"He's not wrong." Abigail gave Jackson an apologetic smile. "It's nothing personal, but the original 5C or not, you are a player."

"I can't take offense at the truth." He resisted the urge to tell them everything about Wendy made him want to be a better version of himself. Instead, he acted on the realization. A better version of himself would do his damnedest to not further damage quirky, beautiful, fun-loving Wendy Travis. With that thought in mind, he gave the president of the Manhattan Knitters' Club his full attention. "I'll see you the night of the event."

"Oh." The word spoke volumes. "Not before?"

"It's nothing personal. I'm afraid there are matters concerning my family that I must focus my attention on for the foreseeable future. And if I recall, there was a clause in our contract that allowed for such an occurrence." Thank God she'd put that in their contract.

She nodded. "There was."

"Then we're good. I'll see you the night of the ball." He turned and left before he could change his mind.

Wendy deserved a guy with a heart capable of forever love. Not seasonal love.

Monday spa night was a shell of its former fun self. A fault Wendy laid at Jackson's feet. She hadn't seen or heard from him since he had ditched her at yesterday's dance lessons.

"Quick, someone tell me something to make me laugh." She spoke to Eddy and Abigail, who'd dropped by thirty minutes ago. Since her couch wasn't big enough for all three of them, they'd taken the party to her bedroom.

She'd placed a sheet over her comforter to keep everything clean and then the three of them had climbed on top of her bed. Now they were flat on their backs with cucumbers on their eyes, charcoal masks on their faces, and spinning thoughts in their heads.

At least Wendy's were spinning and making her slightly nauseous. Who had Jackson been talking to when he'd said she was more boring than vanilla yogurt?

"Sugar, I can't be funny on demand," Abigail said.

Eddy reached over and laced his fingers with Wendy's. "Honey, I talked with Bobby. He sufficiently groveled. He feels horrible about what he did."

"To my hair or for telling Chasity where to find me?"

"Both."

"Bully for Bobby." The awful hairdresser was the least of Wendy's concerns. Jackson's cruel words had caused her self-confidence to tumble. And the fact she gave a damn about his opinion gnawed at her. Since when did she care what others thought?

Get it together. Self-esteem is our schtick.

Not so much right now. What if she never again had the courage to go after what she wanted? What if fear of rejection kept her from asking? What if all of this was the universe reminding her she didn't deserve love? That she'd been wrong to announce to Jackson otherwise?

Eddy squeezed her fingers. "Anyway, Bobby's offered to come here, redo your hair, do all of our makeup, and help us get ready for the ball."

"I think I'll go to School of Hair," Wendy said. "They've never let me down." Even her voice sounded wussy. In less than twenty-four hours, she'd become a pebble of her former rock-the-world self.

"Dollface, you can't tell Bobby no."

"Of course, I can. And consider it done. My answer is no."

"Or we could execute another plan where Bobby is concerned," Eddy said, as if she hadn't spoken. "We'll pay him his top-shelf celebrity fee, using Jackson's card, of course. Then Bobby will reimburse us, as his amends to Wendy, and we'll use the money to pay the registration for all three of us to go to the knitters' conference in New Orleans."

Abigail made a noise of surprise. "Bless your sketchy heart, I like your idea. Wendy, what do you think?"

"Bobby does deserve the pain of getting a big paycheck and then having to lose it. But the only way I can support this plan is if he has to write a check to the charity of our choice in the amount Jackson pays him. As much as I'd like to take the money and hit a knitters' conference, that would be wrong."

"You're right. But for a moment it was fun thinking about helping you get revenge on Bobby," Abigail said.

"I do like the idea of him having to give his money to a charity all about dogs," Eddy said. "He's a true-blue cat person. Can't stand dogs."

"Tell Bobby our terms," Wendy said. "But if he does something to my hair I don't like, I will use my dullest knitting needle to stab him in his testicles."

"Ouch." Eddy released her hand.

"Now that that's settled, can we talk about what we're all thinking?" Abigail said.

"What's that?" Wendy asked.

"That while we're dishing out revenge, we need to dish out a big ol' dollop of the stuff to Jackson for calling our darling *boring*."

A new wave of anger whipped through Wendy. Out of kindness to Jackson, she shouldn't have told them what she'd heard him say. Privacy and all that crap. But she had. She'd blurted it out the moment she'd walked back into the dance studio. Eddy and Abigail were her people. "I don't think—"

"Honey, he called you boring," Eddy cooed.

"Yes, but—"

"Sugar," Abigail said, "revenge ninjas are never called boring. Be a revenge ninja."

Wendy removed the cucumbers from her eyes and sat up. The other two were already sitting. He did deserve a little pain for telling Chasity she was boring. "Let's do it."

Eddy leaned forward and pulled the spacers out from between Wendy's newly painted toes. "Tell us, darling, on a scale of one to ten, how revengie do you want to get?"

She gnawed her bottom lip.

Founding member of the Manhattan Revenge Ninjas has a nice, non-boring ring to it.

"A seven." She resisted the urge to immediately change it to a two. People who founded revenge clubs didn't do level-two revenge. "Make that an eight." That's like a B minus.

We're not boring, and we're certainly not B-minus material.

Wendy had always been a straight-A type of girl. Why should her level of revenge be any different? "Okay, a nine."

Her friends clapped.

She held up a finger. "Ten tops."

They clapped louder.

"My only condition, when the night is over, I have to honor my part of the contract." After all, she wasn't willing to lose her integrity over the asshole. And it's not like he'd broken his end of the contract. He just exercised a loophole that she'd built into the document.

"Honey, if that's your only condition, we can bring him to his knees," Eddy declared.

"Fuck bruised kneecaps, let's slash open his heart," Wendy said, causing them all to break into a fit of giggles.

Bruised kneecaps. The phrase reminded her of Mr. Bruiser. Which reminded her that it had been Pencil Thin's body pulled out of the Hudson. Her office had been all abuzz about it today as two detectives had set up in the conference rooms at Contracts R Us and interviewed the employees one-by-one. Mr. Morgenstern and Wendy had been the first to be questioned. Wendy had not mentioned Mr. Bruiser, or her meeting with him, or the fact he'd been in her apartment building, or the contracts she'd had to sign a false name to. She left that breach of loyalty to the cartel to Mr. Morgenstern. She'd never even mentioned any of it to her friends. No sense in putting their lives in danger.

31

Tuesday night, Jackson glanced out at the view from his penthouse. The sun setting over Manhattan never failed to bring a smile to his lips. The hues of yellows, pinks, and lavenders could take the breath away from a blind man. Even on a night like tonight, when life had left him weary as hell.

He turned to his sister, who was curled up on his couch. "I don't know why you can't get over him." When he had returned from his ten-mile run, she'd been sitting in front of his door, a bottle of wine between her legs and a box of tissues next to her.

"The heart loves who the heart loves. And my heart loved his at first sight." She blew her nose and topped off her wine, her face blotchy and tearstained. "Have you heard from him?"

The correct answer would be no, but it wasn't the truth, so Jackson didn't respond. When he'd left the dance lesson on Sunday, he'd run into Mitch in the elevator in Annie's apartment building. He'd been on his way up to see Annie. Jackson's whole being had gone into call-the-cops-there's-going-to-be-a-brawl mode. He'd managed to subdue the need until after the door had closed. At which time he pushed the stop button and proceeded to, once again, punch Mitch in the nose.

Mitch hadn't reciprocated. Instead, he'd calmly replied he deserved that.

Fucking idiot.

The brief conversation that followed had blown Jackson back twenty-thousand steps. The two men had left Annie's apartment without ever seeing her.

"I can't believe he didn't show up for our non-date Sunday night," his sister wailed. "He could've texted and said he wasn't coming."

"He doesn't deserve you." Jackson glanced at his phone. Something he'd done frequently since leaving Wendy at their dance lesson on Sunday. He kept hoping to get a message from Wendy demanding he make time for a booty call. Yeah, he was the asshole thinking about getting laid while his sister's heart imploded and while Wendy was probably experiencing something similar. That was if he'd read the signs right. Maybe he hadn't. Maybe he'd jumped the gun with Wendy by ending them a week early.

Annie hiccupped and spilled her wine.

He took the bottle and her now half-empty glass from her.

"It's rude to take wine from the brokenhearted." She rubbed at the stain with her tissue.

He wanted to scoff, tell Annie she sounded asinine, but couldn't. "What can I do to make you feel better? Anything I can do, I'll do."

She blew her nose. "Do you mean that?"

"I don't say things I don't mean. Do you want me to hunt him down and drag him to your front door for an explanation of his bad manners?" Maybe he'd been wrong to order Mitch to just disappear. It wasn't like the guy didn't have a decent explanation for everything.

"No woman wants a man who has to be dragged back to her."

"Finally, you said something that makes sense."

Annie leaned toward him and studied his face. Then she sat back. "What I want is for you not to sabotage what is blooming between you and Wendy when your contract is up."

"Not that."

She leaned forward again and poked him in the chest. "You said anything—that's what I want. I'll stop crying and delete Mitch's number if you promise to continue seeing Wendy after the ball."

"You know I'm not capable of forever love so that would just be cruel to her."

"Earth to Jackson, Wendy is the best thing that's ever going to happen to you. It's time to figure this love stuff out on your own terms and not Mom's."

He rubbed his jaw. "Do you really believe love at first sight is a thing?"

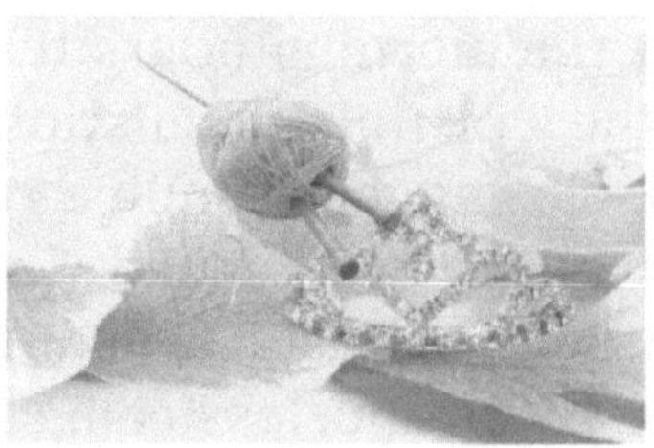

32

T hursday evening, Wendy paced around her apartment while dipping her tea bag in a cup of hot water. Through her open window, she could hear the wind whipping around the buildings and snaking between the cars. The noise gave her apartment an eerie quality.

The atmosphere suited her mood. Or maybe it simply played into her mood. If the sun had been shining and the birds chirping, would she be so on edge? Feeling so scared?

Her agitation had started when Mr. Morgenstern hadn't shown up for work this morning. He had the flu and would be out for a while. Or so the story went.

Wendy didn't buy it. Mr. Morgenstern didn't believe in sick days. He washed his hands on the hour every hour and made everyone stop what they were doing and sanitize their hands as well.

So, if not sick, then why not at work? And why had his secretary taken a box of files with her when she'd slipped out at ten a.m., not to return until six hours later?

Was Mr. Morgenstern missing? Was he the next Pencil Thin? Would Wendy be the one following Mr. Morgenstern?

Wendy spent the morning hours telling herself to stop with all the fanciful speculation. Then, thirty minutes before closing, her landline rang. When she answered, her phone went dead. In all her years working at the company, that line hadn't rung once.

Freaked out by the voiceless call, she had made a point to leave on time. Out of caution, or paranoia, she pulled her jacket hood over her head while exiting the building.

Then, instead of taking the subway, she'd taken a taxi. Had the driver go way out of his way.

Five minutes after getting home, she had another call. This one to her cell. She let it go to voicemail. No message. Blocked number.

When it rang again, she answered. Ten seconds of silence followed by disconnection.

She'd taken a shower with her gun lying on a towel right outside the tub. And for the first time ever, wished it were a Glock capable of doing real harm. Then she'd chastised herself for being a drama queen.

That's when she'd called Eddy and Abigail and invited them over for a slumber party. They were due to arrive, freshly showered, at any time.

More than once today, Wendy wished she and Jackson were talking. Then it could have been him she'd invited over for a slumber party. He would have made a soothing protector. But after telling someone Wendy was more boring than vanilla yogurt, Jackson had failed to drop by with a perfectly reasonable explanation for the insult. That had been Monday, Tuesday, Wednesday, Thursday ago.

Which was fine. He'd told her family stuff had come up and family should come before her. Besides, she didn't need an explanation. What could he possibly say that would make it hurt less? Nothing.

Now, while waiting for her friends to knock, she forced herself to think logically.

There hadn't been any more mistakes on her contracts that she'd been made aware of. And no more messages from Mr. Bruiser to meet him in the dark corner of a restaurant.

So why did everything inside of her scream the non-calls had something to do with the Angelino contract?

Pencil Thin died of a bullet to the back of the head. Mr. Bruiser does more than bruise.

What did Pencil Thin know that had gotten him killed? Whatever it was, Wendy didn't know it. She knew absolutely nothing of any importance. Unless you were a reporter for a magazine with a gossip column, one like *Naked Runway*, and then it would be quite important. At what point would the Angelinos consider her a loose end?

How does one go about surviving if a mob family wants you dead? Was that something she could Google?

The sound of a door opening and then footsteps in the apartment above her caused her to freeze.

She listened. The steps didn't sound like Jackson's. Or did they? What did his footsteps sound like? Should she go up there? Make sure it was Jackson? You know, just in case...

She ran to the window and glanced out. She didn't see anyone exiting, which meant if it had been Jackson, he hadn't left the building. Was he headed down to her place?

On the verge of hyperventilating, she sagged in relief when Eddy and Abigail came into view walking down the sidewalk toward her building.

While watching her friends approach, she noticed a man, head down, collar up, walk by in the opposite direction. A man with a limp. "Holy fuckanolie." Mr. Bruiser had a limp. It had to be him. Did he have her building staked out?

She ran to her door, threw it open, and waited for Eddy and Abigail.

She put a finger on her lips. "You guys are never going to believe this." She pulled them inside, shut and locked her door. "My apartment may be bugged," she whispered.

"Why?" asked Abigail, in a normal voice.

Wendy shushed her and mouthed, "Because I have ties with the Angelino family."

Eddy laughed. "You are such a hoot. How much have you had to drink?"

She dragged them into her bathroom. Shut the door. Turned on the shower and then said, "Remember that booty-call contract I told you about between Jackson and me?"

They nodded.

"Well, I got the idea from a contract I proofed at work." She quickly told them about the work contract between Penelope Angelino and Mitchell Travinni and then waited for the significance of the first last name to sink in. Their eyes popped wide like corks leaving a champagne bottle.

"Your boss has you working on contracts involving the Angelino family," Abigail whispered.

"Why would he do something that stupid?" Eddy asked.

"I don't know. Maybe they threatened him if he didn't? He's not a brave man. More of a weasel. Anyway, he had one of his top proofreaders in charge of proofing their contracts. Then one day, Pencil Thin didn't come to work. Then I was given their contracts to proof and was told to not use my real name on the line where proofreaders signed. But then, one day when I was really tired, I forgot and signed my name. Someone in the Angelino family noticed the discrepancy, and I was summoned to meet with an associate. He invited me to call him Bruiser. Luckily, he liked me and told me to forget the contract ever existed. I did and things were fine until today."

"What happened today?" Abigail whispered.

"Mr. Morgenstern didn't show up for work, and Mr. Bruiser just walked by. I think he's been staking out the apartment and saw you guys coming and left so he wouldn't be noticed. I think—"

Abigail slapped Wendy across the face.

"Why did you do that?" Wendy rubbed her sore face.

"Honey, bless your heart, you were spinning," Abigail said in a sweet tone. "Take a few calming breaths and tell me how Pencil Thin got a bullet in the back of the head."

"He's the guy that was pulled out of the Hudson," Wendy said. "I've been wanting to tell you, but thought I was protecting you by not telling you, but now..."

Abigail held up a palm and pulled out her phone. "It's time for me to call my persons."

"Your persons?" Wendy echoed. "You mean the ones who were going to help us vet potential candidates for the Manhattan Knitters' Club? Or do you have multiple persons for different levels of needs?

Abigail glanced up. "Just the two. They are jacks-of-all-persons."

"I need a person." Eddy had been unusually quiet for him. No doubt, still struggling with his and Bobby's fractured relationship.

"Then we'll get you one." Abigail said with a buttload of perk. "In the meantime, tomorrow night's the ball. Which means tonight we need a plan to get a good night's sleep so we look our best tomorrow night."

"That is a plan I can work with," Eddy chimed in. "We're going to blow this popsicle joint, get us a room at the Marriott, and get a good night's sleep because I happen to have three Ambiens on my person. Tomorrow night, we will attend the ball. Then the morning after, we will celebrate our revenge upon Jackson and turn our attention to worry about Wendy's gangster problem." He stood and turned off the shower.

Wendy turned the shower back on. "We can't take twenty-four hours off from worrying about the problem."

Abigail held up a finger to them and placed her phone to her ear. "Sarah Ann, this is your favorite former neighbor. How are things in Mayhem? Have I called you at a bad time? Is Ruby Rae behaving?"

"I'm doing great," Abigail enthused after minutes of listening. "The yarn store is coming along beautifully. I called because I have a friend who has encountered a slight glitch in her life. I was hoping you could pull a few strings and let us know if she has anything to worry about."

Wendy and Eddy stood silent and intensely listened.

"Yes. Of course. I can do that," Abigail finally replied. "Thanks. Love you, too." She hung up and smiled brightly at Eddy and Wendy. "We're to spend the night at the Waldon. She'll have a room reserved for us. In the nightstand will be a burner phone for me to call her back on. We're to leave Wendy's phone here. Shall we go?"

"Who in the heck is your former neighbor?" Wendy asked.

"A member of Mayhem's 21 Club. Most think of it as a bunch of senior citizens entertaining themselves by running a café. It's more than that." Abigail glanced in the mirror over the sink and checked her teeth. "What do you guys think of this color?" She puckered her lips. "Should I wear it tomorrow night? It's done what it said it would do, stayed on my lips and not my teeth."

"Honey, if you can look fabulous in that hussy color, I say wear it twenty-four seven."

Wendy smacked him on the arm. "It's not a hussy color. It's the color of a proper sexy siren."

"My momma would roll over in her grave if she saw me wearing firecracker red on a Thursday night," Abigail said.

"I thought your momma was alive," Wendy said.

"Oh, she is, but if she weren't, she'd be doing a lot of flipping."

Two hours later, the Manhattan Knitters were settled into a suite in the Waldon, knitting and drinking red wine. Abigail had called her people who told her they should all hold tight and enjoy the night. Despite the instructions to leave her phone behind, Wendy hadn't. What if Jackson tried to contact her?

"This is the most fun I've had since my coming-out party." Eddy drained the second bottle of on-the-house wine. It was called When Pigs Fly. Their suite sat in the corner of the tip-top floor of the old, but very elegant, hotel.

"What does one do at a coming-out party?" Abigail paused her knitting, made a checkmark on a pattern she was following, and then gave Eddy her full attention.

Eddy framed his face with jazz hands. "Come out...of course." Then he went back to knitting. He'd given up on learning to use the double-pointed needles. Said they were made for female hands and his, while capable of softness, were manly hands. Tonight, he'd been jauntily knitting ankle scarves for all of them. Pink for Wendy to match her new wool coat, green for Abigail to remind her of all the money she would make once her yarn store opened, and hooker red for himself...just because. He was also making Bobby a pair. Super chunky, white yarn instead of whisper thin, though. *All the better to make the rat bastard look like he had cankles.*

Abigail's burner phone dinged. She read the message. She bit her bottom lip and didn't immediately share.

"Well?" Wendy asked. "Is it all in my imagination?"

"Not exactly."

Damn. Maybe she should have left her phone behind. She turned it off.

33

Wendy, Eddy, and Abigail juggled to stand in front of the bathroom mirror as they double-checked their appearances before reentering the grand ballroom—a massive space, with a dramatic eighteen-foot ceiling.

"God, we look fabulous," Eddy enthused.

Wendy, once again a strawberry blonde and now sporting hair extensions, decided she could pass as a princess. Bobby's magical touch was in full evidence. What Wendy saw in the mirror was the best version she'd ever seen of herself. "I plan to make the most of tonight." With the contract with Jackson ending, she seriously wanted to find a better quality of man to get involved with next. Maybe she didn't deserve love, but she deserved respect and companionship.

"When you walked in, every man in the room lost their heart," Eddy said. He, on the other hand, had caused quite the ballyhoo when he'd stepped into the ballroom wearing a black velvet Christian Siriano tuxedo gown with matching bolero jacket. "And Abigail, darling, Versace looks divine on your body. You're going to bring all the men to their knees."

"Sweet cheeks, it's not the clothes that bring a man to his knees," Abigail said, before reapplying her red lipstick.

Eddy blushed. "Touché."

"Bobby didn't let us down," Wendy admitted. "I don't think I've ever felt more beautiful." The man had shown up at the hotel this morning ready to devote his busiest day of the week to the three of them. He had apologized profusely the whole time he'd worked on Wendy. And, when it had become apparent Wendy wasn't the forgiving type, he'd sheepishly admitted Chasity had coerced him to turn Wendy into a tawdry version of herself. He'd also admitted to telling the actress where she could find Wendy that fateful night at the Comedy Club.

Eddy opened his purple, leopard-print envelope purse and pulled out his mask. "Ladies, are you ready?" His mask had cost a fortune but truly looked like someone had taken a pair of black lace thongs, cut out the crotch, added a couple eyeholes, and called it a creation. There had been no talking him out of it, although they had done their best.

Wendy and Abigail donned their masks.

Wendy's was made of an intricate black lace with beaded embellishments and a series of feathers that hugged her jaw line and stood a full foot above her head.

Abigail's resembled a black lace spiderweb. One eye was encased in a Middle Eastern-style mask and had a pearl drop hanging on her cheekbone. The other eye was unadorned. The top of the mask was an assortment of intricate swirls that covered most of her forehead. Her eye makeup was smoky exotic and looked stunning with her red lips. She had long sheets of diamonds on her earlobes. Her hair had been pulled up in a series of sophisticated curls. The southern belle looked suspiciously like a harem mistress. That was until you saw the rest of her attire.

"Never more ready." The mask made Wendy feel invincible. Like a superhero in stilettos.

"Sugars, this is going to be fun." Abigail pulled up her dress and stuck her phone in the top of her cowboy boots.

"I wonder if Jackson's here yet," Wendy said.

Abigail's people had checked Wendy's apartment for bugs and found nothing. While Wendy was relieved, it just allowed her brain to go back to thinking about Jackson. About the revenge they were plotting on him for calling her boring.

When he'd said he'd be busy all week, he hadn't been kidding. She'd heard nothing from him. He hadn't even asked why when she texted him and said she'd meet him at the ball. He'd just texted back a thumbs-up. That had been last night.

It had been her plan, if he had responded and insisted on picking her up, she'd cancel the revenge she and the Manhattan Knitters' Club had planned and allow him to pick her up for a *date*. The only one they'd ever have.

Stupid thumbs-up emoji.

While she couldn't sue him for breach of contract, she could and should sue him for breach of good manners...and not having the common sense to be worried about her well-being. God. She was a freaking contract proofreader. Didn't he know that was a dangerous job?

"Thank Gucci you didn't text him this week asking him to squeeze you in for some servicing," Eddy said. "The cad doesn't deserve you."

"He certainly doesn't," Wendy said with more volume than conviction.

"Bring it in." Eddy held his hand out.

Wendy and Abigail placed theirs on top of his.

"Three, two, one, kick ass," they said in unison.

They separated. Obviously, Jackson would recognize Eddy, but they were betting he wouldn't be able to figure out which of the guests was Wendy and Abigail. Especially since they both indulged in a couple of well-placed fake tattoos and colored contact lenses. And kick-ass hair extensions. And as far as Jackson knew, Wendy was still a blonde.

The only downside to their revenge scheme, Wendy wouldn't get to dance with him. She'd been looking forward to having him twirl her around the dance floor. And if she was honest with herself, she really wanted to feel his arms wrapped around her one last time before the contract ended.

Or the Angelinos offed her. She shivered.

"Good evening, everyone. Welcome to the ball." An older gentleman stood on the stage. "Tonight's auctions will happen in segments. Every thirty minutes, a new man will be auctioned off. As soon as our hostess arrives, we'll get started."

Polite applause mingled with hoots and hollers. The hoots and hollers belonged to the Manhattan Knitters.

Their level-ten revenge plan was to bid against each other, driving up the amount of money Jackson would have to shell out for his freedom. When Wendy was satisfied with the amount, she'd give them the signal to stop bidding.

The revenge wasn't just the amount of money. It was also about their disguises. Their masks. Since Jackson wouldn't recognize her, he'd be livid thinking she hadn't won the bid. That she was a contract-breaker. This would drive him crazy because he trusted her. Once the bidding ended, she would take her sweet time removing her mask. Thus, allowing him to thoroughly wallow in anger and humiliation that he'd been taken advantage of by a mere vanilla yogurt.

"Hi," said a deep voice at her elbow, a voice that sounded not at all familiar. She turned to look. A masked man gave her a smile. "Nice ink."

She glanced at the fake tattoo on her shoulder. A butterfly. "Thanks." She started to ask if he came here often, decided that sounded like flirting. Then remembered she wanted to flirt.

"Are you here to bid?" he asked.

"I am." She gave him an assessing glance. Under the mask, was he cute or handsome? "Are you one of my options?"

"Busted. I'm terrified no one will bid on me."

She laughed. That sounded like a guy who skated on the edges of cuteness while trailing his hand along the rail of handsome. "And so now you're chatting up women in the hopes one of them will promise to buy you."

"Guilty." His neck turned a faint red. Had she made him blush?

"I'll tell you what." She smiled. "If you'll go get me a glass of wine, I promise to bid on you." She'd make guys that blushed her new type.

"Red or white?"

Her spine tingled, and she shivered. Not in a good way. Not in a *Jackson's looking at me* way. "Red." What was that all about?

"Good choice." He hurried off but didn't make it far before he stopped and spoke to another female.

"What the heck?" Even her new type lacked commitment. Which was probably why her spine had tingled. A wolf in sheep's clothing had just chatted her up.

She spotted a waiter and raised her hand, giving him an I-need-a-drink signal.

"Hey, gorgeous." This voice she knew. This voice haunted her dreams. This voice belonged to Jackson. Damn it.

Wendy turned. "How did you know it was me?"

Her heart leaped in her throat as she took him in. Black tuxedo. White shirt. Shiny black shoes. Sexy as hell body. Gorgeous face. Cute black dog on a pink leash. No mask.

"I looked for the best ass in the room."

Be still my heart, he's smooth.

"So...you *like* my ass?" she said flatly.

His smile faltered. "I dream of your ass."

"I bet you say that to all your former bed partners." Had he spent the week with Chasity? "Is this your dog?" Wendy reached down and pet the animal, realizing she had a beautiful tiny tiara propped on her head. The addition did funny things to Wendy's stomach.

"She is. All the bachelors have been assigned a rescue dog."

"Was the tiara your idea?"

He nodded and glanced at her shoulder. At the tattoo. But didn't say anything. "I hope you and your friends have fun tonight."

Her heart tried to betray her, but she bolted that shit down. Love couldn't hurt you if you kept it shut away. "What's your dog's name?"

"Shady Bell."

"Hi, Shady Bell," Wendy cooed. The dog rewarded her by moving away from Jackson and sitting on Wendy's expensive shoe.

Jackson placed a finger under Wendy's chin and lifted so that they were staring into each other's eyes.

Everything inside of her went tight. She had no idea why. Definitely not a result of sexual awareness. Well, almost definitely.

"I'm sorry about being out of pocket all week. Thanks again for agreeing to buy me."

"Did you have a top bid in mind?"

He reached out and ran his finger over her butterfly. "What do you mean?"

Who in the hell is he to think of me as boring?

"If someone comes out with an opening bid of, say, five thousand, do you still want me to outbid them?"

A bright mockery invaded his eyes. "Five thousand? Is that all you think I'm worth?"

She shrugged. "My opinion of your worth isn't up for discussion."

He frowned. "Last time I went for twenty-four thousand dollars."

Oh. My. Stilettos.

"You're kidding...right?" No way.

His mouth set in annoyance. "I don't kid about money."

"Who spends that kind of cash on man candy?"

He sighed. "Rich little old ladies and rich bored housewives tend to have a lot of disposable income. As do the parents of rich socialites looking for husband number one for their daughters."

She took a quick breath. Utter astonishment made her sway. "Good grief. Mom used to say men were a dime a dozen. And only a nickel if you bought them day-old."

He grimaced. "Our value has gone up."

This guy was an idiot. "Are you really willing to spend that much to avoid a date with a hooker?"

He coughed. "Excuse me?"

Ordinarily, she'd laugh at the expression on his face. "A lady who wants to get her hooks in you."

"It's all for a good cause. And it's tax deductible."

"Ladies and gentlemen, may I have your attention." Wendy and Jackson turned to the stage. The MC stood there, looking stunning in a form-fitting black dress. And very familiar.

Wendy's eyes widened. "Your sister's the MC?"

Jackson shook his head.

"Our first bachelor is Jackson Adler."

Golf applause rung out.

His sister glanced out at the crowd. "Jackson, come on up and let's make some money for a great cause."

"We'll talk later," he whispered to Wendy before bounding up on stage.

"Ladies and gentlemen, our first bachelor is escorting Shady Bell. She's looking for a forever home. Remember, if you win a bachelor, you are also agreeing to adopt or sponsor the dog. Either way, once a week, your dog will be taken to a senior citizen's home for some senior-puppy therapy. Senior-puppy therapy has been very popular on the west coast, and we're excited to bring it to New York City."

This elicited a more rousing round of applause.

"Shall we start our bidding at twenty-five thousand?"

Wendy glanced around the crowd and found the blusher dude. When would he go up on the auction block? And why didn't he have a dog?

34

Jackson stood on the stage and tried to smile like a man excited about being bought at auction. Thank God he knew the outcome. Wendy would buy him. He hadn't realized just how much he'd missed her this week until he'd seen her. Or, he hadn't allowed himself to acknowledge how much he'd missed her until he'd seen her. My God, she looked sexy as hell tonight. He searched for her, hoping her back was to him so he could get another look at her ass.

She wasn't where he'd left her.

Where had she gone?

No one immediately offered the twenty-five thousand his sister suggested. She'd started that high for a reason. She'd found out Jackson had spoken with Mitch before Mitch's repeat ghosting performance. Of course, he hadn't told her what he now knew about Mitch. Knowledge would only put Annie in danger.

Annie had started the bid so high in the hopes of bruising her brother's self-esteem when no one other than Wendy bid on him.

God. Little sisters were a pain in the ass.

He searched for Wendy. Why hadn't she placed the first bid? He hadn't given her a limit.

"Ladies, standing before you is one of New York City's Elusive Six. They were first mentioned by *Naked Runway* several years ago. Two of those bachelors are now off the market. Tick. Tock." On the surface, it sounded like his sister was really trying to push him, but underneath, Jackson knew she mentioned that bit of fact so she could send the single ladies into a feeding frenzy. One that would haunt him long after the auction ended.

Jackson grimaced. He'd only been trying to save her from future pain.

Shady Bell barked.

"Sorry, Shady Bell, you're not allowed to bid on your own bachelor." His sister tossed the dog a treat.

The audience laughed.

"Twenty-six thousand," said someone in the audience.

"That's a generous bid," his sister said. "Do I hear, twenty-six five?"

"Twenty-six five," said a man's low voice.

Jackson stiffened. He knew that voice. *Eddy*? Why in the hell was he bidding?

"Twenty-seven," he heard Wendy say.

His shoulders dipped in relief. He spotted her in the back row standing on a chair. His heart did a funny little step. A step similar to the waltz. He'd like to dip—

"Twenty-seven one," said a voice.

"Twenty-eight," said another female voice.

"Twenty-nine," said a distinct female voice.

Son of a bitch. Chasity. Why was she here? And why was she bidding on him?

"Do I have thirty?" his sister asked. Her eyes told him she knew it was Chasity who'd just placed that bid. Had she personally invited her?

Silence.

"Going once—"

"Thirty," said Wendy.

"Thirty-one," said Eddy.

"Thirty-two," said the woman he didn't know. Was it Abigail? Were all the Manhattan Knitters bidding on him? Why?

Jackson glanced toward Wendy, willing her to bid higher. A man was at her shoulder, talking to her, distracting her, handing her a glass of wine. Who the hell was he?

"Thirty-two...do I hear thirty-three?" asked his sister.

"Thirty-three," said Wendy.

Jackson glanced at Chasity. Now that man stood beside her. The man dipped his head and said something to Chasity, who shrugged in response. "Fifty thousand," Chasity bid.

Wendy fell off her chair and yelped. Her wine went flying, eliciting several more cries.

Jackson bit back a laugh. God, he loved her. Couldn't wait for the bidding to be over so they could talk. He watched for Wendy to stand.

"Fifty thousand, going once..."

"Slow down," Jackson hissed at his sister. Where was Wendy? Was she hurt? Should they stop the bidding?

"Going twice..."

"Wait." Wendy reappeared on her chair, paddle in hand.

He exhaled. Other than a cockeyed mask, she didn't look harmed.

"Um, what was the last bid?" Wendy asked.

"Fifty thousand," his sister said. "Do you want to go fifty-one?"

Jackson refrained from nodding at Wendy. He didn't want to appear to be leading her along in her bidding.

Wendy slowly raised her marker. "Fifty-one."

Jackson swallowed hard. Thank God.

"Sixty." Chasity walked over to Wendy and tapped her on the elbow.

Jackson watched.

Wendy bent down and Chasity spoke into her ear. And then Wendy spoke in Chasity's ear.

What were they talking about?

After a few more exchanges, Wendy glanced at him, frowned, and stepped down.

The crowd shifted, causing him to lose sight of Wendy.

His pulse kicked up. Were she and Chasity still talking? Why had Wendy gotten off her perch?

"Do I have sixty-one?" his sister asked.

Damn it. He had a bad feeling about this. The seconds ticked by. How long would his sister wait? Not long. She was angry at him. She'd think it served him right to end up with Chasity.

"Sixty going once," his sister said.

He willed Wendy to speak up. She had to buy him. She *had* to be the girl he thought she was.

The girl who kept promises.

The girl he could trust.

The girl who owned his heart. Yes, she owned his heart. And he planned to tell her later this evening.

Wendy couldn't turn out to *not* be that girl, because love could last longer than a season with *that* kind of girl.

"Sixty...going twice... Sold." The gavel came down before Jackson could open his mouth and bid on himself.

Bitterness flooded him. She wasn't *that* girl. He'd been a fool to believe she was. A fool to allow his heart one second of believing in forever love.

Damn it. That girl or not, they had a deal. A contract. What had happened to all the honor Wendy bragged about having? He'd fallen in real love with a sham.

She'd played him. Taken his credit card, gotten makeovers for herself and her friends. Made him take those damn dance lessons. Only to back out at the last minute.

Was it because he hadn't contacted her all week?

He'd been a little busy.

Or maybe she never planned on following through. Maybe the whole thing had been a cat and mouse game. It wasn't like he could sue her for breach of contract.

Chasity squealed, ran up on the stage, and threw herself in his arms, kissing him on the mouth before he could protest.

The audience cheered while his sister led them off the stage. Once they were behind the curtain, he peeled himself away from Chasity. "What in the hell are you trying to prove?"

She pursed her lips into a perfect pout. "Darling, that's not a very nice way to talk to someone who laid down sixty-thousand dollars for a night of romance with you. Plus, another ten thousand to that woman you've been dallying with so she'd let me win."

He clenched his hands into fists. Wendy had sold her integrity for the cheap rate of ten thousand dollars? "I didn't ask you to buy me at auction. I thought I made myself clear the last time we talked."

"I know you think you've fallen in love, but I can assure you, you haven't. And even if you have, I care way too much about you to let you make a fool out of yourself over a nobody. I mean, had she told me no to the question I asked her, I would have walked away and allowed her the winning bid. But she didn't. So, I did what any good friend would do. I offered her ten thousand dollars to stop bidding."

He shoved his hands in his pockets. "What are you taking about? What question did you ask her?"

"If she loves you."

His heart stopped pumping blood to his brain. "You did what?"

"She said she doesn't."

Jackson's throat tightened. "Of course, she doesn't love me. Yet." The words felt like darts coming out of his throat. "A man has to earn a woman's love. Why were the two of you talking about love?"

Chasity gave him a soft smile. "Don't hate me, but I told her I love you, and I was willing to bet my life savings to win you. I asked her if she was willing to do the same. I asked her if she loves you."

Chasity touched her wrist, drawing his gaze to the diamond bracelet he'd given her. A gift given at a time when they had been enjoying each other's company. She laid her hand on his arm. "I'm sorry."

"Excuse me. I have someone I need to talk to." Without waiting for her reply, he stalked into the crowd toward where he'd last seen Wendy. This wasn't over. She had the right not to love him, but she didn't have the right to break their contract. And for what? Ten thousand dollars.

When he realized she was no longer anywhere near where he'd last seen her, he stopped and scanned the crowd. It would have been easier to find her if she'd been wearing the damn tiara. The fact she hadn't worn it to tonight's ball should have been his first clue the evening wasn't going to go as planned. If ever there was an appropriate time to wear a tiara, it would be to a ball. Hell, he'd even bought his dog a tiara that matched Wendy's.

"What do we have here? The Sixty-Thousand Dollar Man," Eddy purred from behind him.

Jackson turned, his hands fisted. "Where is she?" No way in hell was he letting her slip away before he confronted her about her lack of integrity. And what the hell was Eddy wearing? Even for him it was a bit much.

"Who?" Eddy fluttered long eyelashes at him.

"You know who. Tell me where's she's at before I damage your money-maker."

A look of horror crossed Eddy's face, and he took a large step back. "Women's restroom. Second floor."

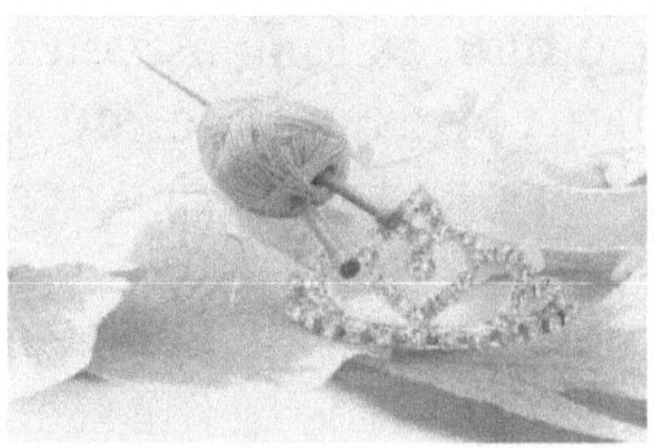

35

Wendy stood in front of the mirror and took several breaths. How had everything gone so wrong? She turned on the cold water and filled her hands, prepared to splash her face. Anything to cool off, if even just a fraction.

Before she could, the sound of heels clicking against the tile caught her attention. "Well, well, well. What do we have here?"

Wendy glanced up. Chasity. "What do you want, now?"

"I thought I should tell you that Jackson is looking for you, and he's not happy."

"Of course, he's not happy."

Chasity tutted. "Should have never broken that little contract you made him sign. He's such a stickler when it comes to trust."

Wendy straightened and let the water slide through her fingers. "Go away. You won."

"I did, didn't I. And I didn't even have to threaten you. Not much of a surprise coming from a mouse. But now, I'm faced with a dilemma. Should I or shouldn't I tell *Page Six* what I know?"

"Why would you do that to him?"

"I won't do it to him, as long as you make a point of telling him you don't love him, like you told me." Chasity glanced in the mirror and reapplied her lipstick.

"I doubt he'll ask."

"You need to make sure he does ask. If you don't, I will go to *Page Six*. And, let's face it, the scandal would tank Jackson's reputation. He'll become known as someone not afraid to fix the outcome when there's something he wants badly enough. Trust me, no one wants to do business with that type of man."

"Why are you doing this? Even if you do love Jackson, he doesn't love you," Wendy said. "If he did, he wouldn't have agreed—"

"Oh honey. It's not his love I want." With that, she turned and left.

Jackson strode toward the ladies' room. Each step one closer to the certain death of his ability to ever trust in love.

Without knocking, he opened the double-wide doors and marched inside. Wendy stood alone at a mirror, dabbing a tissue at the corners of her eyes. Tears were not going to save her from his wrath. "We had a deal."

"I'm sor—"

His intention to allow her a chance to explain herself evaporated. "*Don't* say you're sorry."

"Jackson, I—"

"You're sorry? You fucking can't be sorry for something you did on purpose."

Her eyes widened. "But—"

"I thought you were trustworthy. I thought you were someone who believed in the sanctity of a..." He snapped his lips closed. He'd been about to say marriage contract. That's not what this was about.

Wendy's face lost its color. "What? Spit it out."

He stabbed his fingers through his hair. "It doesn't matter."

Her nostrils flared. "Earth to Mr. High and Mighty. I'm not the only one who proved untrustworthy."

"I did not break our contract."

"Technically, you kept it, but did you keep the promises it contained?"

"What the hell are you talking about? Which promise do you think I broke?" How did she have the audacity to act like she was the wounded party in their contract? Just because he hadn't been able to see her this week, it wasn't a breach of contract. He'd truly been busy with family. Annie had taken off and he'd gone to look for her. When he'd found her upstate at a cabin the family owned, he'd stayed with her. It had given them both a chance to soul-search. While his searching had made him aware how much Wendy meant to him, her searching had made her aware she deserved a guy worthy of her attention. Now, all his searching had been for nothing. Wendy wasn't the woman he thought she was.

Wendy's shoulders sank, and she exhaled hard. "Never mind."

"Fuck no, I won't never mind. You started it. Tell me exactly which promise you think I broke."

Red blotches formed on Wendy's neck. "You know what, I don't love you, so none of this matters. If you want to sue me for not purchasing you, so be it."

He jerked. Chasity had told him the truth. "I just might," he lied.

She opened her mouth only to slam it shut.

"Darling, there you are." Chasity waltzed into the ladies' room and placed a hand on Jackson's shoulder. "Shall we go talk about what all I get for my money? I'm assuming sex will be a part of the purchase. I mean, we do it so well."

Jackson let his gaze lock with Wendy's. He willed her to say *don't go*. That everything was one colossal misunderstanding.

Her mouth remained shut, but her eyes shouted go to hell.

He turned to Chasity. "Let's get out of here."

36

E ddy and Abigail walked in as Jackson and Chasity walked out.

"What happened?" asked Abigail. "Why didn't you buy him?"

Wendy slumped against the hand dryer. "I was afraid to."

"Afraid? Why?" Eddy dropped an arm around her shoulders.

"There was this guy, he wore a mask, and he said hi to me right away this evening. He said he was a bachelor, but he didn't have a dog with him the way the other bachelors did. Which I didn't think much of until I was bidding on Jackson. That's when Chasity walked up to me and said the guy in the corner—the one without a dog— said he had an acquaintance who wanted to know if I was in love with Jackson."

"That was probably just his way of finding out if you were single," Abigail said.

"Or his acquaintance was Mr. Bruiser."

Eddy adjusted his fake cleavage. "Let's say you're right. Why would Mr. Bruiser care who you love?"

"People like him often hurt people you love to get your attention."

Eddy gasped. "That is how it works in the movies."

"So that's why you didn't buy him?" Abigail pulled her phone out of her boot. "You were afraid Mr. Bruiser might hurt him?"

Wendy nodded.

"Hi, Ruby Rae. There's been a horrible new development." Abigail stepped into a stall and closed the door and started telling her person everything that had happened tonight.

Eddy guided Wendy toward the exit where they stood and waited on Abigail. "This is getting out of hand. If some guy is after—"

"Ruby Rae says we all looked quite lovely in our ball gowns tonight."

Wendy frowned. "Did you send her a picture?"

"She has a person watching us until your hiccup has been dealt with."

Eddy fanned his cheeks. "I wonder if her person is tall, trampy, and tempting? I saw one of those tonight. He could make me forget Bobby."

"Sorry, hon. She wouldn't tell me who he was or what he looked like or anything. Quite annoying." Abigail pulled up the hem of her dress and stuck her phone back in her boot. "Anyway, she says we're to stay and have fun. When we're ready to go home, she'll have a car waiting on us. She would like for all of us to stay at my place. She promises to get to the bottom of this as soon as possible."

"No disrespect intended, but I find it hard to imagine your persons from the haunted town of Mayhem will have the tools to get to the bottom of this," Wendy said.

Abigail laughed. "Don't underestimate my persons. They might be senior citizens, but they're feisty."

A manic laugh erupted from Wendy. "It's bad enough I've dragged the two of you into my troubles. Now, I'm guilty of dragging sweet old ladies into it as well."

"Dollface, leave the drama to me," Eddy said. "Let's get back out there and enjoy this party." He readjusted his tiara. "I didn't get waxed to go home before I've been felt up a few times." He pulled Abigail's tiara out of one of his inside pockets and handed it to her.

Wendy removed hers from her purse and slipped it on. They hadn't worn them earlier so as not to give themselves away.

"You're right, Eddy." Abigail gave them a bright smile. "I think I want to adopt one of those cute puppies. I could use some companionship in my shop, and besides it will be good for business to have a mascot. Did I ever tell you that back home there's a coffee shop that has a porcupine as a mascot? Her name is Miss Pincushion."

At six a.m. on Monday, Wendy's heart, which had been a bowl of hot, messy achiness all weekend, had transformed into a frozen tundra. That was the moment, while waiting on her Keurig to brew her a cup of coffee, she'd read an article on the *Page Six* website.

As much as Wendy knew it was best if she didn't know, she wanted to know if Jackson and Chasity went on their auction date. If *Page Six* had covered the power couple's breakup, surely they'd cover a romantic auction-purchased date.

Stupid decision on her part. But ever since telling Jackson she didn't love him, all her functioning brain cells appeared to have vacated her head.

Anyway, the airy article had left Wendy's hot mess of a brain with frostbite.

Chasity Kennedy and Jackson Adler are once again an item...more in love than ever before...wedding bells...did she buy herself a husband at the doggy charity event? Or was their whole breakup a charade...

Now at work, the words *wedding bells* kept repeating in Wendy's head as she did her best to proofread contracts. Combine that annoyance with the frostbite, and, well, she wasn't having a good day. To make matters worse, concentration and perfection weren't possible when your brain was emotionally damaged. For every mistake Wendy found on a contract, she made two of her own.

But she tried. Really hard. All day. Thank God, it was almost time to go home. She glanced at the digital clock on her computer screen to see if it was too early to start shutting her computer down. Ten fifteen a.m.

How was that possible? Surely, at least a century had passed since she'd arrived to work at eight. Hell, it felt like five centuries.

She forced her gaze back to the contract. An Angelino contract. One which should have had her on full alert. The dissolution of the booty-call contract between Penelope and Mitch. It didn't.

Were Chasity and Jackson ring shopping this morning? Or enjoying a lazy breakfast after a night of—

An icy tear dropped off her lashes, landed on her cheek, rolled downhill until finding its final resting spot on, not her neck, but the contract. "Son of a—" She'd just defaced an Angelino with bodily fluids. A shudder whammed her insides.

Damn. What should she do? If she signed it with the smeared print and sent it off, would the shoddy quality warrant another summons from Mr. Bruiser? Probably. Which meant she couldn't. She had to obtain a new copy of the last page of the contract.

Unfortunately, the only way to do that was through Mr. Morgenstern. On the bright side, he had shown up for work this morning, looking pale but all in one piece.

Wendy blew her nose, grabbed the defiled page, and strode toward her boss's office.

"Hello, Mrs. Highly, I need to speak to Mr. Morgenstern," Wendy said to his secretary, who appeared to be gathering her stuff to go to an early lunch.

Mrs. Highly sighed like Wendy had just asked her to donate a kidney. "He's busy. Can't it wait until I return?"

Wendy smiled pleasantly but firmly. "Afraid not. It's about the Angelino contract."

The woman's scowl cracked. "Oh. Well. Of course." She picked up the phone and pushed the intercom button.

"I told you, I'm busy and not to disturb me," Mr. Morgenstern barked in a slightly out-of-breath, ill-tempered tone.

"Ms. Travis needs to see you about the Angelino contract."

"Christ. One moment."

Two minutes later, his door opened. A beautiful lady walked out first, her hair tousled, her skirt wrong side out, and her eyes cast to the floor, followed by him. His frown wide, his shirt wrinkled, and his gaze fully on Wendy. No more pale cheeks. Now they were a rosy red.

"Mrs. Highly, please see my ten o'clock appointment out. Thank you."

No words were spoken until Wendy and Mr. Morgenstern were alone.

"What is it?" Mr. Morgenstern said to Wendy, his voice scraps of fury and frustration.

Wendy swallowed the rising bile in her throat. Had he been having sex with a woman while his secretary sat in the outer office?

Eww.

Wendy evicted the thought. "I need another copy of the last page of the Angelino contract. I'm afraid there's a water stain on mine."

He took a step closer and eyed her carefully. He smelled of cheap cologne and expensive perfume. "How did the water stain get there?"

She refused to look away. "I'm not sure." No way would she tell him it was the result of a tear. That would send him over the edge. But, then again, she wasn't telling a bold-faced lie, either.

He held out a hand, and she handed him the page. He put on his spectacles and gazed intently at it, holding it up to the light as if he were someone cool enough to figure out the origin of a stain. "Have you been crying? Is this a tearstain?"

Well...hell. Maybe he *was* cool enough. "My eyes have been watering today."

He huffed out a breath, glanced at the door as if sorry the woman had left, and then folded his arms across his belly. Not quite a beer belly, but not a six-pack either. "You realize this is your second strike."

Wendy startled. No freaking way. Would he? "That's not a mistake. That's an unfortunate incident. It's not strike-two worthy. I caught the problem and am remedying the situation. I'm not guilty of sending out a contract with an error. I just need for you to print off another copy of the last page for me to sign. Not give me strike two." She spat it all out, not taking a breath for fear she'd breathe in uncertainty, and she couldn't afford to sound uncertain.

He shook the page in her face. "In my boss book, this is a mistake. The manner in which you handled this contract constitutes gross negligence."

"Gross is a bit harsh."

"Is it? Julie told me you and your boyfriend broke up."

Since when were he and the mail clerk extra chummy? "That would be correct."

"You're obviously letting your personal life interfere with your ability to concentrate this morning."

"I dis—"

"When I granted all your demands to continue to work on the Angelino contracts, I trusted you would live up to your part. You'd be stone-cold accurate. You didn't. You know the rules. Two strikes and you're fired."

She swayed from shock. If she got fired from this position, she really would be a loose end in the eyes of the Angelinos. "Of course, you have alternatives. You're the boss. That gives you the right to not only fuck on company time, but to also ignore the rules you set up for your employees when those same rules are counterproductive to what's best for Contracts R Us."

Mr. Morgenstern's face turned twenty-three shades of red. And one unfortunate shade of gray. "Gather your things. I will send security to escort you out of the building."

Wendy pointed to the page in his hand. "But what about the Angelino account? They want consistency in who is handling them. Aren't you afr—"

A smirk lifted his lips. "Let me worry about the Angelino account. Leave your work phone on your desk. And, per the employment contract you signed, you'll have one week to vacate your company-owned apartment."

Ten minutes later, Wendy sat at her desk, staring at her work phone. Her only phone. How would she afford yarn in the future if she had to pay for an apartment and a personal phone?

One-by-one, she erased all her text messages. All her apps. Then Eddy's phone contact information. And Abigail's phone contact information. And Jackson's phone contact information. Then she proofed what she'd left on the phone, taking the time to scroll through the remaining numbers to see if there were any personal ones she'd missed.

At the bottom, she came across one she didn't recognize. Ziggy.

Who in the hell was Ziggy? There was no record of an outgoing or incoming with that contact. About to simply move on, her brain registered the words written in red at the bottom of Ziggy's contact page—Stop Sharing My Location.

What? How was it she'd been sharing her location with someone she couldn't even remember? Had the number been in the phone when it had been given to her? Was it some trick Mr. Morgenstern used to keep track of his employees? To know where they went on their lunch hours? What an ass. No wonder he'd encouraged her to use it as a personal phone.

"Ms. Travis, I was asked to escort you from the building."

Wendy glanced up. Tom, from security, stood at her desk. She'd watched him escort many an employee out of the building over the years. Employees who had incurred strike two. In all the times she'd watched him, not once had she ever thought *someday that will be me*.

And now it was her. Without fair warning, she broke down into loud, sloppy tears.

"Umm." Tom awkwardly patted her back. "I can give you a few more minutes."

She blew her nose. "I'm okay." She grabbed her box that held a picture of Mom and Dad, the butterfly figurine Dad had given Mom on their honeymoon, and a jar of black licorice, and stood. Biting her lip, she allowed him to escort her out of the building. Several of her coworkers waved goodbye.

"Will you be okay?" Tom hailed her a taxi. "Is there anything I can do for you?"

Sniffing, she gave him a wobbly smile. "There is. Would you please tell Mr. Morgenstern I said to go fuck himself?"

Tom barked out laughter. "I'd be happy to do that for you."

Sitting in the back of the taxi, she stared out the window. *Oh look. The restaurant where I met Mr. Bruiser.*

That was either the one bright spot in all of this or not. Mr. Bruiser was either no longer her concern, or she was on his radar more than ever.

38

It's hard to imagine how a week could go by hot-streaker-dude fast and simultaneously ancient-streaker-dude slow. The Manhattan Knitters had spent their nights at Abigail's apartment until Wednesday. That's when Abigail's person called and said she'd taken care of everything. Wendy was most definitely no longer considered a loose end.

But she wouldn't tell Abigail what exactly she'd taken care of or how.

Now it was Friday, and the Manhattan Knitters were at Wendy's apartment. Packing.

"What kind of asshole fires you on a Monday and expects you out of your residence within a week?" Eddy grumbled for the umpteenth time. His mood was so dark you could hide in its shadows. The Broadway show he'd performed in had abruptly closed. Plus, he and Bobby had engaged in a terrific public fight at Bobby's salon. And, to kick him while he was down, Eddy had lost his tiara on the subway.

"The kind that owns Contracts R Us." Wendy stuffed a stack of folded pajamas into a box. She didn't have the energy to try and yank him out of his funk.

"In Mayhem, none of this would have ever happened," Abigail said. "Mommas raise their boys with more manners in Missouri."

Wendy sniffed. "I take full responsibility. If I hadn't added sex to mine and Jackson's contract, I would have never fallen in love with him. And if I hadn't fallen in love with him, I would have never cried onto an Angelino contract."

"Hmm," Abigail said through tightly pursed lips. "Darling, I—"

"Can we change the subject?" Wendy asked. "I need something to laugh about."

"I think you should at least tell Jackson what really happened at the ball," Eddy said.

"I can't. If I do, you know what will happen." Wendy was no longer worried about Mr. Bruiser placing a hit out on Jackson, but she was still worried about Chasity making good on her threat.

"Chasity and Bobby are dead to me," Eddy declared. "I can't be bothered loving vicious bitches."

"Sugar, you know you can stay with me as long as you like," Abigail said to Wendy.

"I don't do charity. But thank you for the offer," Wendy replied.

"Why don't you at least change your flight? Put it off for a week," Eddy said. "It's more fun to wallow in misery when you do it with another."

Wendy shook a finger at him. "After tonight, you're not allowed to wallow and neither am I. The Manhattan Knitters' Club does not allow crybabies in its membership."

"You're not wrong," Eddy said. "But will our club even survive without you at the helm?"

"Of course, it will. And, besides, with any luck, I'll find another job in the city and be back in the club in no time." Wendy had quickly landed a job with *The Boston Globe* as a proofreader. The pay wasn't as great, and there wasn't a free apartment, but at least it was a job until she found something better.

Abigail picked up the bottle of wine and refilled all their glasses. "Let's toast."

"What shall we toast to?"

"To friendships that can survive distance," Abigail said.

Ker thump.

The noise came from upstairs. The sound of a door closing. They jumped up and ran to the window. After about three minutes, they watched Jackson, dressed in a tuxedo, get into a black town car.

"He could've at least looked up," Abigail said.

"I'm glad he didn't," Wendy lied. Did he have another gala to attend? Was that why he'd been all dressed up? Would Chasity be his plus one at the event? Would they come back to Jackson's love shack afterward?

At least she wouldn't be around to listen to them. Wendy glanced at the boxes. Brown and pink. The pink ones were going with her to Boston. They were her must haves. The brown ones were going into storage. "I think we're done here. The movers will be by later to pick up the boxes."

Eddy massaged her shoulders. "Look on the bright side. I bet he doesn't think you're boring anymore."

Wendy laid her head on his shoulder. Not-boring didn't feel like much of a victory. Especially, when her heart hadn't survived.

"Sugar, we could discreetly set the record straight. Let him know you love him."

Wendy shook her head. Why embarrass herself in that manner. It's not like Jackson had any feelings for her. "I don't want to do that."

Her night in shining Armani had been a bust.

39

Jackson didn't realize he'd returned to apartment 5C until his penthouse key didn't work. "Fuck." He switched keys and opened the door. Whereas before, having a place close to Wendy had soothed him, tonight, simply stepping through the entry infused him with a potent dose of anger. Not so angry, though, that he turned and left. Instead, he stayed. Stayed and allowed himself a last trip down memory lane.

He'd kissed Wendy up against that wall. And on that couch, they'd talked about her parents and their accident. And, on the kitchen island, they'd kissed like teenagers. Neither going beyond second base, just enjoying the moment. On the wine rack were three bottles. They'd picked them out at the corner market. All with ridiculous names that made her laugh.

Shoving away the memories, he checked the time.

What was today? Thursday? No, Friday. God. A full week had passed since the ball, and he'd heard nothing from Wendy. No explanation. No apology. No, I really *do* love you.

A week in which he'd stayed mostly drunk.

A week in which a chunk of his heart broke off every time he envisioned her standing in front of him and saying I *don't love you.*

A week in which his sister had nagged him continually to fix his and Wendy's relationship.

"I didn't break us, why should I fix us?" he muttered.

The bottom line, Wendy had kept her promise not to fall in love with him, and he had broken the promise not to fall in love with her.

"Why couldn't we both have fucking kept the no-love promise?" He walked into his bedroom and glanced around. The sight of his bed where they'd shared their last night of passion almost undid him. He sat on the edge, picked up her pillow, and inhaled the scent of her on its crisp white pillow slip.

How ironic that he, known by some as a womanizer, had turned out to be the one who did the falling in love.

He heard a noise downstairs.

Was it Wendy's night to host the infamous Manhattan Knitters? Or was she preparing to leave and go to Eddy's or Abigail's? Not that her whereabouts mattered. He had a date tonight. With Chasity. For charity.

She'd left a message with Annie this morning threatening to go to the press if Jackson didn't take her out tonight. Annie had offered to refund her donation, but Charity had insisted on the date. A date scheduled to begin in thirty minutes.

He glanced down at his wrinkled T-shirt and faded jeans. Did he even have clothes here that he could wear on a date with Chasity?

He walked into his bedroom and was pleased to see several suits in his closet. And a tuxedo. The one he'd worn the night he'd met Wendy at her company picnic. Was that the night he'd lost his heart? The night they first sat and simply chatted. He recalled the elderly lady sitting in the café wearing her tiara, and he'd imagined that being Wendy in sixty years and the image had made him happy. He hoped like hell Wendy never lost her love for the whimsical. Not that Wendy viewed herself as whimsical, but she definitely was. She had a hard outer cover that protected her until she trusted you enough to let you inside. But under that cover was a Disney Princess not afraid to slay dragons and rescue the prince.

Another noise from downstairs caught his attention. Movement of some sort. The Manhattan Knitters were definitely down there, doing what they do on Friday nights. Wasn't that a kick in the head? His life had been flipped topsy-turvy, and nothing had changed for the tenacious threesome.

Part of him, his broken and bitter part, wanted to go downstairs and shake Wendy until she gave him a reason for not buying him at auction. A reason that made sense. The other parts of him, his brain and pride, wanted to move on and forget the blue-eyed heartbreaker.

Laughter filtered up through the vents. He really should have upgraded the insulation in this building sooner rather than later. He gave the pillow one last sniff before tossing it back with the other. It was time to get on with his life.

Ignoring the memories, he quickly showered and changed. Then he called for a town car. At least the building now had a doorman. Because, even if he was upset with Wendy, he wanted her to be safe.

The sound of footsteps out in the hallway caused his heart to jump into his throat. Shit. Since when did his heart jump around?

Since he'd started hoping Wendy would come to him with an explanation.

He glanced through the peephole. No one was there. It must have been a neighbor. He glanced at the clock. If he didn't leave now, he'd be late. He didn't show up late for dates.

40

The Manhattan Knitters decided to walk from Wendy's former apartment to Abigail's loft. It would be their last trek through the city together.

"I can't believe you're leaving," Eddy said.

The three of them stood at a crosswalk, waiting for the light.

"I know." Wendy couldn't believe it either. So much had happened so fast. "I haven't completely wrapped my brain around it either."

"The club just won't be the same without you as president."

The light turned, and they crossed.

"On the bright side, now you'll be able to add not one but two members."

"That is not a bright side," Eddy said. "Don't you agree, Abigail?"

"Don't look but do you guys get the feeling we're being followed?" whispered Abigail.

Wendy stumbled. "I thought you said we were safe." She reached out and linked hands with her friends. This wasn't some dime-store drama she'd found herself in the middle of. It was the Angelinos. So what if Mr. Morgenstern had shown up alive? Pencil Thin was still very much dead.

"Maybe something new has developed," Abigail said.

"This way." Eddy tugged Wendy's hand, who then tugged Abigail's, and they made a sudden turn. One they wouldn't normally take to Wooster Street.

"Shouldn't we stay on the busy roads. Get a taxi?" Wendy asked. "Stay visible. Stay alive." For some reason, the name *Ziggy* popped into her head. She'd forgotten about the mysterious phone contact. But now...now she wondered.

When she'd met with Mr. Bruiser, the hostess at the restaurant had taken her phone. Did she work for the Angelinos? Was it she who had added Ziggy's name to her contact list?

Had Mr. Bruiser been following her ever since? Had there also been a listening device in her phone?

A silver lining in being fired was she'd given up her phone and no longer lived in her apartment. No way for the guy to continue to track her. Unless he'd been watching her apartment. Followed them when they left.

She stopped walking. All the stress of the past couple of weeks caught up with her. "I say we stop running. Take a stand. Fight the bastards. Are you with me?"

Abigail gave a short laugh. "You know what, I'm sure I'm just being paranoid." She let go of Wendy's hand, made a U-turn, and went into a corner coffee shop.

Wendy and Eddy followed.

They chose a seat close to a window and people watched. "I'm sorry. I should have never put you two in this kind of situation."

"What are friends for if not situations exactly like these?" Eddy asked.

"Exactly," Abigail responded.

They spent the next ten minutes in silence. Not once in those six hundred seconds did anyone suspicious tiptoe in front of their window.

"Like I said," Abigail announced, causing Wendy to startle. "No one was following us. I was simply being paranoid. It comes from living in a town where asshole ghosts spy on you."

Wendy wasn't so sure about that. "I have my gun on me. Are you guys carrying?"

Abigail pulled a small purple instrument out of her boot. "I have my Taser."

"I didn't want the bulge," Eddy said. "I left Marilyn Monroe at home." Marilyn Monroe was Eddy's silver Glock.

The reflection of a man off a taxi window caught Wendy's attention and her breath hitched. "Did you guys see that?"

"What?" they both asked.

"A guy's reflection in the taxi window? I think he's standing on the other side of the window. Out of our line of sight."

"Should we call the police?" Eddy asked.

Abigail shook her head. "Remember, Sarah Ann said it would be best if we didn't get them involved in any of this."

Wendy hadn't liked that suggestion the first time she'd heard it, and she sure as hell didn't like it now. New York's finest should know if the Manhattan Knitters were in danger.

"Besides," Abigail continued, "maybe it's a coincidence. He could be waiting on an Uber or something."

"It's not a coincidence. I'd bet money that is the guy who has been following us," Wendy said.

"Let's not take a chance. We can slip out through the employee exit." Eddy stood. "It's right past the restrooms."

One-by-one they nonchalantly made their way toward the restrooms. Once they were out on the streets, they grabbed a taxi and had the driver take a convoluted route to Abigail's loft.

"Now what?" Wendy asked while Abigail secured the alarm system.

Abigail gave them a bright smile. "I'm going to call Ruby Rae and let her know of our suspicions, and then, unless she has other plans for us, we're getting drunk."

"Drunk?" Wendy echoed. "Have you lost your common sense?"

Abigail shrugged. "Darling, this is your last night in town. We need to enjoy it. Not worry about the boogeyman."

"She has a point." Eddy said. "I do wish, though, you had curtains on your windows."

They all glanced at the large expanse of windows.

"Let's go upstairs," Abigail said. "No one can see us up there from the street." She walked toward the stairs.

"I hope you've got chocolate," Eddy said. "Eddy's going to need a whole lot of chocolate to go with his wine."

Abigail paused. "I don't. I've been trying to shed a few pounds. But I have plenty of wine."

Eddy sighed. "I'll go buy us some divine chocolate at the café on the corner. You girls stay here and call the cops if I'm not back in five minutes."

"Oh Eddy, I don't know if that's safe," Abigail wailed. "Wait until I've called my persons."

Eddy gave a masculine laugh. "Honey, no one messes with Eddy."

Wendy pulled out her gun and gave it to him. "Here. Take this. Just in case."

"If you insist." Eddy checked to make sure the chamber was full of BBs and then hurried out into the night.

Wendy started the stopwatch on her phone.

Abigail called her people. Two minutes and a lot of whispering later, she hung up. "Just as I suspected. She still has someone following us just to be on the safe side. She was not happy that the guy had made himself known to my spidey senses."

"That's good to know, but—"

"Wendy, Abigail," they heard Eddy holler. "Open the door."

Abigail got to the door first. She quickly unlocked the dead bolt and pulled the door open.

When Wendy got there, what she saw caused her eyes to widen and fear to wrap huge hands around her throat. She gasped and took several steps back. "What the—" No other words would come out.

"Look what I found," Eddy said.

"Why did you bring Mr. Bruiser here?"

Eddy had one hand in the small of the guy's back. "I felt him following me. I think I might be a little psychic. Anyhoo, I pretended to stop and adjust my shoe strap. Thank God I'm wearing my new sassy, strappy sandals. Then, quick like a ballerina, I twirled. You should have seen the surprise in his eyes. Anyway, he turned and walked the other way. I was having none of that. I scooched up behind him and stuck my gun in his back. Thank Gawd you sent it with me," he said to Wendy. "And then I told him to walk where I told him to walk."

"We meet again." Mr. Bruiser scowled at Wendy. His voice had a low dangerous vibe. "Under the most unfortunate of circumstances."

Oh God. Were they all going to die because she had told her friends what had happened? Told them about the contracts?

"Don't just stand there, get him in here," Wendy said, once she came out of her shock.

Eddy shoved the gun in the guy's back, and Mr. Bruiser stumbled inside.

"You're making a big mistake," Mr. Bruiser said directly to Wendy.

"Shut up or I'll shoot you," Eddy said.

Wendy wrung her hands. "Maybe he's right. Maybe we should just let him go."

"Listen to the little lady."

"We can't let him go. He knows where I live. Let's get him restrained," Abigail said. "And then we can talk about our options."

"You," Eddy said to the man, "put your hands on the wall."

Wendy saw the canister of BBs on the table at about the same time Mr. Bruiser noticed them. He spun around. Glared at Eddy. "Are you packing a BB gun?"

"N...no," Eddy stammered.

The guy shook his head. "Then fine, go ahead and shoot me and prove it."

"Aim for his balls," Wendy said. "That's where you'll do the most damage."

Mr. Bruiser gave her an incredulous look. "And to think, I liked you." Before Wendy could respond, he snatched the gun from Eddy and had it pointed at them. "You guys are more trouble than you're worth." He pointed at the wall. "Up against it."

"If that gun's not going to hurt you, it's not going to hurt us," Wendy argued.

The guy raised an eyebrow. "You're right." He reached behind his back and pulled out another gun. "But this one will."

"Eddy? You didn't frisk him?" Abigail squeaked.

Eddy shrugged. "I was going to once I got him here."

"Why exactly did you bring him here?" Abigail asked. "Why didn't you just let him walk away?"

"Because Wendy is leaving tomorrow, and I don't want to have to worry that this guy quietly kills her off, dumps her body, and we never know about it because we're too busy thinking she made it to Boston and couldn't be bothered to return our calls because she was too busy with her new life and—"

Without warning, Abigail leaned down and pulled her Taser out of her cowboy boot. She raised it, pushed it into Mr. Bruiser's chest, and pulled the trigger.

He fell with a loud thud.

"I didn't know those things could do that," Wendy said.

"It's a hopped-up version," Abigail said. "Now, hurry, get me some yarn. We need to get him hogtied before he comes to his senses."

Wendy grabbed a ball of yarn, apple green, and threw it at Abigail. "Maybe you should let Eddy tie him up. He's had the most experience with bondage."

"I was Knotty County goat roping champion three years running." Abigail made a lasso twirling motion over her head. "I know how to capture them and then execute a tie that holds."

Eddy and Wendy watched while Abigail tied Mr. Bruiser's hands and legs behind his back. "Help me pull him over behind the couch. We want him out of sight."

"Why do we want him out of sight?" Eddy asked.

"Because while you were buying chocolate, I ordered us a pizza. It'll be here any minute," Abigail answered.

They pulled him behind the couch and then wrapped a whole container of cellophane tape around him for good measure. And stuffed a tea towel in his mouth right as he was coming to.

"How long do you think that's going to hold?" Wendy asked.

Boy, did his eyes look angry.

41

Three long hours later, Jackson found himself standing in front of apartment 4C. He scraped in a breath and ran a jerky hand through his hair. For fuck's sake. He couldn't remember the last time he'd been anything but calm, cool, and collected while standing outside a girl's door.

He sure as hell couldn't remember the last time nerves made him feel like the shy boy about to grope second base with the popular girl. Of course, he wasn't standing outside just *any* girl's front door. This was Wendy's door. He would be a fool not to be worried.

Three hours ago, instead of picking Chasity up for their date, he'd knocked on the actress's door and, when she answered, handed her a check for sixty-thousand dollars. His plan had been to turn and leave. Politeness had caused him to accept her invitation inside so they could talk.

For an hour, he listened to her rant about Wendy not keeping her end of their bargain. Unfortunately, he'd been unsuccessful in discovering what Chasity meant by *their bargain*, and knowing Chasity, it meant nothing. Just something she'd said to throw him off his mission.

After leaving Chasity's apartment, he'd done something he absolutely hadn't wanted to do. He'd gotten a tattoo. A feat that had all but caused him to pass out every time the needle stuck him.

He'd marshalled through his fear for a girl. A girl who had his skittish heart, but who might not want to give him her heart in trade. And if she didn't, who could blame her? His heart came with a warning label: *is probably not capable of forever shit.*

While sitting through the tattoo, he'd busied his brain with images of how this part of his plan might go down. One image was of her telling him to go fuck himself. And one was of her giving him an opportunity to prove he was worthy of a second chance. He really hoped for the second vision to prove true.

Annie had told him it would take something big for Wendy to give him the time of day. She referred to the big as a kick-ass grand gesture. Of course, she hadn't told him what the gesture should be. He'd had to come up with that one all on his own.

Now, he was about to discover if his gesture was grand enough. Before he could talk himself out of his half-ass plan, he rapped his knuckles on Wendy's doorframe.

No answer.

He raised his hand to knock again and was interrupted when a couple of guys surprised him by stopping at her door. They wore white jumpsuits that bore their names. "May I help you?" he asked the tall one.

"If you're here to see someone, you're too late. They've moved," the short one said, taking out a key and opening Wendy's door.

"Moved? Where?"

The tall one glanced at a clipboard. "Can't say. Against the rules."

"I'll make it worth your while." Jackson peered inside and saw plastic over the couch and lots and lots of boxes. His stomach lurched.

The short guy shrugged and held out his hand.

Jackson gave him a fifty.

"We're taking everything to a storage rental."

The tall one laughed.

Jackson left before he did them both bodily harm. He immediately called Wendy. It went to voicemail.

One hour later, he stood outside Abigail's loft and knocked. He didn't care that it was midnight.

Abigail, wearing her tiara and holding a glass of wine, answered on the third knock. "Well, aren't you just an annoying midnight gnat?"

"Have you seen Wendy?"

Her frown turned to a scalding stare. "Sugar—"

A light flicked on. "Jackson?"

He jerked his gaze past Abigail and saw Wendy curled up on a couch. Relief rushed through him as he attempted to step inside, only to be blocked by Abigail's small frame. "I tried to call," he said to Wendy. "Why didn't you answer?"

"Well, duh," Abigail answered.

"I had to turn my phone in," Wendy countered.

He again took a step toward her only to have Abigail shift into his path. "Move. Please."

She didn't. "Now's not a—"

Eddy strolled around the corner, wearing a flowy robe of some type. "Oh, my Ga-Odd, look who's here."

He floated to a stop and wagged a finger in Jackson's direction. "I don't know what you think you're doing, but it's not—*not*—happening."

Eddy took a seat on the couch and draped an arm around Wendy's shoulders in a protective manner.

Jackson took a moment to glance around the dance studio as he regrouped. Instead of empty space now there were lots and lots of bins of colorful yarn. Where he'd once spun Wendy at the end of a waltz, there was a couch and a rug and two rocking chairs.

While in the middle of his regrouping, Abigail attempted to shut the door. Jackson snapped back to the moment and put out a hand, preventing that. "I'm not leaving." He returned his attention to Wendy. "May I talk to you, please?"

"You heard Abigail. It's not a good time," Wendy answered brusquely.

"When exactly will be a good time?"

Again, Abigail tried to shut the door.

Frustrated, Jackson picked her up and moved her out of his way so he could step inside.

When he set the spitfire down, she poked him in the chest. "Listen mister, I have a Taser. Touch me again and I will fry your cupcake. *Comprehend-o?*"

He dragged his gaze from Wendy and gave Abigail a quick glance. "Noted."

Wendy stood and walked toward him. "If you're here about the contract, there's nothing more to say. I can't be trusted. Now, please leave."

He shook his head. "That's not why I'm here." He heard a noise. Some type of thumping. "What's that noise?"

"It's nothing."

"It sounds like something."

She sighed heavily. "If you're here to give me flirting lessons, I'm no longer interested."

Hell. He'd forgotten about the flirting lessons. Who did she have lined up? "Why didn't you tell me you were moving?"

She looked surprised. "Why would I tell you?"

He winced.

"She lost her job because of you," Abigail accused. "Which means she lost her apartment because of you."

Again, Jackson glanced at Abigail. She now had a Taser pointed at him. Hell, she hadn't been kidding. He took a step back. "What are you talking about?"

"She—"

"Put that thing down," Wendy said. "It's not his fault I lost my job."

"Not true," Abigail said. "If you hadn't been so preoccupied with him, you wouldn't have made your second mistake at work."

He hooked gazes with Wendy. "Is that true?"

She stared straight into his eyes. "My mistakes are my fault. No one else's."

"Is that why you're moving? You can't afford the rent because you lost your job? I can he—"

"I don't want nor need your help." Pride punched each word with a black belt wallop.

"Bless your heart," Abigail said to Jackson. She planted the Taser against his chest and attempted to push him back toward the door. "The lady doesn't want to talk. It's time for you to leave."

He didn't budge. He wasn't leaving without saying what he'd come to say, even if it meant getting zapped. "Wendy, may we talk in private?"

For the longest moment of his life, Wendy didn't respond. Then she sighed. "Abigail and Eddy, please give Jackson and me three minutes alone."

Eddy harrumphed and stalked to Jackson. "You hurt my Wendy, and I will crush your nuts."

Jackson nodded. There was another loud, unexplainable noise from behind the couch. "What was that?"

The Manhattan Knitters looked at him as if about to be caught with stolen goods.

"A dog," Wendy said. "Abigail adopted one at the auction." Her voice was high pitched.

Another thud.

"That's not a dog." Jackson walked to the couch and looked behind it. He had no idea what he expected, but it absolutely wasn't anything close to what he found. Laughter bubbled out of him. "You?"

Mitch lay on the floor, his hands and feet hogtied behind him. A rag stuck in his mouth. Jackson leaned down and pulled the rag out.

"You can laugh later, just get me the fuck untied," Mitch said. "They've tased me four times."

"You know him?" Wendy said.

"Why the hell do you have him bound and gagged?" Jackson's gaze moved from one knitter to the next. They all stared at him with the same expression. Too bad he couldn't interpret their countenance. Something between panic and pride and pissed. "Did he hit on one of you? Is this like revenge of the girlfriends or something?"

"Why would we hogtie a guy for hitting on us?" Wendy asked. "We're not prudes."

Abigail strolled out of sight.

"Then why?"

"*He* wants our Wendy dead," Eddy said.

Jackson didn't know how to respond. How in the hell had the Manhattan Knitters concluded Mitch wanted Wendy dead?

Abigail came back holding a Glock. She aimed it at Jackson. "How do you know him?"

"Long boring story."

"Get my damn piece from her before she hurts someone," Mitch snapped, as he strained against his bondage.

Jackson glanced at the man and raised an eyebrow. "You're telling me they stripped you of your weapon?"

"Fuck off."

Jackson laughed. "Are you sure you didn't get fired from the FBI instead of quitting?"

Mitch remained silent.

Jackson walked to Abigail. "The guy you've got wrapped in yarn and tape is a former FBI agent."

"Oh." Abigail surprised him by handing him the gun.

Wendy's brain spun faster than the *Wheel of Fortune* in the hands of a giant. She took a breath and tried to put on the brakes so she could focus. "I don't know where you get your information, but I can tell you for a fact he's the muscle for a cartel."

"That was his cover. I've seen his badge," Jackson countered. "He's former FBI."

She rolled her eyes at her ex-booty-call man. "Earth to Jackson, you can buy fake FBI badges on the internet. You know that right?" No way was Mr. Bruiser on the up and up. Then again, he hadn't broken any of her fingers. He'd just threatened.

"His was real." Jackson pulled a pocketknife out of his tuxedo pocket and undid the guy's hand bindings. "I can't wait to tell Annie the Manhattan Knitters got the drop on you."

"Fuck you," Mr. Bruiser said, rubbing his wrists.

Jackson laughed. A deep, hard belly laugh. "What did they do, attack you with their knitting needles?" He freed the guy's ankles.

"Trust me. They're a lot cleverer than they look." Mr. Bruiser struggled to stand.

"If you're FBI, why did you pretend to be the muscle for the Angelino family?" Wendy asked.

"Contracts R Us launders money for the Angelinos. The ones you proofed were the ones used to launder their money. For over a year, we've intercepted their contracts." Mr. Bruiser pinched his nose. "When we came across the one where you signed your name instead of John Smith, it gave us the opportunity to arrange a meeting with you, which gave us a way to plant a bug in a company phone. The case wrapped up the night of the ball."

"Why in the hell were you at the ball?" Jackson asked.

"Keeping tabs on Wendy in case she proved to be a part of the bust instead of an innocent pawn."

"Of course, I'm an innocent pawn. Why would you think otherwise? I've never even gotten a parking ticket."

"You don't own a car." Mr. Bruiser walked to the door.

"Fine, I've never even gotten a jaywalking ticket."

"No, but you did send a message from a company phone that you had *gotten rid of a body*."

Sweat popped out on Wendy's nose. "Oh. That. I can explain."

"Not necessary. You've been cleared. Mr. Morgenstern sang like a canary."

She wiped the sweat away. The message had been another thing on her list: Things to Do Before Turning 30. Send a weird message to a stranger. All the Manhattan Knitters had done it.

"If that's the case, why were you following us tonight?" Abigail asked.

"Protection of Wendy in case the Angelinos decided she was a loose end they needed to clean up before the laundering charge went to court."

"If you're former FBI, who hired you to protect me?" Wendy asked.

He glanced at Abigail. "I suggest you give Ruby Rae a call."

"You know Ruby Rae?" Wendy asked.

"Who is Ruby Rae?" Jackson asked.

"One of Abigail's people," Wendy said.

"Abigail has people?" Jackson asked.

Abigail placed a call. "Hi Sarah Ann, I know it's late and all, but I got a guy I want you to see." She turned the phone around and aimed the camera toward Mr. Bruiser. He waved. Then she spoke into the phone again. "Do you know him?"

One minute later, Abigail hung up. "She advises all of us to let him go and to never speak of this again."

"He killed our bon voyage buzz, and we're to just let him waltz out of here?" Eddy complained. "That's not fair. There must be something in it for us."

The mention of what they'd been getting buzzed over caused Wendy's stomach to clench. She glanced at her watch. In less than six hours, she'd be leaving Manhattan. Why exactly had Jackson come?

"It's been real." Mr. FBI picked up his Glock and slipped out into the night.

Abigail glanced at Eddy. "As much as it pains me to say this, let's take a walk. Give Wendy time alone with the man who crushed her—"

"Nothing. He crushed nothing," Wendy quickly interrupted. The last thing she needed was for Jackson to know she'd fallen for him. It was one thing to mention to her friends that she might have given him her heart—a totally other thing for him to have that information to do with as he pleased.

"Darling," Eddy said to Wendy, "your gun is fully loaded. Do Eddy a favor and empty the tiny balls of terror on him if he says one thing that hurts you."

"Deal."

Once they were alone in the room, Wendy said, "How is it you know Mr. Bruiser?"

"Once upon a time, he asked my sister on a date and then stood her up. Then he called one day and wanted to cash in an IOU." Slowly, he unraveled a convoluted story to Wendy. A story that ended with Mitch being the original Mr. Upstairs. "When I punched him in the nose for the second time, he showed me his badge."

The story was tragic. "I hope you told Annie all of this. She deserves a guy who doesn't sleep with women as part of their job assignment."

"According to him, he didn't really sleep with Penelope. She had reached out to the FBI, ready to turn on her family. It was all a ruse. All those voices you heard were porn turned up loudly as a cover."

Wendy gave the man who thought of her as lackluster a sad smile. "Now that we've gotten that all cleared up, I think it's time you left as well." She glanced out the picture window. Eddy and Abigail stood across the street, staring at her and Jackson.

"If that's what you really want," Jackson said. "I'll leave, but I'd like to stay and talk."

Not that he deserves it, but let's be generous and listen to what he has to say.

"About what?"

"For starters, about how I miss you."

"You miss someone who is more boring than vanilla yogurt?"

His eyes widened. "I'm sorry you heard that."

You notice he didn't say he's sorry he said it, just sorry you heard it. Move closer and kick him.

Wendy stayed where she was. "I bet you are, asshole."

"I didn't mean it." He stepped closer to her.

"Then why did you say it?"

He took another step closer, moving into her space. Close enough she saw a pulse ticking in his jaw. "To keep Mitch from hitting on you."

He'd been talking to Mitch...not Chasity? "Why in the hell would he hit on me?"

"I didn't know he was FBI at the time. At the time, I thought he was a guy leading my sister on, and who had the audacity to hint that he might hit on you as well."

Her heart, which had been tucked away since the moment he showed up tonight, came out of hiding. He'd said those ugly words out of some sort of misguided need to protect her. "Then you really didn't mean it?"

He stared at her. "No, I didn't mean it. I've had more fun with you than I've ever had with any woman. You were my dose of fresh air and fun."

She adjusted her tiara. The one he'd given her. "You think I'm fun?"

"I do."

Slow your oars. There's more we need to know. Go ahead. Ask.

Ugh. What if she asked the next question and didn't like the answer? Would she be able to get her heart to go back into its bubble of protection? "Were you with Chasity tonight?"

"I saw her briefly to give her back the money she spent on me."

Wendy blanched. That was the worst possible answer. No, Chasity would make good on her threat. "Why? That was so stupid. She bought you fair and square."

He grabbed her hands and held them tight when she tried to pull away. "Did you let her win me at auction to get even with me for the yogurt comment?"

"Of course not, but I did have Eddy and Abigail help drive up the bid as a form of revenge."

He didn't reply right away. When he did, he said, "Well played."

Jackson exhaled a deep breath and pushed with the next question on his mind. "Why did you let Chasity win? Was it because she offered you ten thousand dollars to stop bidding?" Call him a glutton for punishment, but he had to hear it from Wendy. He desperately wanted her to be *that girl*. The one he could forever love. But he wasn't sure she could be if she was so easily bought off.

Wendy's reaction caught him where it hurt. In the shins. She kicked him.

He grunted but didn't release her hands. "What the hell did I do to deserve that?"

"I did not take any money from that woman. Did she tell you that?"

Relief flooded his heart, making room for the love he'd been desperately trying to hold at bay. He nodded.

Wendy kicked him again.

"Damn it, stop that."

"You deserve every kick you get. I can't believe you believed Chasity. That you believed that of me for even one second, let alone a week."

He dropped her hands and sidestepped to avoid another kick. "I didn't know what to think," he admitted.

Wendy stalked to a bin of yarn. She picked up a ball of yarn and threw it at him. "Mr. Bruiser, whom I believed worked for the Angelino family, had a guy ask Chasity to ask me if I loved you." She threw another ball.

The woman had great aim. At least the balls didn't hurt when they hit him. "What does that have to do with the price of an Armani down?"

"The only reason I could think he would ask was if I said yes, I love you, then he would kill you as a warning to me to keep my mouth shut. So, I told Chasity I didn't. And then, I didn't dare buy you."

He took a seat on the couch. "I see. Any other reason?"

She put the new ball of yarn she held back in its bin. "None I want to share."

He tried to interpret the look in her eyes. It was intense, sad, and a whole lot of something. Something he couldn't identify. The something bothered him. "What does that mean?"

She walked back to the couch and sat next to him. "It's nothing. Never mind. Did you come to get your tiara back?"

He stared at her, pretty sure it wasn't nothing. He scrubbed a hand over his face and resisted the urge to bolt. "I came to tell you, I..." Damn it. What was he saying? He couldn't just tell her he loved her. Declarations of love should occur in a romantic setting. He had to play this carefully. "I want to keep seeing you."

"Not happening."

"Why not? I like you. You like me. The sex is great."

"Yes, but it's over. We're no longer under contract."

Time for his grand gesture. He carefully shrugged out of his jacket and removed his tie.

She gave him a look of horror. "Keep your damn clothes on. Don't think for one second I am about to have goodbye sex with you."

"I'm not after goodbye sex." He unbuttoned and cautiously removed his shirt.

"Stop it. I'm serious."

Fuck. None of this was going right. "I don't want break-up sex." He turned slightly so she could see his bicep and removed the bandage. "I wanted you to see this."

Wendy glanced at his arm. "What I don't see anything."

"Look closer."

She leaned in and did. A gasp escaped her sweet lips.

He couldn't tell if it was a happy gasp or a pissed-off gasp.

"Why did you get a butterfly tattoo?" she whispered.

Relief filled him. She hadn't said get out. "Because you have one, and I love you."

Her brows wrinkled. "I don't have one."

"Yes, you do. I saw it at the fundraiser."

She looked startled. "Oh, that." Her eyes searched his. "It was fake."

He groaned. He'd been needled for nothing. "I see."

"Why did you get one? You're afraid of needles. It's real...right?"

He glanced at the red, angry skin surrounding his tattoo. This was all Annie's fault. "It's real." He put the bandage back in place.

Out of the blue, a fat tear rolled down her cheek.

"Why are you crying? Please don't cry. I'll leave if that's what you want."

She shook her head. "After the ball, when I realized I was beginning to fall for you, I asked my parents to send me a butterfly if it was okay to have feelings for you.

When none came, I thought it meant I'd been right all along thinking I didn't deserve love."

He wiped away her tears. "I'm sure they tried to get it to you sooner, but I wasn't the most willing to do what they had in mind. Are you saying you love me?"

She nodded and another tear slipped down her cheek. "But we can't be together."

"Why the hell not?"

"Because Chasity said she'd go to the press. Tell everyone about our contract. Our contract wasn't exactly on the up and up for a trusted member of the business world to have been involved in."

He gently swiped the tear away with his finger and then went down on one knee.

Her eyes widened. "Didn't you hear me? What are you doing?"

"Chasity Kennedy is a non-issue. Trust me. She's been dealt with." He pulled a small velvet box out of his pant pocket, opened the jeweler's box, showing off a square cut diamond surrounded by sapphires. A box he'd been carrying with him since the auction. "Wendy Travis, it would be my greatest accomplishment if I could talk you into signing yet another contract."

She tilted her head and studied him. "What kind of contract?"

He grinned. "I'm open to ideas on what should be included as long as there is one iron-clad paragraph that promises you will someday marry me. You know, after you've given me a chance to properly court you and give you a reason to love me."

She laughed. "I don't have sex with a guy until at least the fifth date."

"Then we will have five dates in one day."

She giggled, leaned forward, and placed a kiss on his lips. When she pulled back, she replied, "If I say yes, I will want Eddy and Abigail as my bridesmaids."

He took a moment to imagine his parents' reaction when they saw Eddy come down the aisle wearing a bridesmaid dress. Dad would be beside himself. Mom would worry he'd outdressed her. This was going to be fun. He slid the ring on Wendy's finger. "I wouldn't have it any other way."

42

Epilogue

Six months later, at exactly six o'clock on a Friday night, Wendy opened her door to Apartment 5C. Eddy, Abigail, and Jackson's sister Annie spilled inside.

"I brought the spirits." Annie, being the newest member of the Manhattan Knitters' Club had been tasked with bringing the wine. She pulled a bottle out of her bag and held it up. "Look, it's got the cutest little hippo on its label."

Eddy grabbed the wine, peered at the label, and gasped.

Everyone went silent.

He placed one hand over his heart. "Out of all of our applications, we chose you to be our newest member, and you repay us by bringing a wine called Fat Bastard to our Friday night gathering?"

"But the hippo—"

"Do you believe us to be uncouth? Uncultured? Unsophisticated?" Eddy asked.

"Ummmm…I thought you were unconventional."

Wendy bit back a laugh. That was an understatement if ever there was one.

Eddy slapped a hand over his mouth, shook his head, and then lowered his hand. "You naughty, naughty bitch. I love it. You're fabulous. I hate you. Shall we?" He motioned toward the living room.

"Damn straight, fat bastard," Annie replied.

"Speaking of fat bastards," Abigail said. She headed toward the living room and everyone else followed. "I have it on good authority, we have a candidate who has offered to sponsor us in our quest to get our PI licenses."

"PI license?" Wendy asked. Everyone took a seat on Jackson's L-shaped couch. "What exactly did I miss while away on my honeymoon?"

Eddy pulled out a new skein of hot-pink yarn and began rolling it into a ball. "Honey, there will be plenty of time for that story later. First, tell us everything about your trip, and don't leave out any of the juicy details."

Wendy glanced at the bedroom door. Her husband was in there taking a shower. They were staying in this apartment while his condo was being renovated. "Umm. The honeymoon was nice." She still wasn't walking straight. Nor gotten used to the gorgeous ring on her finger.

Annie squealed. "Eww, I don't want any of the details of my brother's honeymoon."

The door to the bedroom opened. Jackson stood there wearing jeans and a muscle-fitting white T-shirt. "Did I hear you refer to our honeymoon as nice?" He strolled over to Wendy and dropped a lingering kiss on her lips. "Nice is for the weather. Not hot sex."

Wendy shivered. *Holy Devil's Kiss.* The sex had indeed been hot. Hot on the beach. Hot in the hot tub. Hot on the balcony. Hot. Hot. Hot. And loud. Very, very loud.

"It's knit night. Want to join us?" Abigail patted the open cushion next to hers. "I promise I left my Taser at home."

Eddy fanned himself with his hand. "Please say yes. And wear that T-shirt every Friday night. Your pecs are like magnificent." With his free hand, he patted the open cushion next to him. "I spy an added butterfly."

Jackson laughed. "Wendy thought the first one needed a mate."

"That is so sweet," Annie said. "Who would have ever thought you'd turn out to be a pushover in the hands of the right woman?"

Wendy smiled. She loved her new, big happy family. "Please, do join us."

Jackson shook his head. "Thanks, but I don't think this group can handle more than one man."

"You may be right. Would you mind taking our picture before you leave?" Wendy stood and handed him her phone. "We need a new one that includes Annie for our Instagram account."

Jackson took the phone, and they all squished together. "Abigail, your tiara is crooked."

Wendy helped her adjust it. Thanks to Jackson, they all had new tiaras decked out with stones that matched the color of their eyes. That had been his gift to them for being Wendy's bridesmaids.

Jackson's heart pounded with happiness. "Ready?" he asked the crazily posed group. He zoomed in on Wendy. Her eyes were a lazy-day shade of blue. The color of satisfaction. The color they always turned after an orgasm. He fucking loved that shade of blue. He zoomed out and prepared to take the group picture.

"Everyone say, 'Not Cupcake,'" Eddy said, right before Jackson took their picture, sending the Manhattan Knitters' Club into a fit of giggles.

1. If you'd like to learn more about the town where Abigail grew up and a little about *her people*, I invite you to read my quirky paranormal romcom series: Singles Town. Start with HEXES AND O'S. https://books2read.com/HexesAndOS

2. Sign up for my newsletter to learn when the next book in the: MANHATTAN KNITTERS' CLUB series releases. http://eepurl.com/hDXCiL

**OTHER BOOKS BY
LISA WELLS**

PARANORMAL ROMANTIC COMEDY
Singles Town Series
Hexes and O's
It's a Curse Thing
Cup of Spirits

PARANORMAL WOMEN'S FICTION
Magical Midlife Moonlighting Series
The Undead Life of Molly Thorn (Book 1)
The Magical Midlife of Molly Thorn (Book 2) (June 27,
2022
The Bewitched Life of Molly Thorn (Book 3) (Coming
late 2022)

CONTEMPORARY ROMANTIC COMEDY
Manhattan Knitter's Club
Her Night In Shining Armani (Book 1)

The Impromptu Nanny Contract (June 2022)

Aggie the Horrible Vs. Max the Pompous Ass

An Off The Wall Proposal Series
The Seduction of Kinley Foster (Book 1)
The Attraction of Adeline (Book 2)

NONFICTION
How To Add Humor To Your Novel: Learn To Write Funny Scenes

How To Add Unforgettable Dialogue To Your Novel (2023)

ABOUT THE AUTHOR
Lisa Wells writes romantic comedy with enough steam to fog your eyeglasses, your brain, and sometimes your Kindle screen. On the other hand, her eighty-year-old mother-in-law has read Lisa's steamiest book and lived to offer her commentary. Which went something like this: You used words I've never heard of...

She lives in Missouri with her husband and slightly-chunky rescue dog. Lisa loves dark chocolate, red wine, and those rare mornings when her skinny jeans fit. Which isn't often, considering the first two entries on her love-it list.

To learn more about all of Lisa's books, visit:

Newsletter:

http://eepurl.com/hDXCiL
Website:

www.lisawellsauthor.com
Facebook:

https://www.facebook.com/lisa.wells.737
Instagram:

https://www.instagram.com/lisawellsauthor/
BookBub:

https://www.bookbub.com/authors/lisa-wells
TikTok:

https://www.tiktok.com/@lisawellsauthor